AF270791

Race
To The
Finish Line

Aisha Yusuf

Published by Abāyo House

Visit our website at www.abayohouse.com

ISBN: 978-1-7771151-0-4

Disclaimer: The author requests the N-word not be used by non-black people when reading this book out loud in classrooms, book clubs, or anywhere else.

Thank you.

*To Xafsa and Salma.
I wrote this for you*

Chapter 1

My heart sank as soon as the words left my dad's mouth. I had no idea how to react. My body felt numb, and I could barely think. When my parents said family meeting, this did not cross my mind. I didn't even think it was a possibility.

My father looked at me worried. "Leyah, say something."

"Sorry, I'm just shocked. I'm really happy for you." I got up to hug him. He had been working hard for this promotion. I've watched him struggle for years to get to where he is now.

"It's only twelve months, it's a pilot project I'm starting up. We'll move right back when it's over," he reassured me.

I nodded at my dad and smiled. I didn't want him to sense how sad I was because he'd turn down the job offer and I couldn't let that happen.

"What about your job mom?" I asked, concerned. "Will you be able to practice law in America?"

"No, but I got a teaching job at the University of Arkansas," she said.

I frowned. "How can you teach law if you can't practice it?"

"I can practice law," she clarified. "But the process is very complicated and since I have a Ph.D. in Environmental Science, I decided to teach instead."

"But you love being a lawyer," I said looking at my mom.

"I think it'll be a nice change," she smiled.

I let out a deep breath and nodded. "But why America? Why not Europe or Asia?"

Moving to America seemed terrifying.

"Aaleyah, I know moving to a new country when you're about to start senior year is hard for you, but we can't leave you here alone." Dad paused for a moment deep in thought.

"I can turn down the position if you're worried about moving. You're right. At a time like this, it's not safe for us. Especially for you two," he said hanging his head low unable to look at us.

"No." I shook my head. "You're not going to turn down this once in a lifetime opportunity for me. I'm stronger than you think. How hard can handling some racists be? I just need to endure for a year." I put a brave smile on my face. Showing any signs of uncertainty would make him turn down the job.

"I love you guys and you don't have to worry about me. It's only a year, it's not a big deal," I said firmly even surprising myself.

I hugged my parents, and went up to my room to get ready. Too much was happening at once and I needed to go for a drive to clear my head.

I put on a pair of jeans and a sweater to escape the rainy July weather. It's been chilly for the past few days, but I'm not complaining. The scorching hot weather was not good for me. I grabbed a black *hijab* and carefully wrapped it around my head. Putting on a *hijab* was harder than it looked.

I ran downstairs to the living room.

"I'm going for a drive. Is that okay?" I asked my parents.

"Yeah, but don't be out too late," my mom replied.

"I won't!" I grabbed the keys from the key rack beside the door.

I stepped outside and the aroma of the rainy weather filled my nose. I inhaled deeply appreciating the fresh air.

I pulled out of the driveway, and drove down the streets of Vancouver not having a destination.

Questions flooded my mind, and anxiety overwhelmed me. I had so many worries that I couldn't tell my parents. I didn't want to leave my friends. I didn't want to start over at a new school. I wanted to finish my senior year here. I knew if my parents knew how I really felt they'd change their plans because of me, and I couldn't let that happen.

I sighed my stomach churning in knots just thinking about the idea of moving.

My parents have sacrificed so much for me and I just had to suck it up.

"Easier said than done," I mumbled.

I slowed down approaching a red light. I stared out the window soaking up everything I was seeing. It wouldn't be much longer until I would be absent from these streets. My eyes landed on a Tim Hortons, and suddenly my heart ached.

I pulled up to the coffee shop and went inside. The smell of freshly baked goods and the rich aroma of dark roast coffee welcomed me. I would definitely miss this. There wasn't a day I didn't have my Iced Cappuccino.

"Hello, what can I get for you today?" the person behind

the counter asked.

"A medium Iced Capp please."

I went towards the other side of the counter and waited for my order. The cashier handed me my drink. I smiled and thanked him.

I sat down beside the window and watched the trickles of rain trailing down the glass. It was making a slight tapping sound. It was calming—almost hypnotizing. I looked out the window sipping my drink savouring every sip.

My phone rang suddenly startling me.

"*Asalamu Alaykum,*" I answered my mom.

"Can you pick up your brother? He said his friend ran out at practice, and he doesn't have a ride."

"Okay, I'll head there right now." I hung up the phone and went to my car.

"How was practice?" I asked Aamir as he put on his seatbelt.

"It was good, but I don't understand why we're practicing when school didn't even start yet."

"It gives you guys an advantage."

He yawned. "I guess."

I felt Aamir's gaze poking a hole through my face.

"Why are you staring at me?"

"I'm guessing you heard the news. You have a gloomy look on your face," he paused staring out the window. "You okay?"

I sighed and shook my head.

"I mean I'm sad, but there's nothing I can do," I said. I turned to look at him when I stopped at a red light. "You're really lucky Aamir. You start university this year and you get to live in the dorms."

"Awe, are you going to miss me?" he teased.

I rolled my eyes. "Don't be stupid. Nobody cares about you."

I chuckled at the dirty look he shot back at me. I turned up the volume of the music playing in the background. We drove in silence bobbing our heads both of us deep in thought. We had new chapters starting and our lives would change drastically. I was going to miss him. I don't know how I'm going to survive without him. He was my best friend. The thought of saying goodbye left a sinking feeling in the pit of my stomach.

We gathered around the living room later that night.

"When are we leaving?" I asked my dad.

"In three weeks *InshaAllah*. We need to start packing soon."

"Where are we going exactly?"

"A town called Anderton, but I'm going to be working an hour outside of town. Your mom and I are going to have to commute to work."

"A town? How come you're going from a big city to a small town?" I asked confused.

"If we lived in the city, we would be separated," he explained. "The town is closer to the facility."

"I am going to be the director of the company there. We're developing a new medicine, and one of our facilities is in Arkansas—it's bigger than the one here. Anyway, I'm going to be overseeing the project in that facility," he continued.

"Woah, that's cool!" I exclaimed beaming with excitement.

"How's the pay?" Aamir grinned.

"Bigger than what I'm getting now," my dad laughed.

I smiled. This would be huge for him. Maybe this won't be as bad as I was telling myself. Everything would probably be okay.

Chapter 2

My best friend was unable to look at me.

She pouted. "You're actually leaving Leyah?"

We were sitting on the floor of my room. I folded my clothes, and placed them into a suitcase. Seeing my room slowly become empty was making everything surreal.

I looked up at Iman fighting the heaviness weighing on my heart.

"I don't want this to be real either."

"But we were supposed to make this year our year. We were going to look for universities, and take a road trip across the country," Iman said.

"We can still take the trip and search for universities. Maybe I can come visit during winter break."

"Just one year." I squeezed her hand. "I'll be back before you know it."

"What if you like it there and you forget about us?"

I laughed at her ridiculous statement. "I highly doubt that."

"Oh my God, do you remember this song?" Iman jumped up and cranked up the music that was playing in the background.

We have a habit of abusing a song we liked, and this song was no exception.

We danced letting the beat take over our bodies.

We yelled at the top of our lungs singing along with the song. I grabbed a hairbrush off the floor and used it to mimic a microphone. I let go of all my worries and sadness enjoying the moment with my friend.

We collapsed on the floor breathless after the song ended. The music continued to blare from the speakers. I got up and turned it down letting it play in the background.

I looked at the mess I had to make disappear by the time my parents came back home. I bobbed my head to the music while I packed my makeup. We cleaned my room for hours until the only things left were my bed and dresser. All the posters on my wall were gone. The clothes lying around were packed up. Everything that made my room mine disappeared. I sat on my bed and Iman sat beside me.

"What are you doing for the next few days?" Iman asked breaking the silence.

"Tie up a few loose ends and say bye to the city." I thought about how I would spend my last few days in the country a lot.

"Tie up a few loose ends?" Iman chuckled. "You sound like a criminal."

My brain could not fathom exactly how much I would miss her.

I wish I could fast forward the year.

I wiped away the beads of sweat dripping from my forehead.

"Come on!" my coach yelled. "You're not going home until you get this right."

I nodded trying to catch my breath.

He held the pads and yelled combos.

I punched the pads as quickly as I could following his fast-paced instructions.

"You can hit harder than that!" he instructed.

I ignored the burning sensation in my muscles, and hit harder even though my body was about to give up. This was the last time I would be in this gym and the last time in this ring with my coach. I needed to give it my all.

"Mind over matter." I tapped into my mantra.

"Okay we'll stop here," he said after what felt like the longest twenty minutes of my life.

I nodded panting heavily unable to get any words out.

"You're really leaving us Aaleyah?" coach asked after our training. "You're one of my best fighters. I'm sad to see you go.

"I'm sad to be leaving you guys," I told him. "I'm only going to be gone for a year."

I tried to sound cheerful. This gym was like a second home. I came here every day after school since I was eleven years old. I had way too much energy as a kid, and my parents put me into this sport to channel it into something beneficial. They tried soccer and basketball, but running back and forth just wasn't for me.

Coach patted me on the shoulder. "Good luck with everything. And Aaleyah, I hope you never stop fighting."

"Thank you." I smiled. "You don't have to worry about that. I'll always be fighting."

I looked around the gym a lump forming in my throat.

"I really will miss you guys."

I walked out of the gym with a box of my belongings. I opened the trunk and set my things inside. I sat inside the car for a few minutes before I drove. My mind had a hundred and one things running through it—like an endless marathon. I played my music to drown out my thoughts and drove home.

I walked inside the empty house, and set my stuff beside the door. I went to the living room picturing where the furniture once used to be. Without it, the place felt cold and unwelcoming. I ran upstairs to my bedroom and jumped onto my bed—the only thing remaining in my room.

I stared at the ceiling visualizing how things would turn out once we got to America. Maybe I was being a drama queen, and things would not be so bad. I was always curious about how high school was over there. Was it like the movies where everyone was separated into groups? Was there such a thing as the popular kids? I hope not. I didn't need my life turning into a dramatic teenage movie.

I hugged my brother tightly as tears streamed down my face. This was the furthest he could come with us in the airport.

I let go of him letting my parents hug him next. My mom rambled on about all the things he should do when we're gone.

"Make sure you eat all your meals, and just because we are not here with you doesn't mean you can go crazy. Remember, God is watching you." My mom was trying hard to stay strong, but the crack in her voice gave her away.

Aamir walked over to my mom, and gave her another hug. "I promise I'll be good. You guys make sure you're safe."

We are sad to miss your soccer games, but make sure you tell us everything that happens." My dad put a hand on my brother's shoulders. "Don't forget about your studies."

"I promise dad I'll have a 4.0 GPA *InshaAllah*."

My dad gave him one last hug. "I know you will."

"Just because you're in university now doesn't mean you're cool. You better call us Aamir," I warned him, crossing my arms over my chest.

"I will and that goes for you too," he said hugging me.

"I won't come home for Thanksgiving break, but I will for winter break."

We waved at Aamir before we made our way to our gate.

This was really happening.

Chapter 3

We landed after a long flight to Anderton, Arkansas. I could already feel the hostility, and it was almost suffocating. The stares we were getting could burn holes in our backs. We ignored everyone, and grabbed our luggages. We made our way outside to find a taxi.

After waiting twenty minutes, we finally got a taxi to stop for us. The inside smelled like cigarettes and sweat. My dad gave the man the address. The driver looked at it, and grunted furrowing his eyebrows. He started to drive towards our destination saying nothing.

I looked at my mom confused, and she shook her head at me signalling me to not pay attention to the man.

I turned my attention towards the window taking in the scenery. One thing that shocked me was the pride that American people had. The American flag was everywhere. Most houses had the American flag and some even had the confederate flag—which made me want to rip it off their doors. The town was a small one. No tall buildings, one small mall and a movie theatre. I counted every non-white person I saw while driving. Five, alongside the many,

many people walking around. I saw nobody wearing the hijab, and I realized I would probably be the only one in my school wearing it.

The taxi driver pulled up to a suburban neighbourhood with rows of gated mansions. The driver grew more suspicious as he glanced at the address again.

"You sure this is the right address? These houses are way out of your league." He showed the paper to my dad to double-check if it was right.

I scoffed and rolled my eyes. I opened my mouth to fire back, but my mom pinched my leg to shut me up.

I bit my tongue the entire ride to our new house to keep myself from snapping at the man.

The cab driver shrugged, and continued to drive down the neighbourhood until he pulled up to the largest house amongst the bunch. I had no idea why we needed such a big home for only three people.

My dad got out of the taxi and punched the code into the keypad. I watched in awe as the gate opened. My eyes widened, and my mouth dropped open. It was huge. There was a fountain in the middle, and the driveway curved around it. It looked old, but I could tell it was newly renovated. There were two pillars around the entrance, and there was a big brown oak door. The windows were enormous, and if the house was not gated, it would have been open for the whole world to see into. Looking from the outside, the windows were somewhat tinted. You couldn't get a clear view inside.

My dad paid for the taxi, and we made our way towards our new house with our suitcases trailing behind us. The inside of the house was more jaw-dropping than the outside. The polished tiles on the floor were literally sparkling.

I didn't want to walk on it even though I was wearing my socks. Two spiral stairs led to the upper level, and climbing up and down those stairs would probably be a hassle. There was a dazzling chandelier dangling from the ceiling that lit up the foyer.

I ran into the kitchen first and to my surprise, it was already furnished. The windows in the kitchen overlooked a beautiful man-made pond. There was a dining table next to the windows, and there was a grey marble island table in the kitchen with black stools pushed up against it.

The appliances were all sleek and black matching the dynamics of the kitchen. Three black lamps hung from the ceiling. I could already tell I would spend a lot of time in there. I loved to cook. I cooked with my parents every time they were in the kitchen. Since my dad was the chef of the house and my mom was the baker, I got the best of both worlds.

We inspected every inch of the house. I decided that the theatre in the basement, the kitchen, and the gym were my favourites. My parents set it up like a boxing gym which made me thankful. They put in a small ring, a heavy bag, and a double end bag; it also had weights and other training equipments.

Next, we were standing in front of my room.

"Whoa." I stared at my room overwhelmed.

My new room was twice the size of my old one. The bed was a California king bed. I didn't understand how one person needed that much space to sleep in, but I appreciated it anyway. The walls were painted dark royal purple and white. The colours complemented each other beautifully. There were two nightstands with lamps on either side of the bed. To the left was a white study desk with a black wheelie chair tucked in. On the floor was a fuzzy black carpet that covered the entire room.

The windows were covered with a white curtain, and against it was a window seat where I could enjoy the view of the town—even though there wasn't really much to look at. The empty walls made me excited to hang the posters I brought with me.

There was a spacious washroom inside the room. Then I opened the closet, and automatically decided that more than the kitchen, this closet was my favourite place. I couldn't stop grinning when I saw the small pink carpet and full-length mirror at back of the closet.

After what felt like hours running around the house, we finally sat down in the living room, and drank iced-tea to cool us down.

When the shock of the house wore down, my anger came rushing back by the way he treated us.

"What a complete jerk. Who does he think he is?" I breathed out in frustration. "I should have just knocked his teeth out."

"Aaleyah, you can't beat people up every time they piss you off," my dad warned.

"I know," I groaned.

I looked at my parents surprised at their lack of frustration.

"Why didn't that piss you off?"

"Because Aaleyah, if I got upset every time something like that was said to me, I'd spend my entire life angry. It just isn't worth it sometimes. It's easier to let some things go. I learned how to pick my battles because I can't fight every one," my dad explained.

"He still deserved to be slapped," I mumbled.

"And get a lawsuit? I don't think so," my mom said, shaking her head.

"He would have no proof. It would be a light slap. Enough to teach him a lesson, but not to leave a mark."

"Violence is not the answer Aaleyah."

"I know that..." I trailed off. "But how do you deal with people like that?"

Dad thought about it. "By not being like them. By continuing to move ahead."

"I knew moving here was going to come with a lot of challenges and struggles. With us being who we are, we need to work twice—if not three times as hard—to succeed or to gain half of what they have."

"Is that why you got us this house?" I asked.

He looked around the living room. "It was one of the only houses available. It was either this or living in those white picket fence houses beside a racist with a confederate flag as a neighbour, which really wasn't an option. This neighbourhood is also gated which is a plus."

I nodded. "Makes sense."

"Besides, I love seeing their reactions when they realize that one of the few black families in this town live in the biggest house. You saw how the taxi driver reacted when he realized this house was ours. Things here will be difficult for us, but we must not forget who we are, and we must remember that *Allah* will always be on our side. We'll be okay."

I thought quietly about what my dad said. I don't think I could be as calm as my parents.

"At least they furnished the house nicely," I said changing the subject.

Dad smiled and turned to mom. "That was all her."

Mom got up and walked around the living room admiring her work. "If being a lawyer didn't work out for me, I was going to become an interior designer."

I got up and stood beside mom. "I think we'll be okay here."

She put her arms around me and smiled. "*InshaAllah* I think so too."

I took my stuff up to my room that night. I had to unpack my clothes, and the thought of it was dreadful. I had three huge suitcases filled with clothes and shoes, and a few boxes filled with some of my makeup and other things.

"Tomorrow I will clean this mess," I promised unable to keep my eyelids open.

I went to my duffel bag and took out my pyjamas knowing I would not have found it in my suitcase. Along with it were my toothbrush and skincare products. I went to the bathroom and took a shower, brushed my teeth, and washed my face.

I jumped on my bed and yawned allowing the marshmallow-like bed to engulf me. I wondered how I was going to get out of this comfortable bed every morning. It was only after *Maqhrib*, but since we were travelling, we prayed *Maqhrib* and *Isha* together—I could sleep peacefully.

I took out my phone and messaged my brother and friends I arrived safely. I scrolled through my social media until a call from my brother interrupted.

"Hello?" I answered.

"I already miss you guys."

"We miss you too. How is it without us?"

"Honestly kind of lonely. How was your first day?"

Aamir asked.

I told him about our day. All the stares we were getting, the stupid taxi driver, and about the mansion.

"Wow that's a lot."

"I know," I sighed.

We talked for a few more minutes until I was yawning every other sentence.

"You sound tired, go to sleep. I'll call you guys tomorrow," Aamir said.

After saying goodbye, I hung up the phone. It didn't take long until the tiredness overtook my body. Immersed in a world of darkness, I was pulled into a deep sleep.

Chapter 4

I woke up the next morning sore and groggy. I rolled around in my bed stretching and yawning trying to peel myself away from the comfortable soft bed that was keeping me hostage. I went under the duvet preserving the warmth before my mom barged into my room telling me to get up.

A few minutes later, I heard mom's footsteps coming closer. I hugged the blanket tighter knowing she would rip it off me.

"Aaleyah wake up! We have a long day ahead of us." She ripped the blanket off my body as I braced myself for the cold air.

I sat up annoyed not wanting to move. I rubbed my eyes and yawned trying to wake myself up. I looked around my room trying to figure out the unfamiliar surroundings until it dawned on me where I was.

"Oh," I said realization hitting me. We actually moved. I thought it was a bad dream, and when I woke up I would be back in my old room. I groaned accepting this was my new reality, and I would have to deal with it.

I got up from my bed and walked to the washroom. I

turned on the light and looked in the mirror. I had dark circles around my eyes the jet lag clearly showing. My hair was all over the place. I was too lazy last night to maintain it, and this was the result. I turned on the faucet and splashed my face with cold water to wake me up. I looked at my curls to see the mess I was working with. My curls were severely tangled and the only way to fix it was to wet my hair. I went to my room to search for the suitcase that held all my hair products.

I cursed myself for not labelling everything. I searched in every suitcase and box until I finally found it. I took out my spray bottle, hair products, hairbrush and walked back to the bathroom. I filled my bottle and sprayed my hair with water dampening it to make detangling easier.

After fifteen minutes of detangling and applying the products in my hair, I was finally done. I looked at the end result and was satisfied with what I saw. My hair no longer looked like a bird's nest. I tied my hair in a loose ponytail and got ready for the long day ahead of me.

After breakfast, I went back to my room to unpack my belongings. I stood in the room not knowing where to start.

"Clothes first," I said wheeling all my suitcases into the closet.

I decided instead of throwing all my clothes out at once that I would do one suitcase at a time. I started with the big ones first. I wanted to colour coordinate my clothes to make getting dressed easier. I hung up all my shirts and sweaters shading from darkest to lightest. I did the same with all my pants and skirts. I dedicated a whole section for my hijabs separating by materials instead of colour. I hung up my *abayas* and dresses near the mirror.

Next, I pulled up the boxes containing all my shoes. I separated them into three sections, heels, every day wear, and sports shoes–colour coordinating them from darkest to lightest. By the time I was done, I was ready to collapse. My closet was almost done. All I had left was to set up my vanity, and I would be finished.

I resisted the urge to take a break, so I got my make-up and set them on the vanity trying to organize them the best I could. I took all the empty suitcases and boxes and put them in the storage closet beside my room. I set up my study desk putting my laptop, books, pens and pencils, and other stationery items.

After the longest two hours, I was finally done.

"I should probably eat," I whispered to myself not ignoring my grumbling stomach any longer.

I ran downstairs to the kitchen and opened the fridge. I smiled happily to see that the refrigerator was packed with food. My parents must have gone shopping while I was unpacking. I closed the fridge and went to check the window to see if the car was there, but it wasn't.

I went back to the kitchen to make myself a turkey sandwich, a fruit smoothie, and some sliced apples on the side. I headed back to my room and sat on the floor with my laptop in front of me. I decided to do some research on this town to see what we were getting ourselves into.

I searched the Internet to find anything that would give me insight about this town, and nothing interesting popped up. It appeared to be a regular boring town, but I continued digging. I searched the depths of the world wide web until I came across an article titled "An Inside to the Most Racist Towns in America". I was intrigued by the title, so I clicked right away.

The article was about the prominence of white supremacy in these towns. It gave a brief history on how the African American population of some of these towns were chased out during the race riots between 1907 and 1910–each for something different. It mentioned that these towns were a stronghold for the KKK, and young people today are joining the KKK because they identified themselves as the alt-right.

I set my laptop down shocked by all the information I read. I knew this town was racist, but not to this extent.

"Crap," I muttered.

After the initial shock wore off I picked up my laptop again.

The statistics stated that 98.2% of Anderton's population were white, 1.6% were Hispanic and Asian, and 0.2% were black. I continued scrolling the web until I saw one particular article that stood out: "The Alarming Disappearances of African-Americans in the United States," the article read. I clicked immediately. The article highlighted black people going missing at an alarming rate. The end of the article contained a list of states and towns where the disappearances were most common, and there, at number three, was Anderton.

"Although a majority of Anderton's African-American residents were run out of town during a race riot in the early 1900s, it is believed that many of these people are indeed missing. Anderton, as well as surrounding towns, have one of the largest disappearance rates of African-American people in the country. These towns have been under investigation for a while, but no evidence have been found. The disappearances continue until today; although Anderton's African-American population ceases to exist, it is believed that the town is somehow involved. In what way is yet to be determined," I read aloud.

"Damn," I said letting out a shaky breath.

I clicked on the list of names of the people who disappeared since 2000, the latest person was a fifteen-year-old boy who disappeared just two years ago. Lewis Wiremen was his name. I shook my head realizing that the boy would have been seventeen like me.

I was stunned as I continued the article. I closed my laptop a little while later feeling disturbed not wanting to read anymore. These people vanished without a trace, and nobody was looking for them. Nobody cared. If this list contained a majority of white people, there would have been a national outcry and the whole world would have been shut down. Black bodies were disposable to these people.

I knew from the very moment we stepped foot here we were unwelcome. Being black and Muslim in a place where 99% of the people were white and Christian made us immediate targets. These people hated us and who we are.

I became worried about my parents suddenly. They've been gone for a while, and it was making me nervous. I called them on WhatsApp, but no answer.

I picked up my dishes and ran downstairs. I set my dishes in the sink and looked out the window. The sun was already setting, and I was beginning to panic. It was not safe to be out this late.

To distract myself from the anxiety brewing, I decided to get dinner started. I opened the fridge to see what I should make.

"Lasagna sounds good." I opened the pantry to see if my mom bought any, and thankfully she did.

While the pasta was on the stove, I started preparing

my sauce. I chopped up the vegetables adding them to the ground beef. I sprinkled a generous amount of spices and stirred everything together, and left the pot on simmer.

I inhaled deeply enjoying the delicious aroma of my sauce. Hunger began to set in again. I took out the glass dish for the lasagna and oiled it up, so it wouldn't stick to the bottom, and I waited for a few minutes for everything to cool down. When it was time, I layered everything.

I checked the time feeling anxious. Reading that article really got me paranoid, but how could I not be?

I put the lasagna in the oven and sat on the stool scrolling through my phone, but my mind kept going back to those articles. To shake the thoughts away, I decided to make dessert. After confirming I had all the ingredients, I decided on a simple apple pie—we also had vanilla ice-cream which was the perfect combination.

"Mmm, what smells so good?" mom said.

I jumped back startled.

"You scared me!" I wiped my hands on my apron and went to help them with the bags they came in with.

"I was really worried about you guys, and I couldn't even call you." I set everything in a corner.

"Where were you guys?"

"We were running a bunch of errands, but we will tell you all about that later." My dad reached into his pocket and handed me a sim card.

"Perfect." I took it and pulled out my phone. I looked around for a pin, and went over to my mom and pulled it off her *hijab*.

"I need to use this for a second." I put the new sim card in.

"Dinner will be ready in thirty minutes. Go change and

freshen up. I'll call you when everything is ready."

I set up the dinner table.

"This looks very delicious," mom said cheerfully skipping into the kitchen.

I laughed at her youthfullness. Sometimes people thought we were sisters. Both of my parents looked very young, and they were both in good shape and are health freaks–so I guess that kept them young. And you know what they say, black don't crack. I just hope I age as well as they did.

We all sat around the table and dug in. This would be our first dinner without my brother. It made me think of how lonely he must be.

"What happened today?" I asked when we were finished.

"Wait, before you answer, let's get dessert and move to the lounge room," I said jumping from my chair setting my plates in the dishwasher. My parents not far behind me.

We grabbed our pies, and sat around the coffee table. I looked at my parents waiting for them to tell me what happened while they were gone.

"It's quite interesting how much people stare. What's even more shocking is that when you catch them staring they don't look away," my dad said in irritation.

"Today has been very eventful," he continued.

"What happened?" I asked getting curious.

He chuckled shaking his head. "Well, let's start from the beginning. While you were unpacking, we decided we should run errands. It was not supposed to take as long as it did."

"There's only one high school in this town," he continued. "When we went to the front office to register you, we felt the energy shift. It wasn't good. The lady at the front didn't give us the time of day. We waited for almost an hour to speak with the principal. We were getting very impatient, so we decided to leave. Finally, he came out of his office, and we spoke to him about registering you in the school."

"It took us two hours," he said. "They tried to pressure us to place you in a lower grade to get you accustomed to their curriculum. Anyway, he gave us a lot of trouble, but that's done now. We got you registered in school as a senior. I am learning people in this town will be difficult to deal with."

"We found out the KKK is still very present here—they're actually celebrated." He leaned back getting lost in his thoughts.

Mom nodded. "This lady yelled at me to take off my hijab," she said amused twirling her spoon between her fingers. "I guess these things are expected. We live in a time so full of hate and anger. We will pray and do our best to stay safe. Aaleyah, you need to keep both eyes open at all times."

I listened quietly to my parents' worries. They experienced this much racism in one day. I can't imagine how the rest of our time here would be like. I closed my eyes trying to control my nerves.

"I don't get why they hate us so much," I mumbled resting my chin on my hand.

"Oh sweetie," my mom said stroking my back.

She sighed. "It's much easier to hate someone who looks different from you than taking the time to understand them. Instead of celebrating our differences, we detest each other for it."

"All we ask of you is to keep your head high. I wish I could tell you it gets easier," dad said.

"It doesn't get easier?"

"It gets tolerable," he said truthfully.

I nodded feeling my blood boil. "That sucks."

"Aaleyah, you know your mom and I are against violence."

"Yeah," I said slowly not understanding what he was getting at.

"But, God forbid, if you are ever put in a situation that calls for you to defend yourself, you have our full permission. We pray you don't ever come across any violence, but the reality here is different. If it ever comes to it, don't ever be scared to defend yourself," dad said sternly.

"Don't worry, you guys have nothing to worry about," I said trying to force a smile.

Chapter 5

The next few days were slow. I unpacked and got settled into our new home. There was nothing else for me to do. I was getting bored just staring at the walls. I've been able to keep myself busy by watching movies and training in the gym.

I walked around the lonely house exploring it once again thinking maybe I had missed a secret room. That wasn't the case; the house was still the same. Being all alone in a huge house was terrifying. Someone could be hiding in here, and I would never know.

My parents left for work, so I was home alone. School didn't start until next week and I had to figure out what to do until then. I wanted to explore the town, but I was afraid. I needed to buy school supplies, and I knew eventually I had to leave the house. Better now than never I guess.

I ran upstairs to my room and got dressed. I grabbed a black shoulder bag and threw my wallet and house keys in there. I grabbed my phone and car keys and ran downstairs. I dropped my shoes on the floor and slipped them on. If my mom caught me wearing shoes around this spotless house, I would be dead meat. I walked to the garage excited to finally drive the car my parents got for me. Even though I could walk to school, my parents said it would be safer if I drove. It was a shiny black Nissan Altima. I got inside admiring the interior, and I pressed the start button.

I sat back while the car roared to life. I put it in gear and drove to the front gate of the house. I put the password in the keypad and watched the gates slowly open. Taking a deep breath, I ventured into the scary unknown world where I have been sheltered from in my safe gated castle. The town was small. I could count all the shops on my fingers. It took ten minutes to drive around the whole town— okay maybe not ten minutes, more like twenty-five, but still.

After driving around to familiarize myself with the town, I went to a bookshop. I was hoping the supplies I needed could be found here.

"They should have school supplies," I muttered.

I parked in the nearest spot closest to the store. The less space between my car and the store, the less time I'd be exposed to people.

There were a few people gathered around the small store talking and laughing. From inside the car they seemed like friendly people, but I knew as soon as I stepped outside it would be a different case.

I braced myself as though I was stepping into a battleground. I shook my head at the ridiculousness of it all, but my heart was still pounding a little faster than normal. I took another deep breath and got out of the car. I felt like I was a sheep in a lion's den, and I had to stay alive. I got out of the car, and as soon as I was visible to the few people standing around, I could feel the energy in the air shift. I closed the door and walked towards the store not making eye contact with the rude ones who were shooting lasers out of their eyes.

I continued to avert my gaze feeling uncomfortable from their scrutinizing stares. It shocked me how bothered they were that I was there, as if I had killed their pets. Man, if looks could kill. One man was staring at me like I had murdered his whole family. His stare was so intense it sent chills down my spine.

I tried to ignore their stares and walked closer to the store. I was able to get a better look at the man. He looked like he was in his twenties, and was well-built and tall. He had a black baseball cap covering his eyes, but I could still see the colour of them. They were dazzling emerald with golden specks that were sparkling in the sun. I was captivated by how striking his eyes were—nothing like I have ever seen before.

"Pull yourself together," I thought. I can't be out here distracted by crazy racist people's eyes.

I opened the door of the bookshop the bells chiming as I stepped inside. The lights were dim, and the store was empty. I was afraid if I walked any further some crazy person would come and lock me in somewhere. Call me paranoid, but I've watched enough movies to be cautious.

"Hello?" I quietly called out.

I waited for a few seconds until I saw a figure emerge from behind one of the bookshelves.

"Well what are you just standing there for, come on in," the man said.

I hesitated until the person became visible. I felt my tension ease as I saw the man.

He was a tall, slender elderly man. You could tell old age had not slowed him down. He was well dressed in a vintage walnut coloured suit. His aesthetics matching the bookstore.

"Do you have any school supplies?" I nervously asked.

"I do. Follow me," he said disappearing behind the bookshelves once again.

I quickly followed not wanting to get lost in the sea of books.

"Wait here. I'll pull some things from the back. I haven't had a chance to pull them out yet. I keep forgetting that the new school year is about to start soon." He walked towards the back and disappeared behind a door.

I took the time to look around the store admiring the high shelves packed with neatly organized books.

The bookstore was old, but it made it no less pleasing to be in. It provided an authentic vintage feel. I walked between the shelves running my hands through the books. I walked up and down the isles until I reached a part of the store with a desk and chairs. I walked towards the desk and saw tucked further away—hidden—was a hanging chair, and on top of it was a wool blanket.

I smiled. I knew this would be a place where I would spend a lot of time.

"Where did you go?" His voice snapped me out of my thoughts.

"Coming!" I rushed towards the back of the store where the man was waiting for me.

He had taken out two boxes. "Look inside to see if there's anything you like."

I nodded and kneeled in front of the boxes and went through it.

I took out five binders for my subjects. Six notebooks and a few pencils and pens.

"I think this is it." I stood up with all the supplies that were threatening to spill out of my hands. The man quickly grabbed some of the supplies before I dropped them.

"Thank you," I said a bit surprised. I wasn't expecting anybody to be kind.

He smiled kindly. "Well of course."

I frowned a little second-guessing this man's politeness.

I placed my stuff on the counter, and the man rang it up.

"What is the oldest book you have here?" I asked curiously.

"I have diaries from the 1600s."

"Really?" I looked at him surprised he would have something that ancient.

"Yes would you like to see them?"

I nodded cracking a smile.

The man walked from behind the counter towards a shelf and picked out a few diaries.

He put them in front of me. "Here."

I studied the worn-out books. I gently picked up one scared if I handled it roughly it would fall apart. I opened the book to a random page. I ran my hands across the words. I admired the black ink, and the handwriting displayed on the page.

I felt like I was being transported in time holding something so old in my hands.

"Are these for sale?" I asked.

"No, but I lend them out to customers sometimes."

"Can you lend it to me?"

"Yes I can."

I smiled. "Thank you."

"Wait, do I need a library card or something?"

"No, just your name and number so I can reach you."

He paused. "This is a small town, and I know everybody–though I have never seen you before. I am guessing you are new here."

I nodded. "Yeah, my family moved here because of my dad's work."

The man frowned. "What kind of work is here in this small town that a whole family moved here. I didn't even think this place was on the map."

I laughed at his confusion. I thought the same.

"My dad doesn't work in town," I clarified. "He works an hour out at a lab. He chose this town which was closer to his work rather than us living in the city, and being separated."

"Mmm." He nodded to himself.

He put a card in front of me. "Put your name and number here, and how long you would like to borrow the book for."

"Okay." I took the card from his hand. "Do you have a pen?"

"Oh, yes." He reached into the front pocket of his jacket.

He handed me the pen. "Here."

"Thank you."

I filled out the information and handed it back to him.

He continued to bag my stuff and read the total out to me.

"$13.50 is your total. How would you like to pay?"

"Cash," I said as I reached into my wallet.

I handed him a twenty and waited for my change.

"$6.50 is your change."

"Thank you," I said as I took them out of his hand. "Have a great day sir."

"Come back again." The man waved from behind the counter.

I waved back and walked out of the store, and thankfully there wasn't anyone around. I took out my phone and saw a missed call from my dad. I went inside the car and called him back.

"Hello?" he answered after the third ring.

"Sorry I missed your call."

"Aaleyah when are you coming home?" dad asked.

"Right now. I'm in the car."

"Okay. Be safe."

"I will."

I hung up the phone and started the car. I put on my seatbelt, and drove away from the plaza.

The drive home was therapeutic. I looked at the rear-view mirror and saw the sunset behind me. I smiled admiring how beautiful the scenery was.

Maybe things would not be as bad as I was making it out to be. Maybe I was overreacting, and being here would actually be okay.

"I guess we'll see."

Chapter 6

My alarm clock blared signalling that it was time for me to get up. I groaned and turned it off. I was awake all night twisting and turning. The churning in my stomach kept me awake. Today was the first day of school, and I was so nervous. I mean, how can I not be since I was about to go to a school full of racists and Islamophobes?

I sighed knowing there was no way I could magically teleport myself back to my old school.

I snuggled back into my bed just to gather the warmth it radiated. I looked at my clock and decided that I had to get up or my mother would storm in yelling.

I forcefully dragged myself away from my comfortable bed already feeling the cold air attacking me. I put on my slippers and made my way to the bathroom. I looked at myself in the mirror. I had dark circles under my eyes, but it was nothing a little concealer couldn't fix. I splashed cold water on my face and got myself ready for the long day ahead of me.

I walked out of the washroom into my closet and got dressed. I looked at myself in the mirror evaluating my outfit for the day. I knew it was the first day back, and people buy new back to school clothes, but I was trying to minimize the attention I was about to receive.

When in doubt, wear jeans, I thought.

I put my *hijab* on securing it with a pin.

I smiled sadly at my reflection realizing this simple cloth on my head angered people so much to the point of violence. Why? I could never understand. There has been a rise of Islamophobia and xenophobia here in America, but it also happens in Canada.

I was devastated when I found out that my country was allowing a ban on all government officials in Quebec from wearing all religious symbols–including the *hijab*. Even though it wasn't happening in the province I lived in, it still hit close to home. I couldn't believe something like that was happening in my country. I couldn't believe our rights could be so easily taken away.

"Aaleyah!" I heard my mom yell.

I quickly grabbed my school bag and phone. I checked myself out in the mirror one last time before heading downstairs.

"I'm here, I'm here," I said setting my stuff down on the stool

I ate the breakfast my mom so kindly prepared for me.

"You have ten minutes to eat."

My mom got up, getting ready to leave the house.

She kissed me on the forehead and walked away.

"Love you!" I called after her.

"Love you too sweetie. Have fun at school."

"Fun?" I scoffed. "I highly doubt that."

I slowly ate my food, and scrolled through Instagram to see what my friends were up to. I smiled looking at their pictures. I felt a pang of sadness realizing how much I missed them.

I looked at the clock to see how much time I had left.

I placed my dishes in the sink not having time to wash them. I grabbed my keys, put on my shoes, and ran out the door.

My hands were tightly gripping the wheel. The nerves I was trying so hard to suppress were surfacing, and I was having a difficult time controlling them.

My heart was pounding so loudly I could feel the pressure ringing in my ears.

"Turn left in 1km."

I took a deep breath and followed the instructions on the car's navigation system. I drove for a few more minutes finding solitude in my thoughts. I would have to be mentally and physically prepared for every possible outcome that would occur when I entered that school. Maybe I was being over dramatic, but I didn't care.

I pulled into the school and drove around the parking lot until I found an empty parking spot. I parked the car and took a few deep breaths before I got out of the car. I looked at my watch realizing that I had only five minutes until the bell rang. I walked inside expecting the office to be beside the main entrance, but it wasn't. I walked around the enormous school looking for the office.

"Whoa," I said, surprised by the interior of the school. The inside of the school looked newly renovated.

After walking down the main hallway, I found the office.

I pulled open the office door and walked to the front desk. My parents warned me about the reception lady, so I wasn't expecting much from her.

"Hello," I said awkwardly to get the lady's attention.

She stared up at me saying nothing, wearing a bored look on her face.

"Ookay," I said.

"I'm a new student," I continued.

She proceeded to ignore me.

I frowned in confusion. "I thought that I was supposed to come to the office?"

She gave me a long stare before typing something on her computer.

"Name?" she asked without looking at me.

"So she speaks," I muttered to myself.

"Aaleyah Ahmed."

"And how do you spell that?" she asked as she peered at me through her glasses.

"A-A-L-E-Y-A-H, A-H-M-E-D"

I spelled my name slowly, so she didn't have room to make mistakes, and partly to piss her off.

"Weird name," she mumbled to herself quietly.

"Not weird at all." I looked at her straight in the eyes.

Her face turned crimson pink. I didn't know whether it was because of embarrassment or anger.

I waited patiently as she printed out a few pieces of paper. Another student walked into the office, and I saw the rude lady's face light up with a big smile.

"Hi, Emily! How was your summer?" she asked enthusiastically.

I rolled my eyes at the sudden change in attitude. I zoned out their conversation, and looked at my phone waiting for her to finish.

"Sorry Emily, give me a second." The Grinch handed

me my schedule, my locker information, along with other documents without giving me a glance.

I walked out of the office shaking my head. She didn't even give me instructions on how to get to my class.

I walked up and down the hallway looking for classroom 234. I'm guessing I was close since I was at classroom 229. Thankfully the halls were empty, and I didn't have to worry about prying eyes. I decided to find my locker after class since I was already late.

I turned the corner and walked a little bit until I found my classroom. I was dreading walking in late and having everyone's eyes on me. My stomach was eating itself thinking about introducing myself in front of the entire class.

I took a deep breath and knocked on the door before I opened it. I walked inside the class and stared at the teacher standing at the front.

"Hi, I'm a new student," I said nervously.

I ignored all the peering eyes drilling a hole through me, and kept my eyes on the teacher.

"Yes, I was wondering where you were." He looked around the classroom looking for an empty seat for me to sit, and the only open one was a seat in the front.

"Take a seat there," he directed me.

I nodded and made my way towards the desk still avoiding eye contact with my classmates. I did notice I was the only non-white person in the classroom. No shocker there.

I zoned out while the teacher talked about the course syllabus. He had such a monotone voice it could put an insomniac to sleep. I kept glancing at the clock waiting for the bell to ring, but every time I looked it seemed as if time never moved.

"We have twenty more minutes left of class. I want

to hear about your summer, and what you guys did," he paused. "I am aware that some of you might not feel comfortable talking, so if you don't talk today I expect a written answer on my desk next class. Who wants to go first?"

I sat there quietly while some students talked about their summers and all the things they did.

Finally, it was my turn.

"Would you like to go next?" Mr. Smith asked suddenly.

I looked up at him thinking whether it was a smart idea to speak and decided that it was. Ain't nobody got time to do a writing assignment on the first day of school. Actually, all I had was time, but not any I wanted to waste on this. I could be spending that time watching Netflix.

I nodded my head.

"My summer was great. I went to Hawaii with my family in July. I spent the first half of August packing, and the second half settling here."

"Where did you move from?" he questioned. "If you don't mind me asking."

"B.C., Vancouver," I answered.

"Where is that?" someone asked.

"Um Canada," I answered shocked that someone would ask me such a stupid question.

"Welcome. This is a wonderful town. Couldn't have picked a better place," my teacher said.

I could think about a thousand better places.

I listened while frantically looking at the clock waiting for the signal of freedom. It honestly felt like this class was going on for eternity.

Finally after what felt like forever, the bell rang and the students stormed out of the classroom.

I felt my heart pace quicken as I walked down the packed

hallway. I could feel everyone's eyes on me—I mean everyone. Some people stopped what they were doing to stare at me. I felt like an alien, but I didn't show it bothered me. I kept reminding myself that I needed to keep my head high and my back straight. I couldn't show any sign of weakness, because that would mean death. Not literally, but if I did, they would see me as weak and I couldn't let that happen.

As I walked, I couldn't help noticing that a lot of the students were avoiding accidentally touching me. I thought little of it at first, but some were taking the extra measure of walking around me leaving a noticeable distance between us.

I ignored the pang I felt in my heart. I was being treated like a contagious disease. I bit my bottom lip hard blinking back tears. I kept walking each step feeling heavier and heavier. I tried to keep a straight face, and kept looking ahead.

At this point might as well call me a terrori—

"Terrorist!" someone shouted finishing my thought.

I bit the inside of my cheeks to keep myself from saying or doing anything. The day had only started, and I was already done. I have never been called a terrorist before, and honestly, I was still processing what was just said. I always heard on the news or saw on Twitter that these things happen, but I never imagined it happening to me. I was mad at myself for being blindsided. I should have expected this. I'm in a small town full of white supremacists—why did I expect anything less?

I looked up and down the rows of lockers looking for my locker, but it was difficult to do while all the students were surrounding them. I could barely see the numbers. You would think since this is a small town the high school would be small as well. But no, it's freaking huge. It has three stories, and the hallways seem to have no end.

I guess since this was the only high school in this place they needed it to fit every student, but the number of students who attended the school and the school's size didn't match. I'm not complaining, because that meant there were a lot of hiding places for me to find. I was not looking forward to eating in the cafeteria. Mostly because I didn't want to become the source of lunchtime gossip for these people.

I sighed with relief as I noticed the students clearing the hallways as they rushed to their next class. In a matter of minutes, the halls were completely deserted.

"Finally." I quickly went to my locker and opened it.

I put the English book that Mr. Smith handed out to us in the locker, and some of the school supplies I have been hauling around all morning.

I looked at my schedule and realized I had a spare next, and lunch after that. I had two hours and twenty minutes of free time on my hands every other day. I needed a quiet place to spend that time. After dealing with hostile people all morning, I needed a safe space for me to recuperate.

I walked aimlessly looking for a place to spend my free time. I didn't know if there were rules for students with spare blocks. Was I allowed to leave the school? Am I supposed to spend my time in the library? Cafeteria?

I decided the best and safest choice was the cafeteria. It was big enough for me to stay away from the other students, and I didn't have to worry about the restrictions of a library. Now the only thing to do was find the cafeteria.

I opened the double doors, and it echoed loudly through the space capturing everyone's attention. They were all staring at me, some people looked away immediately, and some continued to stare.

It was hard to ignore them, but I managed. I didn't show them the slightest hint I cared, or that they intimidated me. Even though I knew I could protect myself, and that I had the strength to defend myself if anything happened–I still couldn't stop my heart from beating fast. I couldn't stop my hands from sweating, and I surely couldn't stop all the crazy thoughts going through my head. I hated that I felt this way. The tears were threatening to spill all day, and it was physically and mentally exhausting keeping these barriers up.

I sat at an empty table in the corner away from everyone else. I took my phone out and looked at all my missed notifications. I had a thousand texts on the group chat with my friends. I scoffed at the thought of scrolling through all those messages and actually reading them.

I opened it to see what the gist of it was. The newer messages were asking me about how the first day of school went. I smiled remembering that even though I was alone here, I still had people who had my back. I texted the group chat to let them know I was okay.

Heey guys!! I miss you all so much. This school is honestly something else. Let's have a group call later so I can fill you in on everything!

I put my phone away so I could focus on my English assignment that my teacher had assigned for the semester. There was a big term paper we had to do when we were finished. I was happy and surprised to see the book was about two black women. I mean who would have thought?

It made me like my English teacher a little bit after seeing the book he had chosen. Maybe he wasn't like the rest of them. But I was still annoyed that he assigned readings on the first day of school. Not only did we have to read two chapters, but we had to answer the questions he put on the board. Who wants to do homework the first day back?

I flipped through the pages of the book to see how long chapter one was. If it was too long, I would have to use my laptop and search for the answers. I was just too tired to read.

I closed my book in frustration. I had to read each line at least ten times before understanding what I read. I stopped forcing myself to focus and decided to do it at home.

I pulled out my phone and responded to everyone's messages and checked what's been happening on Twitter.

I spent the remaining time of my spare block on my phone until the bell rang for lunch.

A few moments later the cafeteria filled with the chatter of excited students reuniting with their friends.

Nobody sat at my table. They avoided it like the plague. I took out my lunch mom packed for me. I didn't want to buy food from the cafeteria in case they poisoned it.

I leaned back in my chair and watched all the students in the cafeteria. It was interesting watching the social dynamics of the school. There were the loud boys with their jerseys sitting in the middle of the cafeteria. Next to them were the cheerleaders. There was a clear divide between the cool kids and everyone else. The rest of the students gravitated towards those most similar to them.

Two boys in jerseys plopped down at my table. "I thought I heard rumours of a dirty terrorist at our school."

I looked up at the boys in front of me my mouth wide open at what he just said.

Silence quickly spread through the cafeteria.

"Oh, don't look so shocked." The kid in front of me sneered as he leaned in closer so no one could hear what he was about to say.

"We don't like niggers here. So watch your back," he said putting emphasis on the *er*.

They got up and walked back to their tables. I continued staring at them with my mouth wide open.

I looked around, and everyone was staring at me whispering. I quickly packed up my things needing to escape. I rushed out of the cafeteria ignoring all the stares. I continued to walk until I was outside.

I stopped under a tree and lowered myself on the ground before my legs gave out on me. I took deep breaths to calm myself down, but my brain was scattered, and my breathing was coming out in quick breaths.

I put a hand over my mouth in shock. I closed my eyes and shook my head. I kept taking deep breaths until I could feel my heart beat normalize. I leaned against the tree my face in my hands trying to calm myself down.

After a few moments, I opened my eyes and looked up at the sky letting the tears flow.

I wiped my face and leaned back on the tree trunk. I needed to collect myself before the bell rang. Everyone at the school probably heard about what happened. All I wanted to do was run home and sleep this day off, but I knew I had to go to class. I had to force myself to finish the rest of the day or else they'd think that they chased me off. I couldn't let that happen.

I reluctantly peeled myself away from the grass that was holding me captive. I took a deep breath and walked back into the school.

I had to convince myself that I was okay. I could already

feel myself breaking, and the first day hasn't even ended. We were only halfway.

I couldn't imagine myself surviving a week here let alone a whole year, but I didn't have a choice. I needed to survive. I needed to blend into the background. That was the only way to get through this crap.

"You got this," I said hyping myself up.

Finding my biology class wasn't as difficult as finding my English class. It didn't seem like it at first, but all the subjects were clumped into one hallway, which made things a lot easier.

Had that secretary lady only informed me of this earlier, she would have saved me lots of time.

I sat in the class half paying attention and half zoned out. I was sitting in the back of the class this time which allowed me to observe the people around me. I was surprised by how much people in this school played into the stereotypes of American high schools. It was almost comical.

I pulled myself back before someone caught me staring shamelessly at them—though that didn't stop them from doing the same. Every once in awhile someone would turn around and stare at me, and they didn't care when I caught them staring. Some were intrigued trying to study me, and others gave me disgusted glances. They knew they hated me despite not knowing me. For some, I was probably the first Muslim they've ever seen in person. I found it funny that in a place where we were supposed to be educated was the place I saw the most ignorance. The irony.

I guess someone being educated doesn't mean they're not ignorant. These teachers have university degrees. Despite the fact they've pursued higher education somewhere other than this town, they were still most likely racist and xenophobic.

I was snapped back to reality when I heard the teacher already assigning homework. It was literally the first day back. Do they not have mercy?

I sighed and took out a pen writing down everything he was saying.

"Okay, class dismissed."

I made it to my last class of the day, and I have never been happier in my entire life. In less than an hour I would be freed from this place. I couldn't even contain my excitement. I sat at the back ignoring everyone's stares. I kept my eyes on the teacher in front of me. Only twenty minutes left until freedom availed.

I was feeling appreciative of how time went by quickly. Much to my surprise, I actually made it. I had survived my first day!

It was probably unhealthy the way I was staring at the clock. Every tick it moved sent waves of happiness through my body.

As if everything wasn't going so great already, my teacher's sleep-inducing voice was washed out by the announcement that came blaring through the speakers.

"Ladies and gentlemen! Congratulations for making it through your first day. Wasn't it great getting to see everyone? Just a few announcements before the bell dismisses you. Cheerleading tryouts will be next Monday, so those of you interested start preparing! Football—both junior and senior—tryouts will be held this Thursday at 4:30. Come prepared boys. And finally, Club Days will be held in the cafeteria next Thursday, so bring your questions. See you all tomorrow!"

The bell rang, and I jumped out of my desk and ran out of the classroom as quickly as humanly possible. I had stopped by my locker earlier, so I could escape before anyone could see me.

I was one of the only students in the parking lot. As soon as I pulled away from the school, all the students poured out.

I smiled to myself proud that I just pulled off such a perfect escape. From here on out, I would not stop by my locker unless necessary. I would just keep everything in my backpack.

I got home not even ten minutes later. I was probably one of the few students who drove to school. Everyone else walked since this town was so small, and everything was within walking distance. But for me, this car was for security measures.

The house was empty when I walked inside. I remembered that my mom would not be coming home until later.

I walked into the kitchen and made myself a sandwich and went straight to my room. I changed my clothes and sat on my bed to eat my food.

I lowered myself onto the pillow, and before I knew it I was falling asleep.

Chapter 7

The next week and a half went by rather smoothly, and thankfully there were no more incidents. Mostly because the only time people saw me was during class.

I avoided the hallways, and I barely went to my locker. I also no longer ate in the cafeteria. I eat outside under a tree where no one could see me. I dreaded winter because that would mean I would have to find a new eating place inside, but I decided not to think about that today—one problem at a time.

I looked at the clock and second period was almost over. When the bell rings I would have to dash out of class and escape before the hallways filled up. So far the school had football and cheerleading tryouts. It was such a huge deal, and there were posters everywhere counting down the days until tryouts.

"Today is Club's Day, so head to the cafeteria at lunch and go check that out." My teacher looked at his clock, and just a few seconds later, the bell rang. "Okay, class dismissed."

It was finally lunch, and I was about to head outside until I passed the cafeteria and saw the tables set up for Club's Day. They completely transformed the place.

I backtracked a little and entered. I knew it wasn't a good idea because I would be showing myself to everyone, but curiosity got the best of me.

I wanted to know what kind of clubs a school like this had. I looked at each table to see their clubs. They had typical clubs like reading, debate and dance club.

The ones that caught my eyes the most were The Young Republicans club with lots of pictures of Donald Trump, but that wasn't even a bad one. It was the Confederates club that shocked me the most. They had a huge confederate flag in front of the table.

I decided not to go anywhere near them, and thankfully they were distracted by the many students who wanted to sign up.

I shook my head in disbelief. The fact that they were allowed to have a club like that boggled my mind.

Then I remembered where I was.

I walked away from where I was standing before they saw me staring. I did not want to draw their attention.

"Hey, you should come join our club," someone called.

I frowned at the invitation until I saw the person inviting me.

I walked over to their table intrigued it was the only one who had kids who weren't white. Which is crazy because this school did have kids of colour. I'm sure I saw like three, well five now.

The JOURNALISM CLUB the poster read.

"Tell me about your club," I asked interested.

"This is our journalism club, and we run the school newspaper. I'm the president."

She extended her hand.

"My name is Brianna Garcia," she introduced herself with a big smile on her face.

I shook her hand and smiled back.

"And this is the vice president Matthew Lee."

He also shook my hand smiling warmly.

I examined their table and poster. "What kind of things do you guys write about?"

"The topics we write about has to be school related, so sadly we don't have that many options. Do you know how hard I had to push to get a social justice column on the paper?" Brianna shook her head annoyed.

"Okay I'll join," I announced.

"Wow, I didn't know my pitch was that great."

"You had me at social justice column." I picked up the pen on the table and signed my name on the empty sign up sheet.

"Yes! We got someone to join. That's one more than last year. We can finally shut this down and go eat!" Brianna said with enthusiasm.

"Aaleyah, right?" Matthew asked, reading the sign-up sheet.

I nodded.

"Let's go. We'll show our headquarters," Matthew said.

"You know you're the first person to pronounce my name right since I've been here," I told him.

He chuckled shaking his head. "They do it on purpose. They pronounce my last name wrong. I didn't know there were so many ways to pronounce Lee. Like seriously how do you mispronounce Lee?"

I listened understanding his frustration.

"I'm sorry," he apologized. "It gets me really heated you

know."

"A hundred per cent. I roll my eyes every time they mispronounce my name, and I don't got the time to correct them each time," I said getting heated too.

"Sorry to interrupt you guys, but we're here." Brianna opened the door to the club room.

I looked around the unfamiliar hallway. I hadn't explored the school, so I had no idea this place existed.

"Nobody really comes here," Matthew said. "This is the only room here."

"What's that?" I pointed to a corner that had a construction sign on it.

"That leads to the new wing of the school they've been trying to build, but they said they ran out of funding—it's been like that for the past few years. Which is weird since they haven't tried to raise money for it ever since," he shrugged. "It's off-limits since it's dangerous."

I nodded and walked inside the room appreciating it's hidden location. There were no lockers meaning no students would come here.

"Perfect," I said.

"I know," they both replied simultaneously.

The room was impressive. It was painted burgundy and white showcasing the school colours. There were six computers, and a long oval table which I guess was for their meetings. There was also an office probably for the teacher who oversaw the club. The other side of the room had couches and a TV. It also had a small kitchen with a sink and a fridge.

I was pleasantly surprised, because they had Mac computers. I don't know why I expected they wouldn't have any funding.

"No wonder I've never seen you guys before," I said, sitting down on the soft leather couches.

"Nice huh?" Brianna said as she took out three cokes from the fridge handing us the drinks.

I nodded taking a sip of my drink. I looked around the room again my eyes landing on the office.

"Does that belong to the teacher?" I asked turning back to Brianna.

"No," she shook her head. "Come on. I'll show you."

She got up and walked towards the room, and I followed.

She opened the door and ushered me in. It was much bigger than I anticipated. It had two desks with computers on each one. It also had a couch with a coffee table that had a few magazines stacked on top of each other.

"It's ours," Brianna explained pointing between her and Matthew.

"How?" I asked surprised. "Where is the teacher's office?"

"There is no teacher. Not anymore anyway. This used to be the printer's room, and where the kitchen used to be was the teacher's desk."

"What happened?"

"We stopped printing papers because it was a waste, and we became environmentally conscious," Brianna said as she air-quoted environmentally conscious.

"We moved everything online, and the room got renovated. This all happened during the summer between sophomore and junior year. Sophomore year is when I became president, so naturally this became my office. This is where we watch the rest of the students write. We need an escape within our escape, because nowhere is safe," she continued.

I nodded understanding what she was saying.

"How many writers do you guys have?" I asked.

"Four," Matthew said joining the conversation.

"With you here, it's five," he corrected.

He looked at his watch. "We should get going. The bell will ring soon."

We followed him to the couch outside the office where he picked up his book bag.

"By the way," I started as we walked out of the room, "I don't have classes second period every Monday, Wednesday and Friday. Can I chill here?

"Yeah. That's the best part. You don't have to go to the cafeteria anymore. You can just come here." Brianna smiled.

"Will I get in trouble?"

"No," she laughed. "Who's gonna stop us?"

"Yeah," Matthew said. "No teacher comes here, and I doubt they'll start now."

"Don't they need someone to check what you guys are doing or writing?"

Matthew shook his head.

"We submit all our articles, and she tells us which ones we can post and which ones we can't. No need for her to be here physically."

We walked back into the main hallway joining the sea of students.

"They stare so damn much," I said annoyed when I noticed everyone looking at us.

"Ignore them," Matthew advised.

I looked up at Matthew. "I wish it were that easy."

He nodded.

"I should get to class. Bye guys." I waved at them.

"Wait," Brianna called out after me. "We didn't give you

any information about the club. I'll text you the details."

I gave them my number, and we parted ways.

I spent the remainder of the school day replaying the events of lunch in my head. I was not anticipating that I would attend the stupid Club's Day let alone actually sign up, but my curiosity got the best of me and I didn't regret it. I didn't want to attend because I was sure the clubs would be filled with unwelcoming students. However, I was still interested in what kind of clubs they had at this school. I was always a part of clubs in my old school. My parents taught me to be involved in extracurricular activities, but I shut out the possibility of joining a club at this school. To my surprise I joined the journalism club, even though I never thought of myself as a writer, but I always loved reading.

I was excited to join the club, but the thought of chasing stories in this incredibly boring town would be a challenge.

At least now I don't have to worry about finding a place to spend my spare block when winter comes. A big burden has been lifted off of me. I never realized how important finding a safe space was until I came to a place where my existence posed a threat.

Maybe I could write about that in the school newspaper.

Chapter 8

"I made two new friends," I told Mr. Moretti as I stacked the shelves with books.

"That's great Aaleyah! I told you you'd find people at school." Mr. Moretti peered at me through his glasses.

"Yeah, yeah," I said rolling my eyes.

"I'm going to grab more supplies from the back. Watch the store."

"I can go," I offered.

"No, no," he said quickly. "It is a nightmare in there."

"Okay." I frowned slightly. He never wanted me to go in the back. I wondered if it was that bad in there.

I sat behind the counter scrolling through my phone. Generally—at this time—or any time for that matter, nobody comes inside the store. A few regulars come in here, but other than that, it was always empty.

I was pulled away from my thoughts when I heard the bell chimes coming from the door.

A tall man walked up to the counter slowly. He was wearing a black baseball cap covering most of his face.

"How can I help you?" I asked the stranger.

He stared down at the counter tracing the wood with his fingers.

"Excuse me?" I stared at him confused by his lack of response.

"I'm looking for Mr. Moretti," he replied in a deep gruff voice.

"He's in the back. I can call him."

"No need, I can just wait," he said without looking up.

"Alrighty then," I said quietly.

What a strange man I thought to myself shaking my head. I sat down and went back to my phone, but I couldn't concentrate because he was just standing there with his eyes burning a hole in my face.

I looked up from my phone and glanced up at him, and this time I could see his face.

"I heard someone come in," Mr. Moretti called out.

"A customer is waiting to see you," I yelled back ripping my eyes away from the strange man's face.

Mr. Moretti's footsteps came closer and closer until he was standing right next to the man.

"Good to see you again Liam. I haven't seen you in a while," he greeted the man.

The man took off his cap respectfully and shook Mr. Moretti's hand. "I've been...working."

"It's good to see you back."

The man nodded and smiled.

I frowned at the strange interaction happening in front of me. The cold man I was dealing with suddenly disappeared, and was replaced by this polite gentleman.

I scoffed realizing that he was probably racist. I shook my head and chuckled to myself. It was funny how quickly his attitude changed when he was speaking to me, and when he was talking to Mr. Moretti. Just like the secretary.

Mr. Moretti and the man looked at me with a frown on their faces.

"What happened?" Mr. Moretti asked confused.

"Nothing, absolutely nothing," I said smirking a little.

Mr. Moretti nodded slowly not believing me, but he turned back to the man in front of him.

The man, however, didn't look away. He kept staring at me frowning his eyes so intense that it forced me to look away.

I saw his face fully now. He had golden-brown hair and intense emerald eyes. I've seen him before, but I wasn't sure where.

"Here for a new notebook?" Mr. Moretti asked the man. The man nodded.

"You sure do write a lot."

"Yes..." the man said scratching the back of his neck awkwardly. "I need it for my job, and there's a lot of things I need to remember, so I write them down."

Mr. Moretti nodded at the man. "I have bigger note-books in the back. I'll go find them for you."

"Thank you," the man said.

Mr. Moretti disappeared to the back leaving me with the stranger.

I looked away quickly before he saw me watching him, and pretended to be occupied with my phone.

He walked towards the counter and leaned against it. He traced the desk with his fingers this time staring at me. His glare was so intense it felt like he was shooting lasers out of his eyes.

I shuddered in my seat not liking the way this man was making me feel. I forced myself to look at him to show I wasn't intimidated by him. He didn't look away.

"I've seen you around here before," he confessed. "You were new here then."

I frowned not remembering.

"You were wearing a white shirt and black jeans. I think it was your first time coming to the store."

I tilted my head to the side trying to remember what he was talking about.

"Ah," I said suddenly remembering. He was the man outside the store the first time I came here. The man with the striking eyes.

"It's weird that you remember what I was wearing," I said creeped out.

He laughed, a deep sound erupting from the pit of his stomach. "I have a good memory. I'm not a creep or anything."

"Yeah sure," I said raising my eyebrows not believing him.

He smirked at my comment but said nothing back. Instead he continued to analyze me.

"Mr. Moretti has been gone for a while. I'll go see where he is." I got up and sprinted to the back. The thought of spending one more second with this man sent chills down my spine. I walked between the shelves and saw Mr. Moretti walking my way.

"Found them," he said holding the notebooks high.

"I came to find you. You were gone for a while."

"I'm an old man. Climbing up and down the latter is not as easy as it once was," he stated.

"I can help out," I told him.

He shook his head quickly. "There's no need, but thank you."

I shrugged. "Okay."

We walked back to the front where the man was standing exactly where I left him.

"Weirdo," I muttered to myself.

"What?" Mr. Moretti asked turning to me.

"Nothing," I said quickly shaking my head.

"Here you go." Mr. Moretti handed the notebook to the man. "Would you like a couple? It would save you the trip of coming here every time."

"No, no," the man said. "I like coming here. I'll take one for now."

"Sounds good. Let's ring you out shall we?"

I leaned against the counter thinking about the man who came into the store earlier.

"That guy is creepy," I told Mr. Moretti.

"He's mysterious, but he's a nice kid, a smart kid."

I laughed. "He's not a kid. He's old, and he's really creepy."

"No offence to you. You're old, but a kind old man," I said quickly.

"Being old is not offensive. Old is just another word for wise and prodigious. I lived longer, therefore I am more experienced in life than you. Yet these young people try to undermine us," he said jokingly.

I laughed.

"Wouldn't you say when you were young you undermined the elderly?" I asked.

"No. I understood the knowledge that elders held. So, I respected them and went to them for guidance. It's more prevalent now when someone becomes old, they get thrown aside.”

I nodded understanding what Mr. Moretti was saying.

“My parents always taught me to respect the elders,” I told him. “That’s why I always come here, so I can learn from you. A man who has spent all his life surrounded by books must be brilliant.”

He paused pondering what I said.

“Intelligence is a funny thing,” he said. “How do you determine intelligence? Who decided how intelligence is measured?”

I was silent not knowing what to say. I’ve never thought about it.

He smiled slightly, “I believe that intelligence is not defined by the number of years you have spent in school, nor the number of books you have read. The intelligence we speak of is a concept that has been created to quash our creative mind. This idea of what intelligence is has become a tool to separate people into sections. Sections that determine their worth and their potential, not considering anything else but only what they’ve learned in school.

“Yes, someone might get straight A’s in school, but that does not make that person smarter than the kid who fails every class. Because knowledge is infinite, and intelligence cannot be measured by the few subjects they teach in school. All that does is limit the brain to seek out only what it already knows; it limits the mind to think only within the box. They even limited the ability to think in the confinements of a box. They tell us to ‘think outside the box’ but why is there a box at all?

“We are losing the ability to think freely. There is nothing wrong with asking questions. Curiosity is how we learn, yet people hate questions. That’s why most people have become zombies. All thinking the same way because they don't allow themselves to question anything. They don't even know why they think what they think, because they were told what to think. That's why people don't read anymore because schools have embedded that learning is a thing you will be tested for, so any knowledge you seek will eventually result in a test.

"It has become a punishment. They all think the same, 'what's the point of reading when I have to read in school anyway?' it has become unenjoyable. Intelligence and knowledge are subjective. Don't let them limit your brain to the things you are taught, but teach yourself. Seek knowledge for yourself not because you have to, but because you want to. You are a bright young woman, and I see you have fire behind your eyes. You are one to watch out for."

I sat in my bed that night thinking about what Mr. Moretti said. This is the third time I have been left sleepless because of him. He always says things that make me question everything. Like how the concept of time is measured. Who decided what ten minutes feels like? What does me getting 80% on an exam even mean? What does that calculation entail? Who decided? I actually want to know. Who decided that two hours had gone by since I first got into bed?

"Ugh," I groaned.

I hated that I was questioning everything. I felt crazy even thinking about these things.

I shook my head in annoyance. My brain was in overdrive, and it wouldn't calm down.

"I really need to stop hanging around that man," I said.

I looked at the clock on my bedside table.

"Crap," I muttered.

The clock read 2:30 am and I only had five hours left until I had to get up for school. Eventually, the dizzying thoughts in my mind were silenced by the strong presence of sleep.

Chapter 9

I looked at the blinking cursor on the blank screen in front of me. "So exactly what am I supposed to write about?"

The way it appeared and disappeared every second annoyed me more than it should have. I felt like it was taunting my lack of ideas.

"Anything about social justice," Matthew replied.

"That was very helpful. Thank you for the insight," I said rolling my eyes.

"You're welcome. Don't think anything of it," he trolled.

"Come on Matthew, how the hell am I supposed to write about social justice when I'm only allowed to write about the school. There are no stories here. It's stale, no seasoning, dry, bori—"

He laughed leaning back in his chair. "Okay I get it."

"How about you talk abo—"

"I know!" I sat up suddenly excited that I finally had an idea.

"You're welcome."

I rolled my eyes at his comment.

"Okay," I said to myself facing the blank page that was

mocking me.

I planned out my article for the next hour not stopping once, because of the fear that my ideas would scatter. I already missed the first two weeks of publishing because I had nothing. Thankfully, I got away with it because my column was not as crucial as the "weekly events" or "sports" columns that were the most popular in the newspaper. They weren't interested in social justice, and they didn't care– but I would make them care.

"We're going to have to change the template for next month." Brianna entered the office and sat on her desk.

"Deadline is October 3rd. So, we have exactly a week to come up with ideas."

"Aren't we just going to make it Halloween themed?" I asked.

"Well yeah, but it can't be anything we've been doing. It needs to be nice. It needs to be aesthetically pleasing. Do you guys have any ideas?"

"Keep it simple, minimal, make sure there aren't any colour clashes. White background, black headlines, orange subtitles. A pumpkin and a bat on the corners of the pages."

"Okay, Aaleyah will take care of changing the theme this month then!" Brianna exclaimed.

"Sounds good." I looked at the clock realizing that it was almost five. "I'm gonna get going guys. See you tomorrow."

"Bye," they both said in unison.

I waved at them as I left the room. I walked down the deserted hallways enjoying the peace and quiet. I wasn't being scrutinized by anyone's gaze. The school wasn't bad when no one was in it.

I opened the double doors of the school and walked towards my car. The parking lot was deserted other than a few other cars waiting for their owners. I could see there were people inside the car beside mine. I hoped they didn't look at me. Today was oddly peaceful, and I wanted it to stay that way.

I watched the passenger door open, and the guy who terrorized me in the cafeteria my first day stepped out. He slowly walked towards me giving me a menacing smirk.

"Well, well, well. Look who it is," he said as his two minions walked behind him.

I closed my eyes bracing myself. He was lucky I didn't knock his teeth out that day in the cafeteria. I opened my eyes my stomach churning at the sight of their faces. The only reason I held myself back was because people were watching.

"I've been waiting to find you alone." He lowered his head slightly bending over and looked at me dead in the eyes. "You've been hiding."

I pulled back.

"First of all, your breath smells," I said, scrunching my face in disgust. "Secondly, don't concern yourself with me."

He looked at me startled that I said anything back to him. I don't blame him. He misread me the first day. Which is my fault, because I kept my mouth shut. Not that I was scared–okay maybe a little–but I was more shocked than scared. I've never been in a situation like that.

I walked past him only to feel myself getting yanked back.

I bit the inside of my cheek and stared at his hand tightly gripping my wrist.

I wrenched his hands off my wrist and twisted his fingers. Pulling hard enough for him to shriek in pain, but not enough to cause any actual damage.

"So what we're not gonna do is grab people unless you want your fingers broken." I twisted a little bit more to make a point.

"Okay okay!" he cried out in pain.

I let go and crossed my arms giving him a firm stare daring him to try anything else.

"This isn't over," he spat.

I rolled my eyes. "Whatever."

He stomped away like a child with his two minions following.

I walked towards my car quickly. I didn't have time for any more altercations. I knew I probably shouldn't have challenged him like that, and his fragile ego was probably in shambles right now—but I couldn't help it. How dare he lay his hand on me?

Now I knew I had to watch my back. He didn't seem like the type to back down easily.

"Maybe I should include this in my article," I said out loud feeling anger rush through me.

"Not a good idea. You'll start a war," Matthew said.

I was on a three-way call with Brianna and Matthew. I called them as soon as I got home to ask them if it was a good idea to include today's events in the school paper, and they both decided against it.

"You can generically talk about the treatments you've been getting since you moved here, but nothing specific. You don't want too much attention on you during your first submission. Ease into it," Brianna advised.

"Okay. Sounds good. Thank you Brianna. Ever the wise woman."

"You know me. I am the best at everything I do."

"Okay, let's dial it back a bit. We're sounding a little cocky here."

Their laughter erupted through the line.

"Gotta go. Food is calling," I told them.

"Mmmm, this is so good." I practically inhaled the food down. I hadn't realized how hungry I was until the delicious smell of my mom's cooking infiltrated my room.

"Say *Bismillah*," mom warned. "And slow down, nobody is going to eat your food.

"So how is school going?" dad asked.

"Classes are boring, but we're reading an interesting book in English. It's called Passing, and it's about two African American women who pass as white in the 1920s. After we read the book, we have to write a book report."

Dad nodded. "Sounds interesting."

"Yeah honestly I would have been mad if we read one more Shakespeare play. The man is dead. Let us move on."

My dad chuckled. "Come on. Shakespeare isn't that bad."

"It's very bad."

"I thought you said you liked Macbeth in grade ten?"

"It was alright, but they really need to expand their literary selection. It's a bit outdated," I said truthfully.

"How's the school newspaper going?" mom asked.

"Good. I finally came up with a topic. I missed two weeks, so I'm glad I finally have something to write about. It's hard though. I barely have room to talk about anything important."

"I'm glad you joined a club. I was worried that your senior year was going to be boring for you." Dad smiled.

"Dad, don't worry. I'm having fun believe it or not. Sure the first week was bad, but I joined a club and met some pretty cool friends. I don't really focus on the people in school anymore. I just mind my own business. I'm also doing well in my classes. Oh, and Mr. Moretti is really awesome."

"You talk about this Mr. Moretti a lot. I'm going to have to meet him," my dad said.

"Yeah he's pretty interesting, and the bookstore is really nice. You would like it," I told him.

"I should check it out," he said thoughtfully.

"You really should," I encouraged.

We spent the next two hours in the living room drinking tea and talking. We also Facetimed with Aamir. It was nice catching up with them, and I was glad I was able to talk to them about anything—even though I didn't tell them about what happened with the football players. I didn't want them to unnecessarily worry. They were already stressed, and I didn't want to burden them with my stupid problems. I could handle it on my own.

Chapter 10

I stared at my car in rage. "I am going to kill them. I swear to God the next time I see his face I'm knocking all his teeth out."

They had spray-painted the word "terrorist" in red and slashed my tires.

I put my hands on my waist pacing back and forth.

"What am I going to do?" I panicked.

"We should go to the police," Matthew fumed, a vain bulging out of his forehead.

I shook my head. "No, I need to talk to my parents first."

"Okay," Matthew said. "Come on, we'll walk you home."

"It's okay guys, I can walk home alone." I appreciated their support, but I didn't want to drag them into this drama. "Thank you though."

"Awkward, you thought we were giving you a choice?" he grabbed my backpack off the ground and started walking.

I watched him walk for a bit waiting for him to realize that we weren't following.

"Why aren't you guys coming?" he asked turning around.

"My house is that way," I said pointing in the opposite direction.

He rolled his eyes. "You could've told me that before I started walking."

Brianna looked around the house in awe. "Whoa, your house is huge."

"Come on, let's go inside. My mom will have some questions."

I opened the front door and called out to my mom.

"In the living room," she called back.

"Let's go," I said to my friends ushering them to follow me.

"*Asalamu 'alakum* mom," I greeted.

"Wa'aleykum salam sweety. Why is your face like that?" she asked.

She looked at Brianna and Matthew. "Are these your friends?"

I nodded and introduced my friends to my mom.

"What's up?" mom asked after we all sat down.

"Well..." I trailed off. "Something happened at school."

She frowned. "What?"

I told her about what happened to my car while avoiding eye contact.

"Start from the beginning, and don't leave anything out," she said going full lawyer mode.

I told her the whole story including what happened yesterday. I didn't think that our little encounter yesterday would have caused them to ruin my car. I'm surprised they took it that far.

"Do you two have anything to add?" My mom turned to

Matthew and Brianna ready to take their statements.

"No ma'am," Matthew said.

Brianna shook her head.

"Okay." My mom nodded.

"Your dad and I will take care of this. You Aaleyah, will under no circumstances engage or retaliate. Do you understand me?"

"Yes, I promise," I said.

"Okay," mom sighed. "Why didn't you tell us this was happening?"

"I know, I'm sorry. I thought I could handle it. I didn't think it would turn out like this."

Mom nodded. "Don't worry about your car sweetie. Thank you Brianna and Matthew for walking her home. She thinks she's invincible and can take care of everything herself."

"No problem ma'am. We're just happy to help," Matthew said.

"You can call me Nawal."

"Yes, ma'am."

Mom finally smiled. "I'm going to call your dad. You two are welcome to stay."

"We should get going, but thank you." Brianna got up along with Matthew.

I walked them to the door. "Thank you guys for today."

"It was really nothing. We're just sorry for what happened to you." Matthew gave me a sad smile.

"Yeah Aaleyah we're your friends," Brianna said as she pulled me into a hug.

"Awe group hug!" Matthew yelled as he joined making us all laugh.

"Call us and tell us what happens." Brianna pursed her

lips. "Do you think it's a good idea for you to publish your story?"

"A hundred per cent. I was worried before, but I have to do it. They can't push me into a corner."

Matthew nodded. "Okay but let us know what we can do to help."

"No Matthew. You guys can't get involved. I don't want you to get hurt."

"You're not doing anything without us. We got your back. Besides, this is our senior year, and I have spent seventeen years sitting back and allowing these bullies to trample all over us. I can't leave this place without a bang," he confessed.

Brianna nodded agreeing. "It's about time someone puts them in their place."

"Okay but you guys are making it seem like we're going to get revenge or run some covert mission. I'm not going to retaliate. I'm just writing about what happened to me."

"Whoever reads it reads it." I shrugged.

"Okay, but you do realize that is retaliation, right?" Matthew asked.

I shrugged. "More like being a good journalist, but it's subjective. You can look at it however you like."

"Aren't you going to get in trouble?" Brianna asked worried.

"I'm going to talk to my parents, but they probably won't want me to do it. They'll want me to remain low key, but I'm not wired that way." I bit my bottom lip thinking. "I just need to convince them."

"Yeah, it'll be alright," I reassured myself.

Brianna looked at me assuringly. "Good luck."

"Thank you." I forced a smile.

"We should get going," she said.

"Bye guys!" I waved at my friends opening the gate to late them out.

I closed the door and braced myself to face my mom alone.

"I talked to your dad, and he'll be here soon. In the meantime go change and eat some food."

I nodded dreading my dad's reaction.

"Come here." Mom pulled me into a hug melting down the barriers I've been holding up.

I let the tears I was holding in run free. I was trying to be strong, but I was overwhelmed with so many emotions, and they released when my mom embraced me.

I pulled away from the hug and wiped my tears. "I'm okay."

Mom stroked my face.

She looked at her watch. "It's *Maqhrib*. Pray, eat and take a nap. I'll wake you up for *Isha*. You don't have to go to school tomorrow, and I won't go to work. We can plan and chill around the house."

"But if I don't go to school they'll think they won," I protested.

"They won't win, because planning and taking the time to make a concrete plan is better than being hasty. Even if that means taking time off. What happened to you was traumatic, and I want you to take at least one day off before you go marching into battle."

"I guess I can do that," I sniffled.

I hugged my mom one more time then ran upstairs to my room. I changed into comfy clothes, prayed, and ate. Then I sat at my desk to write my article. I was feeling very motivated, and I needed to write to vent my frustration.

I needed to see how this would play out for the next few days. I planned my article and uploaded the pictures to my computer.

I looked at the clock and realized it was time for *Isha* and I got up to pray.

After finishing my prayer I retired to my bed. I had the worst headache that would only get better after much needed sleep.

Chapter 11

I stayed at home with my parents, and I'm glad I did. We spent the entire day lounging around and watching Netflix.

"Okay, so what's the plan?" I asked my parents.

"Well, I'm going to talk to the school and find out what happened. Your father will report the incident to the police if the school doesn't do anything about it. Be warned, they most likely won't do anything. We'll have to take matters into our own hands."

"I stopped by the school when I was coming home yesterday," dad said. "There was a camera right where your car was vandalized. I knew it was working because it was a motion detecting camera. I took a video of the camera moving just in case they say it's not working."

"Wow dad," I said impressed.

He shrugged trying to be cool. "You have to cover all your bases."

Mom rolled her eyes.

"Okay fine. It was your mom's idea," he confessed.

"Anyway," mom said. "Aaleyah, your father and I talked

last night. We would like it if you stopped writing on the school paper."

"Mo—"

"Let me continue," mom said cutting me off. "But we both knew how that was going to play out. You would try to convince us saying that 'you need to make these decisions for yourself because adulthood is full of making hard decisions.'"

"That argument is becoming a little redundant," she continued.

"But it works," I said pleased with myself.

She shook her head and let out a sigh. "Aaleyah, you're almost an adult. We trust that we raised you to be smart. Continue with the newspaper and publish whatever you want. We won't stop you."

"Thank you," I squealed as I hugged my parents. "I promise I won't do anything crazy, and I'll be careful."

"I need to go call Iman," I kissed my parents and ran to my room.

"It's only been a month, and your life is already hectic," Iman said when I FaceTimed her.

She couldn't believe everything I was telling her.

"Enough about me, what's going on with you guys?" I asked.

"Girl, let me tell you," Iman said getting excited to tell me about all the drama I've missed.

I spent the next three hours talking to Iman only stopping when I needed to pray or eat. We finally hung up because it was getting late, and she didn't start her homework yet.

I decided that I should probably do my homework too. My mom called the school, and my teachers emailed me the required homework for tomorrow. I thought that maybe they'd give me an exemption, but these people are clearly heartless.

I scrolled through Twitter taking a break from all the homework my teachers assigned. Twitter was always poppin' late at night, so it wasn't hard to get sucked in.

I kept scrolling and only read things that would not disturb me and my sleep.

"Interesting," I muttered.

I clicked on the article that grabbed my attention and read through it. The title read "Annual Journalist of the Future Competition". I continued reading the article interested in the competition. It was geared towards high school students. All they needed to do was submit a story before February 23rd, and the winner would get their story featured on the national news and get published in places like The New Yorker. There was also a cash prize of 10,000 dollars. I saved the link so I could talk to Brianna and Matthew about it.

They always talk about finding ways to set themselves apart when applying to university, and what better way than to win a huge competition that would feature our story.

"Ugh," I groaned when I realized I wasted a whole hour on Twitter.

I quickly went back to my homework, so I could finish at a decent time. By the time I finished all my work and planned the theme change for next month, it was already 11 o'clock. I decided since tomorrow was going to be a long day, I should sleep.

"Your mom is so cool," Matthew said leaning against his locker the next morning.

I filled them in on what had happened yesterday. We met up at their locker since it was closest to all of our classes.

"Everyone is staring at you Leyah," Brianna turned towards me. "Don't let them bother you."

I shrugged. "Don't worry I'm starting to get used to it."

"We should get going to class," Brianna said closing her locker.

I walked to my class with Matthew and Brianna.

Things have changed since we became friends. It wasn't intimidating walking in the halls anymore, and I stopped avoiding my locker. Becoming friends with them ruined my plan of staying invisible, but I was okay with it. Eating under the tree wasn't bad, but doing it every day for the next few months would have been dreadful.

I ignored everyone's questioning glances as we walked to our classes. We walked past the football players. They were leaning against the lockers avoiding eye contact. It took every ounce of strength I had in me to not confront those idiots. I'm not normally violent, but I wanted to knock their teeth out one by one.

"Come on keep walking." Brianna pulled me along because I stopped to give them the death glare.

"They're not here," I told them once we stopped walking. "The three guys who tried to corner me in the parking lot. They weren't with those guys."

I was sure they were avoiding me. Which is smart because if I saw them I might have snapped.

"What time is your mom coming?" Matthew asked pulling me away from my thoughts.

"Around ten," I answered.

"Keep us posted," he said.

"I will." I looked at my phone to check the time. "The bell is going to ring soon. I'll see you guys later."

I sat in class waiting for the call that would set me free.

Meanwhile, I had to force myself to pay attention to the instructions of the book report. I kept looking at my phone every minute waiting for the time to move. It's been only fifteen minutes since class started, but it felt like hours.

"Any questions?" Mr. Smith asked.

"We can say anything we want about the book?" someone called out.

"Yes, but you need to make sure to back up your claims," Mr. Smith answered.

"Any more questions?" he continued.

He waited for a few seconds before moving on. "Okay, let's continue."

Instead of talking more, he put on a video to pass the time. I stared at the screen in front of me not paying the slightest bit of attention. The video had nothing to do with what we were learning in class, and I couldn't text without him seeing me because I sat in the front.

Finally, after ten minutes the phone rang. My stomach churned when the teacher looked at me.

"I'll send her out," he said.

"Aaleyah you're needed in the principal's office."

I nodded and put my books in my bag. I ignored all the questioning looks I was getting from the other students.

I walked down the empty hallway. My hands were shaking, and my stomach was in knots. I had no reason to be nervous, but I was. I was scared things would not go as planned. I had a feeling those jerks would get away with what they did.

I walked through the doors of the front office.

"I'm wanted in the principal's office," I told the Grinch.

She got out of her chair and walked towards a door not instructing me to follow. I rolled my eyes expecting nothing less.

"Come in Aaleyah, have a seat." The principal motioned me to a chair beside my mom.

I went inside hesitantly. This was the first time I've met the principal, and I didn't think it was ever going to be under these circumstances.

"It's nice to meet you Aaleyah. I'm Principal William," he introduced himself.

I nodded and looked at the plaque on his desk, "William L.P.," it read.

"Levi-Pedleford," he said. "It was too long to fit on the plaque. People just call me Mr. William here."

I nodded.

"I'm sorry to hear about your car. Could you please run us through what happened." The principal paused. "It seems rather odd that your car was targeted. It must have been random."

I scoffed.

I knew they would try to twist the story, but I didn't think they'd be this upfront about it.

"It wasn't random. They knew it was my car," I said sternly not blinking.

"I just can't imagine them doing something like that. Those boys are sweethearts, but please continue," he said with a dry tone.

I told him about my first day of school, the cafeteria incident, and what happened in the parking lot–which I knew was the main reason they vandalized my car.

He nodded. "I see."

"I would like the cameras pulled up. It seems as though you don't believe my daughter. The cameras should show you everything," my mom demanded.

"The cameras, uh yes. We have been having trouble with the cameras lately. I'm not entirely sure it captured everything."

"The cameras are working," she challenged him as she pulled out the video that my dad took the other day.

"I'm sure you'll be able to find the footage." She handed him the phone.

"Ah, yes." He took the phone from her hand and watched it.

"We'll sift through the footage and contact you if we find anything." The principal got up and handed back her phone.

He quickly ushered us out of the office. "Again, I am deeply sorry this happened, we will do everything in our power to get to the bottom of this," he said with no sincerity in his voice.

My mom and I stood there stunned at what happened.

"Did he just—"

"Yes, he did," mom said as she walked into the hallway. "Don't worry. Your dad and I will figure this out."

"Okay, but he seems suspicious. They'll probably delete the footage."

"Yes, but the parking lot is adjacent to the street meaning there must be traffic cameras," mom said.

"So?" I asked narrowing my eyebrows in confusion.

"We tried handling this through the school. Now we'll handle it through the police. They'll have to check the cameras."

"Really mom, the police?" I dreaded.

"It's our only option."

"It's not our only option," I insisted.

"What do you mean honey?" she asked

I took a deep breath. "I mean, we can just let this go."

My mom frowned. "Why on earth would we do that?"

"Because sometimes we just have to pick our battles, and this battle isn't worth it," I said feeling defeated.

"They'll think they won," my mom warned.

"I just don't think it's worth it. There's no point in exhausting our efforts when we know what the results will be. You saw how the principal acted. I can't even imagine the police, and honestly, I don't want to get involved with them."

"This is our only option," I continued.

"Look at you." She kissed me on the forehead. "I'm proud of you sweetie."

"What do you think?" I asked my mom.

"It doesn't matter what I think. If this is what you want to do, then I support you." She exhaled. "I agree with you. After talking to him, I don't know how else this will go. Those boys will be protected. If a school principal is like this, then I can't imagine what the police department will say. Clearly, the boys are popular in this town." She gave me a comforting squeeze on the shoulder.

"What are you going to do now?" mom asked.

"I'm still going to write my paper. I can't let them stop me."

My mom looked at me proudly. "I'm sorry you're going

through this honey. It's your senior year, and you should be having fun."

"Don't worry. I'll be fine," I reassured my mom.

"Be careful. I know we said you can make your own decisions, but don't do anything stupid," she warned.

"Mom come on! When have I ever done something stupid?"

"Well, let's see. There was that time when—"

"It was a rhetorical question," I laughed. "I promise, I won't do anything you wouldn't do."

"But that doesn't give me room to do anything," I whispered.

"Hey!" mom pushed me jokingly.

"Kidding, kidding," I laughed.

"Okay, I'm going to get going. I'll see you later."

I nodded. "Okay, love you."

"Love you too."

Matthew and Brianna stared at me wearing a look of shock on their faces.

"Wait. Let me get this straight. You're not going to do anything?" Matthew asked.

I shook my head.

"Why?" he questioned.

"Because they're going to make it impossible, and it's not worth it."

Brianna exhaled sharply. "That really sucks. I'm sorry Leyah."

"It's okay. Now I know what kind of people we're dealing with," I said.

We spent the rest of lunch hanging out in the club room,

and thankfully nobody else came in during lunchtime. I laid back on the comfy black leather seats and zoned out while Matthew and Brianna bickered. I had a lot going through my mind, and I knew these next couple of months would be difficult. I was so over it.

"What are you thinking about?" Brianna asked.

I didn't realize they stopped fighting. Both of them were looking at me curiously.

"I don't know, something was off about the principal," I blurted.

"What do you mean?" Matthew whispered.

"Why are you whispering?" I asked laughing.

He shrugged. "I don't know. I thought you were going to feed us important intel."

I shook my head smiling.

"He was acting...weird. He didn't seem as shocked as I thought he would be, and he didn't defend them that much. All he said was they were nice boys. I don't know. I just feel like he knew they did it. Maybe I'm just crazy," I said.

"You're not. I wouldn't be surprised if he was in on it. They are all a part of the KKK together." Brianna shrugged like what she said wasn't a big deal.

I frowned. "What do you mean?"

"There have been rumours for a long time that the principal is the leader of the KKK, and he's recruiting kids from the school, but nobody knows for sure," Matthew said.

"No way." I couldn't believe what I was hearing. "There's no way."

I looked at them both. "Right?"

"I wouldn't be shocked if it were true. This town is shady. They don't like people asking too many questions. I always thought it was weird how the school newspaper had so many restrictions," he disclosed.

"But don't worry," Matthew continued. "It's all just rumours."

"But are rumours really ever rumours? They always start somewhere," Brianna pointed out.

"What are you saying Brianna?" Matthew asked.

"Him being the leader of the KKK, and recruiting students wouldn't be a stretch if he wasn't already a part of it," she stated.

"Wait, you're saying that he is?" Matthew paused for a moment.

"I'm sure all the adults in this town are," Brianna said.

"How big are they here?" I asked.

"Big," they both said simultaneously.

"Damn."

I thought back to the article I first read when I came to this town. It had been nagging at me for a while, but I never knew who to ask.

"Do you guys know anything about the disappearances that have been happening here and the towns near here?" I asked.

"A little, but nobody talks about it. This place is creepy. They act like it never happened, and the police don't investigate properly. All I know is at least thirty-five African American people have gone missing since 2000 in this town alone. That's a lot of people considering the population of African American people that live here. I don't know about the 1900s though. I couldn't find anything. It's like it's been deleted completely," Brianna said staring off into the distance.

"I wonder what happened to them?" I asked quietly.

"Did you guys know a boy named Lewis? I was reading

an article about this town and saw that he disappeared only two years ago," I wondered

Matthew and Brianna looked at each other, and sorrow washed over their faces.

"Yes we did," she said her voice breaking.

Matthew hung his head low looking at his hands. "Lewis was our friend. He went missing in November during our sophomore year. He vanished without a trace," he explained.

I stared at them shocked. "I'm so sorry."

She nodded. "I tried to investigate it, but they shut me down. It's bothered me that there were so many inconsistencies in the story. They swept it under the rug, and I haven't been able to forget it."

"I'm sorry you guys," I repeated.

I decided not to pry. The look on their faces told me they did not want to talk about it. I needed to wait until they were comfortable telling me.

"They barely covered it in the local newspaper," Matthew spoke up.

I nodded not saying anything more.

"Come on." Matthew jumped up pulling us away from our thoughts. "We should get going."

Chapter 12

That night the only thing on my mind was the conversation I had with Brianna and Matthew.

I researched about Lewis, but I barely found any information. The police closed his file within a week. A person disappeared without a trace, and nobody in this town cared. I guess I shouldn't be surprised. These disappearances were nothing new here.

I tossed and turned in bed all night. My thoughts were keeping me awake. I knew there was an alarming number of KKK activities in this town, but I could not believe that a principal of a school could be the leader. You are an educator for goodness sake. What could you possibly get out of recruiting kids? It just didn't make sense. I wondered if Lewis' disappearance had anything to do with the KKK, but I knew that it most likely did.

I tried to dispel these thoughts keeping me away from sleep.

"Racism in Gregory Thomson High school and the

lack of intervention from the school administration," Brianna read aloud. "Wow."

"Is it too much?" I scrunched up my nose in deep thought. "I should probably change it."

"No. It's perfect," she reassured me. "You said you didn't want them to silence you, and they didn't.

"I feel like I'm asking for trouble," I said.

"We got your back. Don't worry," Brianna comforted me.

I nodded biting my nails feeling nervous.

"I'm just glad I finally have something to write about," I told her.

"You should be proud," she said. "Nobody has ever stood up to them the way you did. Don't let them keep you from speaking up. They've done it for long enough. It's time someone put those bullies in their place."

I smiled. "Thank you. That makes me feel better."

She smiled back. "Come on let's eat. Lunch is almost over."

The next few days went by slowly—a bit too slowly. I needed to get my article out there so I could stop anticipating the backlash. Maybe it would not be as bad as I thought it would be.

"Are you ready?" Matthew asked.

"Do it." I was bouncing my knee up and down trying to calm my nerves.

"This week's article goes live in three, two, one," he counted.

"It's done. You can open your eyes now," he teased.

"Shut up," I said pushing him slightly. "I'm glad that's

finally done. I feel like I can breathe now."

"I don't think this is going to be healthy if this is how it's going to be each time. You're too young to have a heart attack."

"This is my first time my article is going on the school news site, and the topic I chose could get me in trouble," I defended myself.

"I think it's brave. Maybe a little stupid, but that could be overlooked," he noted.

"Thank you," I said sarcastically. "That makes me feel so much better."

He smiled. "You are quite welcome. What are friends for."

I rolled my eyes. Even though I was feeling better, I still couldn't shake the nerves.

"Hey don't worry. We got your back," Matthew reassured me sensing my nerves. "Now eat your food."

"Yes sir." I pulled out my sandwich and ate.

"What are you a mouse? Stop nibbling on your food." He shook his head.

I coughed almost choking on my food. "You sound like my mom," I laughed.

I took a big bite out of my sandwich.

"Happy?" I asked between mouthfuls.

"Much better." Matthew chuckled.

We sat on the couch discussing the aftermath of my article. School went by surprisingly smooth, and it was starting to worry me.

"It's Monday, and nothing happened since we published the article. Do you think they read it?" I asked.

"They read it," they said in unison.

"Nothing strange happened?" Brianna asked.

"Nope. Aside from the stares and whispers, nothing significant happened."

"That's good!" Brianna nodded. "Maybe we're reading too much into it."

"Let's celebrate. You guys want to come over?" I asked. "We can watch a movie or something."

"I can't today. I'm helping my mom out at the hospital, but I can tomorrow," Matthew said.

"Tomorrow?" I asked Brianna.

"Sounds good," she confirmed.

"Okay. Tomorrow it is."

Mr. Moretti read the article and peered at me through his glasses. "You're a brave girl."

"I couldn't just let them get away with it," I whined.

"Brave is good," he laughed.

"It's weird because they haven't done anything. I was expecting some backlash, but I guess I'm being paranoid."

"No." Mr. Moretti looked at me with a serious look. "Just because they have been quiet does not mean they are not going to retaliate."

"Keep your eyes open," he warned.

"Yeah," I nodded. "You're probably right."

Chapter 13

The next two weeks went by quietly, but we were still on edge. Saying we were paranoid was an understatement. It was almost Halloween, and the town was getting ready for their annual Halloween bash. This town took Halloween seriously. The school was also getting prepared for the Halloween dance and haunted house.

Every house was decorated. Even the school was almost unrecognizable. I felt like my article posts have been overshadowed by the excitement of Halloween, and I wasn't mad about it. The Halloween spirit was high which was definitely a good thing for us.

I walked down the hallway on Monday morning listening to everyone chattering with enthusiasm about their Halloween costumes. There were lots of posters on the wall displaying what a "suitable" Halloween costume was and what wasn't. It was mainly focused on what the girls should and should not wear, and there was a lot of emphasis on "modesty". Yet me wearing a hijab was a major problem. Wear too much, that's a problem. Wear too little—that's a problem. A girl can never win.

"You excited for Halloween?" Matthew asked when I reached his locker.

"Not really," I said scanning my surroundings. "My parents call it the devil's holiday."

"In this town it is," Brianna whispered.

"Yeah," Matthew agreed. "The devil in people becomes awakened more than it is now."

"Stay inside your house, and don't open the door for any trick or treaters," Brianna warned.

"You guys are making it seem like it's the purge or something." I leaned against the locker observing my fellow schoolmates.

"Might as well be." Brianna shook her head disgusted.

I turned my attention back to them.

"Every year something happens. People lose control. There's looting, extreme public intoxication and vandalism," Matthew explained.

"We normally do our own thing at home. Far away from these weirdos, and even that isn't safe," he continued.

"I should tell my parents to skip work," I said anxiety creeping in.

"Yeah that's for the best. They don't want to be driving home when all the craziness is happening."

"Don't think about it too much," Brianna said interrupting my thoughts.

"When I think this place can't get any weirder." I shook my head.

"You haven't seen anything yet. You should see the Fourth of July," Matthew chuckled. "Come on. Let's head to class."

"I get my essay back today, and I'm so nervous. I hope I get a good mark," I told them.

Brianna put her arm around my shoulder. "You better get a good mark. Your paper was great."

"I hope so," I exhaled nervously walking away.

"See you later," Brianna said.

"Good luck!" Matthew shouted across the hallway.

I gave him a thumbs up chuckling.

I sat in English class waiting for Mr. Smith to hand back our essays. I listened to my classmates debate about Halloween and Paganism, but I was too preoccupied with my thoughts to listen to what was being said.

"Okay we'll stop here for today." Mr. Smith got up to retrieve the essays from his desk.

"Let's hand these back shall we?" he said holding the papers high.

I bounced my knee up and down anticipating my paper.

"Good job," Mr. Smith said as he placed the paper face down on my desk.

I took a deep breath before flipping to the rubric page. "Wow."

Right there, staring at me dauntingly, was the red marking that read C-.

I stared at my paper in disbelief.

I had a million things running through my mind. Why in the world would he tell me I did a good job if my mark was this low? I flipped to the first page to read his comments, but there was nothing there to explain why I received the mark I did.

I sat there numb until the bell rang, and as soon as it did, I walked to his desk to demand answers.

"What can I do for you Aaleyah?" he smiled.

It took every ounce of strength in me not to roll my eyes. His tone was condescending.

"I have a few questions about my mark. Do you have a moment?" I asked biting the inside of my cheek.

"Yes, but I don't want you to be late for your next class. I suppose I can write you a—"

"I have a spare block," I blurted interrupting him.

"Oh, okay, well then pull up a chair."

"Why did you say I did a good job if my mark was this low?" I asked.

"You did do a good job," he replied.

"For who exactly? It just seems like too low of a grade to be praised for, especially since you don't know about my writing capability. If I were a student who got lower marks then it would make sense..." I trailed off. "But that's not what's important right now."

"I'm sorry if that seemed offensive." He looked at me with what I knew was fake concern.

"It's okay," I said quickly before he could say anything more.

"What did you want to talk about?"

"I would like to ask why I got this mark," I told him.

"Okay, well Aaleyah, your central argument or focus is quite problematic, especially since you assume that Clare is black. When the book, and much of the criticism of the book focuses on the fact that Clare is just as white as she is black. Irene's problem is that she cannot accept this truth —about Clare and, thus, about herself."

"I'm sorry but can you clarify what you mean by 'Clare is just as white as she is black?'" I asked.

"Clare has a mixed heritage. She has European ancestry and African ancestry, and she looks white. As we discussed in class, the author is commenting on the fact that the black side of one's heritage tends to dominate. This is tied to the one-drop rule."

"Yes," I agreed.

"Which is obviously absurd."

I nodded waiting for him to continue.

"What Larsen shows is that race is largely a performance; Clare is only black when she is with other black people, just as she becomes white when with other white people. But there is nothing essentially black about Clare, or Irene - or, for that matter, anyone. Just as there is nothing essentially white about Clare, or Irene—or for that matter, anyone."

I nodded slowly trying to grasp what he was saying.

"In short, the book plays with the fact that most readers—especially in the 1930s, assume that Clare is black, even though there is no reason to view her as more black than white. In fact, in terms of appearance alone, she is more white. It is certainly possible to critique this presentation of race, or even to suggest that Larsen is actually interested in something else altogether. But any such critique first needs to start with the problem of race the novel seems to expose." He paused for a moment. "Make sense?"

A high pitched laugh escaped my mouth even startling me.

The caucasity...

My brain felt like it was being fried. Nothing he was saying made sense—not in the slightest bit. His arguments were flawed, and it confused me why he would pick this book if he didn't even understand the most basic knowledge about race.

"Aaleyah?"

"You mentioned that my central argument is problematic, but I disagree. I understand that Clare may be mixed race, but that's not relevant in this novel. Whether she is half white, quarter white, or one-eighth white, her black side will always be dominant. The topic I chose was 'what does Nella Larsen's passing teach us about race,' and my central argument stated that the ability to pass offers one safety and security in the dominant society, aka white society, and I stand by this argument.

"Clare gained privilege, security, and safety because she passed as a white person. The title of the book itself should be self-explanatory. It's implying that these women are identifying themselves as one thing and passing for something else. In other words, they are black but pass as white."

I grabbed the book from my backpack.

"Quoting the back of the book, it clearly states 'passing tells the story of two black women who cross the colour line,'" I read aloud.

"'Clare, light-skinned, beautiful, charming, has for many years passed for white, hiding her true identity from her racist husband'," I continued reading.

"By saying 'true identity,' the focus is not on the white part because at that time, what mattered was how much black was in you. Any amount of black blood was a problem—hence the one-drop rule."

I stopped talking to read Mr. Smith's expression. His mouth was pressed in a thin line, and I couldn't tell if he was concentrating, or if he was angry. Either way, I didn't care.

"I understand the implications of race and racism, and I recognize that this book is teaching us that being black in America, back in those times, and still today, was and is dangerous. Yes, race should not have mattered, but it did. Race is in the fabric of America. These women were not passing over for a mere performance, but to deal with life-threatening situations," I said my voice slightly breaking.

"Clare passing over as white was for her to gain security, and her reaching out to Irene and attending Irene's parties, were for her to come out and enjoy who she really was. By calling race a 'performance' really undermines and takes away the severity of the climate back then. For example, the lynching of black people, segregation, and the Jim Crow era. Black people were and still are not safe, and having a skin tone that passes as white was a privilege. Clare becoming white when she was with white people was not just a performance, but an act of survival. If the larger society ever found out that she was black, it would result in danger for her. The book always mentioned them as black women or African American women who passed."

I contemplated stopping since he was being unresponsive, but I said this much already. It wouldn't make sense for me to stop now, so I continued.

"The relevance, I believe Clare's mixed heritage had, was to show the readers that the white side did not guarantee any acceptance or safety from white society. We know in the book if Clare's racist husband knew about her true identity, he would not have cared for her being half white."

I stopped to flip through my essay to find a quotation I used from the book.

"In the book, when John found out about Clare's identity, he says, 'so you're a nigger, a damn dirty nigger!' John Bellow is a representation of white society and how they would react if they found out Clare was half black in a setting where she was passing. Her whiteness would never come into question no matter how white she looked because it would not matter at all."

"To be honest, I don't understand what you meant when you said there is nothing black or white about us," I confessed.

I calmed my nerves before I continued.

"I'm going to repeat that race is a social construct and should not matter, and biologically we are all one human race, but that is not the reality. Race had and still has an impact in this world. By saying there is nothing white or black about us is undermining and erasing the hardships and oppression that black people went and still go through. Larsen is making fun of the one-drop rule because in white society, they would never focus on her white side. To them, even if she had one drop of black blood, they would have considered her black."

"You mentioned the 'problem of race' and what the book is suggesting about race. I disagree with you. I think Larsen was trying to emphasize that even though these women were half white, it didn't matter, but their appearance did. That's what granted them to live a life of security. Mentioning that these women were half white would never have mattered to white society. The white was not the problem. In fact, the white was celebrated, but the black was the issue. It was seen as a contamination of white blood."

"I can go on, but I'll stop," I said feeling irritated as he gave me a blank stare.

"Well, thank you for that." He straightened himself out before he continued. "What you offered here was much more cogent than your paper."

"I do have a few reasons why I can't justify a mark

change," he continued.

"Well, for one thing, I have to be fair to all my students. I have to mark the paper, not any defenses that come later. Secondly, the argument problem is only one piece of the problem, there were several other problems that I will not get into. Thirdly, your central argument, for example, that Clare and Irene pass for security reasons is not really the problem.

"The problem is that you seem to assume, throughout, that Clare is essentially black. Such an assumption concerns the very nature of race and identity. Unless you modify your more overt claims–like saying 'Clare is black' or 'Clare's true identity', a reader is forced to assume that you, not society, not the book, but you believe that race is something inherent, something that exists before and outside cultural constructions. I have no problem with you believing this, or with you asserting it.

"However, since this book is very much about cultural constructions of race – and, contrary to your claims, it very much matters that Clare and Irene are half white. With that being said, I must stand by the mark I gave you on this paper. As I said, that mark reflects much more than some problematic claims or arguments, and I cannot take your counter-arguments here into consideration. I have to stop discussing this any further," he said quickly standing up from his chair ushering me out.

"Have a good day!" he said before shutting the door in my face.

I was left in the hallway with my jaw dropped open and in complete shock.

I scoffed in disbelief. Everything happened so quickly that I was having a hard time wrapping my head around it.

"Wow…"

I had no idea where the conversation would go when talking to him, but I didn't expect it to go the way it did. He didn't try to understand what I was saying, and that pissed me off.

I rubbed my face almost believing I was asleep, but that wasn't the case. I was awake, and this for real happened.

I huffed as I walked down the empty hallway.

I walked as slowly as my long legs would allow me. I traced my hands down the lockers trying to make sense of what happened.

I finally reached the club room. I opened the door with the key Brianna gave me, and walked inside the only place in the school that gave me solitude. I'm surprised that it hasn't been trashed yet, but I guess I should count my blessings.

I plopped on the couch and exhaled with relief that I didn't snap at my English teacher. I used my alone time to make sense of everything that happened. I pulled out my paper to go over it again.

I woke groggy to someone shaking me. I opened my eyes to see Matthew and Brianna hovering over me.

"Wake up and move over," Matthew greeted me.

I sat up yawning and stretched my arms. I looked at the clock and realized that I slept for thirty minutes.

"I don't remember falling asleep," I confessed.

"You okay? You look a little…" Matthew waved his hands over his face trying to express how I looked.

I raised my eyebrows and shook my head not knowing where to start.

"I don't even know. I mean seriously where should I even begin."

"The beginning is always good," he said.

Brianna's jaw dropped as she looked at me wide-eyed. "Wow."

"Wow is right," Matthew agreed.

I filled them in on everything that happened with Mr. Smith, and the air in the room was thick with mixed emotions.

"It's not even about the mark at this point. It's the fact that he kept disregarding the themes of racial oppression and inequality. He kept saying that race was a performance. How dare he? Like why choose this book if you can't even understand what it's about?"

"And you know what the worst part is?" I asked facing my friends. "There's nothing I can do. Absolutely nothing. I'm completely powerless. I mean why assign an essay asking for our opinion just to disagree and impose your ideas. I don't get it. It's called an opinionated paper–it's my opinion."

I rubbed my eyes in frustration.

"I'm stuck with this mark, and I can't do anything about it. I thought the class was about exploring ideas. The mark is one thing, but him not trying to understanding anything I was saying really upset me. Or maybe he just doesn't care to understand."

I guess what angered me the most was that a white man was telling me–a black person–my ideas of what it means to be black was wrong.

"You stood up to him and set him straight. You made

sense while he didn't. He acted the way he did because you crushed his ego," Matthew said trying to comfort me.

I nodded.

Brianna leaned over and hugged me.

"Let's change the subject," I said sitting up trying to push away the negative thoughts that were consuming me.

I drove a few laps around town after school needing some space to let my thoughts run free. I missed my life back home a lot–even more at times like this. It sucked because I'm not as close to my friends back home anymore. You know what they say, 'distance is the greatest enemy'.

There was not much to talk about with them anymore. Their biggest concern was gossip and the things going on at my old school, and sadly I cant relate. It made me sad because I grew up with them, and at one point, they were everything I knew. Mom says I was growing up, but growing sucked.

I rolled down the windows to let the fall breeze in. I took a deep breath in letting my worries wash away with every exhale. The sunset was casting a glow on the orange leaves. The scene before me was stunning.

"*MashaAllah.*" I stared in awe at *Allah*'s art.

It's crazy how an awful day can be washed away with a drive and beautiful scenery. I made my way home feeling better than I did earlier.

Chapter 14

"You'll never guess what I overheard!" Matthew exclaimed bursting through the doors of the club room during lunch.

"What happened?" I said looking up at him.

"Don't get mad," he warned.

I looked at him suspiciously. "What..."

"I overheard some of the guys from the football team planning their Halloween costumes, and they're planning to do blackface."

I got up from the couch and marched towards the door.

Matthew ran after me and grabbed my arm stopping me dead in my tracks.

"What are you going to do?" he asked with a puzzled look on his face.

"I'm going to stop them," I said matter-of-factly.

"You have to be smart about this. If you stomp over there, they'll piss you off, and it might end up in a fight. The only person who's going to get in trouble is you," he warned.

"Are we not going to do anything?" I asked infuriated.

"No, but I have an idea. I thought about it while I was walking here," he said.

"What?" I asked.

He grinned. "We sabotage their body paint."

I looked at him confused. "How?"

"Leave it to me. They have practice at 4:30 today. In the meantime, I'll go to the science lab and whip a little something up."

"What are you going to do?" I asked him.

"All I can say is that their faces are going to itch like hell. Don't worry though it's not dangerous."

An involuntary grin spread across my face. "I'll do the honours," I volunteered.

"Are you sure? It'll be less suspicious if I do it," he said.

I nodded. "Oh I'm sure."

"Fair enough," Matthew agreed realizing he wouldn't be able to change my mind.

"This is very risky. You could get caught Aaleyah, and that won't be good for you," Brianna said concerned.

"Let's hope I don't get caught," I said my mind already made up.

"How are we going to do this?" I asked Matthew.

"I'm the lab assistant, and I have the keys to the science room. I'll just do it there. Brianna and I will meet you here after school. Move your car and park it at the back street right across the science lab. Stay there until I call you in—I'll open the back door for you," Matthew instructed.

We met back in the club room right after school.

"So, what are we going to do?" I asked.

"We'll go to the science lab first. Then Aaleyah will put

these on," Matthew said holding up a cap, a hoodie, and a pair of sweatpants.

I took the clothes from him.

"You'll sneak into the locker room while Bri and I are on lookout. You'll add my special liquid to their body paints and all over their clothes. Then we just sit back and watch," Matthew said with a twinkle in his eyes.

"Okay but where did you find these clothes?" I asked holding them up between my fingers.

"The lost and found, but don't worry they seem clean."

I scrunched my nose in disgust while I put them on.

Brianna and I stood outside the science lab while Matthew played mad scientist. I had no idea what he was mixing in there.

Brianna was restless biting her nails and looking around every second.

"Relax Brianna he's almost done," I reassured her.

She nodded taking her nails out of her mouth, and she took a deep breath to calm herself down.

A little while later, Matthew walked out with a bottle of clear liquid. "Come on, let's go to the club room."

"Okay Aaleyah, listen carefully. This is important," Matthew said.

I braced myself. "Okay."

"You only need a little bit—like a drop. Don't put too much." He pulled out black CSI type gloves from his pocket. "Put these on, and make sure the solution doesn't touch your skin or you'll be itching too. We don't want this being traced back to us. There are no cameras in the changing room, but there is one right outside, so you'll need to put your hood all the way down to avoid it. We don't need to worry about them checking the cameras unless they suspect someone sabotaged their face paint, which I doubt they will. We'll be on the lookout. Keep your phone on vibrate so we can warn you if someone comes."

"What do I do when I come back out?" I asked.

"We'll go back to the science lab, and exit from the back door. There's a dumpster right outside the lab. You dump the clothes there, and we run to your car. This is just for safety measures."

I looked at Matthew impressed. "You really thought this through."

"We have to make sure not to get caught. Wear the gloves, put on the cap and avoid the camera," he paused and took off his hoodie. "Put this on too."

"Why?" I asked confused.

"It'll make you look bigger than you are."

He looked at his watch and back at me. "It's time. I'll walk in first. I left my backpack in there earlier, so I can go in and check if it's empty. I'll walk out, and I'll text you if it is."

I waited for Matthew's text hiding in the empty girls' locker room which was right across from the boys'. I inhaled slowly to calm my nerves, but it was hard. My heart was beating so fast I could feel it through my chest.

My phone lit up with a text from Matthew. I closed my eyes and counted to three.

"Okay," I whispered to myself.

I dashed across the boys' locker room. I kept my face down avoiding the camera until I walked in.

I took out my phone to read the rest of Matthew's text.

There are three bags at the back of the locker room. That's where their stuff is.

I put my phone in my pocket and walked to the back of the locker room. I scanned around disgusted at how filthy it was.

I found the bags underneath a bench and crouched down next to it.

I pulled out the paint from the first bag and put a drop of the clear formula. I put some in their jerseys. I decided to spare them by leaving the formula out of their pants. I did two of the bags with ease. I opened the third bag when my phone buzzed in my back pocket.

"Shit!" I cursed when I saw the text.

Hide. Someone is coming!

I quickly closed the bag and put the bottle in my pocket. I looked around the locker room and found an empty locker in the corner. I ran to it, slid in side and closed it.

I heard voices and footsteps approaching, but I couldn't make out what they were saying.

"Where did you leave it?" one of them asked while entering the locker room.

"I don't know. Let me check my locker," the other one replied.

I tried not to breathe too hard, but my breathing quickened as his footsteps got closer.

He stopped right in front of the locker I was hiding in, and I could see him through the vents of the locker door. He opened the locker beside mine and rummaged through it.

"Can't find it," he called out to the other boy.

"Maybe I put it in here," he said putting his hand on the handle of the locker I was hiding in.

I squeezed my eyes shut waiting to be exposed. My heart was beating so loudly I was sure he could hear it.

"Found it!" the other boy called out before he could fully open it.

The boy backed away from the locker and ran to where his friend was standing.

"Where did you find it?" he asked his voice becoming distant.

"In the stall. I don't know why you took it in there in the first place," his friend replied.

Their conversation continued, but I stayed inside until I couldn't hear their voices anymore.

After what felt like an eternity, I squeezed out of the locker and hurried over to the last bag and quickly drizzled the liquid in their paint and clothes. I closed the bag and adjusted everything the way I found it.

I texted Matthew I was done. I waited for a few moments and ran out of the locker room. It was easier this time around because my back was turned towards the camera. I speed walked down the hallway pulling the hood to cover my face. I sprinted to the science lab, and exited through the back door. I took the bottle out of my pocket and chucked it in the dumpster. I took off the lost and found clothes Matthew gave me along with the gloves and tossed it.

I dashed towards my car. I smiled when I saw Matthew and Brianna already inside the car.

"I thought my heart was going to stop!" I shrieked.

"I was so scared. I thought you were going to get caught!"

Brianna exclaimed. "I could have just hacked the camera, and this would have been much easier."

Matthew shook his head. "We don't want to break the law Brianna. Let's go. We don't want the car to be parked for too long," he warned.

I started the car and drove.

"Wow, Matthew you are something else. You planned every detail out!"

He shrugged. "They deserve it."

"I can't believe we pulled it off." Brianna shook her head. "I really thought we were going to get caught."

"I can't wait for tomorrow," I said laughing.

"They're going to be so mad," Matthew chuckled.

Pulling this mission off was probably the most exciting thing I've done since I came to this town. Revenge never tasted so sweet. I couldn't wait to see their faces tomorrow.

Mr. Moretti sat there quietly as I filled him on the events of yesterday omitting the minor operation we carried out today. The adults didn't need to know.

"Why are you quiet?" I asked anxious.

I hate to admit it, but I valued this old man's opinions.

"I'm trying to make sense of everything you just said. You blurted it out not allowing me to digest it," he said with a blank stare.

"Okay," I said making a face.

"Okay," he said after a few moments passed.

"I'm not going to talk about your teacher or the book because he's an idiot. You deserve a better mark, and we both know that. However, I want you to prepare yourself for many more incidents like these since you're going to college next year. Yes, you'll have the choice to appeal, but sometimes that won't work in your favour. Aaleyah, I'm sad to say this, but you'll face many difficulties. There will be people working against you, and there will be roadblocks every time you see success. The world is not kind to people who look like you. In many ways, I'm your enemy as a white man."

I tilted my head and frowned.

He chuckled at my puzzled face, and paused for a long time before he continued. "I've lived a long life, and I've seen many things. The way I thought back then, and the way I see things now are completely different. I benefited from systems at the expense of many, and I still do."

I listened to what he said still feeling confused.

"I'm a man and I'm white. I've seen how this part of the world operates. Its gears are running on inequality, and it's fueled by hate. This won't be the only problem you'll experience. You will have people trying to silence you. But Aaleyah, when they try to silence you is the time you need to be the loudest. You're already such a confident, smart, and capable young woman. I don't want you to be discouraged."

I pinched the bridge of my nose. "What am I supposed to do? What can I possibly do?" I asked exacerbated.

"Everything and anything. You are going to make great changes, and you'll do great things. I'm just sad that I might not be alive to see it. Keep fighting back, but always remember pick your battles. You won't be able to fight them all, but I guess you already know that."

"Yeah," I said looking up at Mr. Moretti. "It sucks."

He nodded. "It does."

"Thank you. I should get home before my mom thinks I

was kidnapped."

"Remember to go straight home tomorrow when school ends. It's Halloween, and you don't want to be outside," he warned.

"I will. Bye!" I waved.

I made my way home after talking to Mr. Moretti. The conversation we had earlier replayed in my head.

"Ugh," I groaned annoyed that I couldn't get our conversation out of my head.

I drove the rest of the way preoccupied with my thoughts that I didn't even notice I made it home. I opened the gates of the house and parked the car in the garage.

I was glad when I saw my parents' cars were there.

It was almost dark, and I could feel all the crazies coming out of their homes to cause trouble. Halloween was tomorrow, but some people were starting earlier.

"I'm home!" I announced.

"In here!" dad called from the kitchen.

I dropped my bag on the staircase and went to the kitchen. I plopped down beside my mom on the stool and watched my dad cook.

"We were just talking to Aamir. He said he finishes his finals on the 11th of December. He'll be here around the 15th," mom said.

"Finally. I miss him," I confessed.

I laughed suddenly, a funny thought coming to my head.

"I can't wait to see his expression when he comes here. He always calls me dramatic every time I tell him how bad this place is," I explained.

My dad chuckled and shook his head. "He'll be shocked that's for sure."

"How was school today?" dad asked.

"It was good." I said quickly. "Nothing interesting happened. I can't stand looking at my English teacher in the face."

I changed the subject not wanting to spend too much time on what I did today. If they found out, I'd be in big trouble.

"He didn't treat you badly did he?" mom asked concerned.

Talking about Mr. Smith distracted them from asking any more questions about how my day went. My mom knows when I'm hiding something, so it was better to avoid the topic altogether.

"No," I said shaking my head. "He's very fake. He keeps smiling at me like nothing happened, but his eyes tell a different story. I think I angered him because I disagreed with him. He's a grown man. He can take his tears somewhere else."

"Aaleyah, please, keep your cool. Remember, he still has the future of your English mark in his hands," dad warned.

"There's no hope. I don't think I'm going to pass his class. That man is evil. I have to ace the SATs to make sure I get a mark that I can apply to university with."

"I wouldn't say evil Aaleyah," my mom said.

"You didn't see what I saw," I explained.

"And what did you see?" she asked.

"Evil, they're all evil. We're in a place full of devils," I threw up my hands

My parents looked at each other and rolled their eyes. I ignored them.

"Speaking of the devils, you guys should stay home tomorrow."

"Why?" he asked confused.

"It's Halloween, and apparently people here are psychos during Halloween. I don't want y'all out when all the craziness is going down."

My mom laughed. "If someone heard you they'd think you were the parent."

"I'm serious mom," I said my tone urgent. "I don't want anything to happen to you guys."

My mom smiled at me sensing my worry.

"We'll come home early," dad agreed. "You make sure to come straight home. Don't go anywhere else and drive straight home," he repeated.

"I will. I promise *inshaAllah*."

"Don't worry sweetie," my mom said rubbing my shoulder.

"I'm gonna go change," I told them.

We sat in the living room after we ate dinner and talked about random topics.

"How's work going?" I asked my dad. "What are you doing at your new job? I never really understood."

"I'm an engineer," he responded.

I shook my head and chuckled.

"I know that much. What kind of daughter do you think I am not knowing what her dad does for a living. I'm asking what you do at your company? Exactly what are you engineering?"

"To put it simply, a drug that regenerates damaged tissue," he explained.

I stared at him blankly.

He chuckled. "What that means is faster regrowth for damaged tissues."

"That's so cool," I said impressed.

"Why did they move you here by the way? Couldn't you have engineered the drug back home?" I asked.

"Well the company I worked for back home wasn't doing the things I'm doing now. It didn't pertain to the kind of engineering that I wanted to do. We both acknowledged that my talents were being wasted there. Which is the reason I am here now. We are working on different drugs that would benefit us medically in this job. It will completely reshape medicine as we know it. The reason why the facility is in a secluded area is because what we are doing is highly confidential, and if the drugs we are working on falls into the wrong hands, it would not be good. I shouldn't even be telling you guys this," dad said with a serious tone.

"You're a medical bioengineer?" I asked.

"Yeah. I specialize in tissue and genetic engineering," he replied.

I nodded impressed. "Cool."

"Yeah, Aaleyah. Your father is cool," he said shrugging and leaning back.

My mom and I giggled resulting in him glaring at us.

"What about you Aaleyah? Do you know what you want to do?" dad asked.

I groaned. "No."

I threw my head back leaning on the couch. I hated that I had no idea what I wanted to do with my future.

"How am I supposed to decide? I have absolutely no idea."

"Don't worry. You just need to figure out what you like." My dad patted my leg reassuringly. "It's okay to be lost."

"That's easy for you to say. Mom, you said you always wanted to be a lawyer, because you wanted to get justice for people. And dad, you were a science wiz—no surprise you pursued that. Aamir wants to play professional soccer, and is in the sciences like you. I, on the other hand, have no clue." I sighed my head hurt thinking about it. "Maybe I should follow one of your footsteps. I could see myself as a lawyer," I said stressed out.

"Aaleyah, the only person's footsteps you should be stepping into is your own. You're a bright young woman. You can be anything you want to be. Don't stress too much about it, yet don't settle either. Do only what you are passionate about," mom advised.

"Hopefully I figure out what that is soon."

"It'll come to you eventually. There's no point in stressing yourself out," mom replied.

"Yeah you're right." I nodded.

"How's it been being a professor?" I asked my mom changing the subject.

"It's different that's for sure, but I'm enjoying myself. Even though I'm the one teaching, I'm also learning a lot. I miss being a lawyer sometimes, but it's nice to branch out and try different things."

My dad looked at my mom sadness glazing over his eyes.

"Don't look at me like that," mom said to dad. "You'd do the same for me."

He nodded and smiled at her.

"It's late. We should get some sleep," mom said.

"You're right." I yawned and stretched my arms.

I got up and kissed my parents goodnight. I ran upstairs and collapsed on the bed. I was out like a light moments after my head touched the pillow.

Chapter 15

I walked down the hallway the next morning nervous. My heart was thumping loudly, and my stomach was in knots. I was terrified we would get caught.

My friends and I met at my locker since it was in the main hallway. We'd probably be able to get a glimpse of the football players there than anywhere else. I looked around as I walked down the hallway examining everyone's Halloween costumes. There was excitement in the air, and chatter was bouncing off the walls. Everyone was talking about their plans for the evening.

The transformation of the school was very impressive. Whoever was in charge of the decorations went above and beyond. The lights in the school were dim, and people with scary costumes would jump out at you with no warning, and it kept messing me up. I didn't have time to be on edge today. If I were at my old school, this would have been fun because I wouldn't have to worry about someone trying to hurt me.

It was funny because everyone was smiling and looked

so happy that I forget that ninety-nine per cent of them were racist. They looked sweet and innocent, but we all know devils are deceitful.

I waved at Brianna and made my way to where they were standing.

"Hey guys," I greeted smiling.

"You ready?" Matthew asked.

I nodded.

"We can't look suspicious, otherwise they'll suspect us. At the same time, they used actual paint and not body paint sooo..." he said trailing off.

We talked until we heard laughter and whistles coming from behind us. We turned around to see what the commotion was about.

"What up my niggas!" someone shouted.

The hallway erupted with laughter and giggles.

The guys walked down the hallway laughing and fist bumping people. I clenched my teeth in anger at the sight of their costumes.

Matthew patted my shoulder. "Keep your cool Aaleyah."

I nodded reassuring him I would not lose it and fight them.

I took a deep breath and swallowed the lump in my throat. The sight of their faces—smiling and laughing—sent lava through my veins. I wanted to march right up to them and unleash my lethal left hook square in the jaw, but I couldn't. I clenched my fist so hard that I dug my nails inside my palm, almost drawing blood.

I looked around at the students laughing and whistling, and I clenched my teeth hard.

I watched as a teacher came out of a classroom to see what was happening. When they saw the boys, they just chuckled and went back inside.

I couldn't believe it. I don't know why I was expecting a teacher to say or do something. Yet again, I was reminded of where I was. This is why we were taking matters into our own hands. This was something they probably did every Halloween, but this time I was there to see it.

I bit the inside of my cheek to compose myself. My stomach was churning with disgust, and all I wanted to do was scream at them. They had no care, nor saw a problem in what they were doing. The sight of them sent a level of fury I've never felt down my spine.

I closed my eyes and breathed slowly. The only thing holding me together was knowing by the end of the day, they'll be regretting putting that paint on their body, and they'll probably think twice before ever doing it again.

"Come on. Let's head to class," Brianna said pulling my arm to get me to walk.

We walked down the hallway ignoring the chaos around us.

"What up my nigga," one of them said holding his fist up waiting for a bump as I walked past him.

I closed my eyes when I heard what he said. I practically crushed my molars from clenching them so hard.

"God is really testing me today," I thought in my head.

Matthew tugged on my arm to keep me walking, but I couldn't.

"Keep calm Aaleyah," I said in my head.

I pulled out my phone and snapped a picture of all three of them.

"Yeah. Take a picture, people deserve to see how good we look," the boy in the front mocked.

I smirked and walked past them only to be blocked.

"Move," I warned.

"Or what?" he challenged.

"Move man," Matthew shouted stepping up clenching his fist.

The boys looked at us and hollered like hyenas.

"What are you gonna do?" he said lowering himself down until his face was inches away from mine.

"Knock you out that's what," I said stepping closer to him.

I knew I should have just walked away, but my mouth was already open before I even realized.

"I don't want to embarrass you in front of everyone. Now be smart and move out of the way," I warned whispering. "Your choice."

"Come on Aaleyah. Let's go around," Brianna pleaded. "They're not worth it."

I glared at them, but decided that I should listen to Brianna.

We tried to walk around, but they got in our way blocking us again.

A crowd formed, and people were eagerly watching anticipating what would happen next.

"Move." Matthew shoved the boy in the front hard making him tumble backwards crashing into the crowd.

A wave of silence fell over the crowd as the boy steadied himself and glared at Matthew. He signalled his goons to move out of the way.

"You dirty terrorist," he spat as soon as we walked away.

I paused and turned back around slowly. I didn't want to do anything, but my body was moving without my permission. Thankfully, both Matthew and Brianna didn't hold me back this time.

I walked back to where he was standing and stopped in front of him.

"Did that make you feel better?" I asked.

The best way to deal with entitled white boys like them was not to get angry. Even though I wanted to karate chop him in the throat, I decided against it.

"Yes it did," he said trying to act tough.

"But what would make me feel even better is ripping that towel off your head," he sneered.

The crowd cheered loudly for him.

I stepped closer staring directly in his eyes.

"Please give me a reason to beat you in front of all these people," I said loudly so everyone could hear.

"Ohhh!" a bunch of boys yelled.

"You're gonna let her talk to you like that?" someone shouted.

He looked at me shocked his face turning tomato red. I have never seen someone turn so red before. I don't know if it was because of anger, embarrassment, or both. His humiliation was relieving some of the anger I felt.

Lasers were shooting out of his eyes.

He walked towards me slowly. Matthew tried to step in, but I stopped him. I wasn't scared.

I could knock this boy out no doubt, but I didn't want to start a fight unless he came at me first.

"I'll kill you," he breathed his spit coating my face.

I could feel the anger radiating off him. His teeth were clenched, and his hands were balled into a fist. He stepped closer scowling at me with intense hate it almost sent shivers down my spine.

I wiped my face not breaking eye contact. I knew if I exhibited any sign of fear it would ignite his fire even more.

Instead, I glared right back showing him I wasn't intimidated. I stayed silent and just stared at the blue orbs planning my demise. I continued glaring with my arms crossed.

He was acting so tough, but in the end he did nothing.

He furrowed his eyebrows puzzled by my unbreakable eye contact. He stepped back uncomfortable.

I scoffed in his face.

The people watching us were confused at the exchange happening.

The confident guy was replaced by a scared little mouse. I could feel him racking his brain to find the meaning of what happened. He probably has never had someone stand up to him like this, let alone someone who looked like me. These boys walked around bullying whoever they could with no consequences. They were used to walking around the school like they owned it.

I walked towards him, and he stepped back a little. Not enough for anyone to notice, but enough for me to see I won.

"Don't ever try me again," I hissed piercing through his soul.

He clenched his teeth making his jaw moving up and down.

I turned to walk away but stopped and turned back around.

"Just one more thing." I pulled the afro wig off his head.

"Better," I said.

I walked to the nearest trash can, and tossed the abominable wig inside.

I could hear the students' chatter, but we kept walking without looking back.

"Man," I breathed my heart knocking on my chest.

I turned to Matthew and Brianna shaking my head. "I can't believe them."

"They have class with you right?"Brianna asked.

"Yeah two of them do," I replied.

We watched a Halloween movie in English class, and thankfully he let us sit wherever we wanted. I sat in the back of the class, so I could be on my phone peacefully. Everyone grouped up sitting with their friends which left space in the back with a few seats next to mine. The two boys from earlier entered the class. They scanned the room for somewhere to sit. Their eyes landed on where I was sitting. One boy smirked and leaned over to his friend and whispered something. His friend nodded, and they made their way to the seats near mine—even though there were plenty of other spots they could have sat.

They plopped down on either side of my seat, and got loud and obnoxious to disturb me, but the teacher told them to shut up.

I didn't get angry because it was so funny watching them. One guy was itching himself uncontrollably.

"Dude, I think I'm having an allergic reaction to this paint," he said to his friend.

His friend turned to him and inspected the itching boy. "You're fine dude. Don't be a baby."

I watched quietly in my seat. I texted Brianna and Matthew updating them. I spent the remainder of class texting back and forth with them trying to be stealthy so the teacher didn't see me.

"I'm starting to itch too. Shit!" the other boy cursed.

"See, I told you!" the first boy replied. "I need to wash

this off. I feel like my skin is on fire."

"What about the costume contest?!" the other boy asked.

"I don't care about the stupid contest. I'm going to wash this off!" He jumped from his chair, and ran to the front desk where the teacher was sitting. Then he dashed out the door, and shortly after, the other boy followed.

I sat back and watched my revenge unfold in front of my eyes. I wanted to laugh but I couldn't because it would seem suspicious. Especially since everyone seemed worried. I leaned back in my chair and giggled to myself.

"Okay class. See you Friday!" the teacher announced as the bell rang.

I got up to leave, but Mr. Smith held me back.

"Aaleyah, can you please stay behind."

I turned around and gave my teacher a puzzled look.

"Please, have a seat," he said pointing to a chair.

I hesitantly took off my backpack and sat down.

"What's up?" I asked confused.

His cell phone rang suddenly interrupting us.

"Sorry, give me a second." He picked up the phone and walked out the door.

I waited for five minutes until he returned.

"Sorry about that," he said apologizing again. "How have you been Aaleyah?"

"Good," I said feeling uncomfortable.

"I just want to make sure everything is okay regarding what happened on Monday."

I nodded, and fake smiled at him. "Yes everything's fine."

"Is that all?" I asked getting up.

"Wait," he said, stopping me.

"Aaleyah, I know that you didn't agree with the mark

you got, but I don't want that to discourage you in this class. You even sat in the back of the class. I just felt that maybe you were avoiding me," he said.

"Everything is fine. I sat in the back because I wanted to. Not because of anything—."

I got interrupted by his buzzing phone.

He picked up his phone and looked at the notification. He nodded to himself and looked up at me.

"That's good to hear," he smiled not even letting me finish my sentence. "Sorry for keeping you here. You can leave now."

"Okay," I said scratching my forehead.

I slowly walked away trying to understand what the hell just happened. I turned back to look at him, and he was smiling.

I shook my head and walked out of his class.

"Weird," I muttered to myself shaking off the icky feeling.

I walked down the empty hallway. If I'm being honest I was a little scared. The hallways were dark, and the Halloween decorations weren't making it any less creepy.

I shook the thoughts out of my head and continued walking. The hallway got darker once I turned the corner. The club room was in an isolated hallway where not many people visited. There were floating reapers, creating human-like shadows. I took my phone out and put the flashlight on. I had to make sure the decorations were just that—not people waiting to jump out. I took out the keys to the door and opened it. I entered the dark room and flipped the light switch, but the light didn't come on.

I sharply exhaled already over this day.

I walked in further to turn on the lamps beside the

couches, but the dark eerie vibe of the room made me want to leave, and go somewhere that wasn't isolated and dark.

I dropped my bag on the couch and tried turning on the lamps, but both of them were not working.

"What the hell?" I inspected the lamps only to see they weren't plugged in.

I bent down and picked up the cord to plug it in, but froze when I felt someone behind me. The air in the room shifted making the hairs on my arms stand up. I slowly stood up and turned to face the front of the room, and across from me a figure descended from the shadows.

I stood there paralyzed by fear. I moved back as he inched forward. He slowly walked towards me tracing his fingers on the desk. I couldn't see his face because of his ski mask. He was wearing all black. He had on a black hoodie and black sweats.

My heart was beating rapidly. I opened my mouth to scream, but no sound came out. I was numb.

"Who a-are y-you?" I stuttered.

He was silent. He continued to inch forward tracing his long bony fingers on the surface of the desk. He kept walking until he was an arm's reach away from me. I couldn't move back any further because he cornered me against the wall.

"Listen if this is about earlier I'm sorry," I whimpered.
Still nothing.
"I won't publish any more articles."

Maybe this was their way of retaliating. I always thought it was weird that they never confronted me. I was expecting them to rip out my locker or something, but they never did.

"Come on," I pleaded. "This isn't funny."
Silence.

I quickly pulled out my phone. "I swear to God I'm going to call the police!" I yelled.

He ripped my phone out of my hands and threw it across the room.

He leaned closer.

"Watch yourself," he snarled. His voice was low and raspy.

My breath hitched in my throat sending waves of shivers down my spine.

"I swear to God this isn't funny. You've won okay?" I said my voice cracking.

He didn't answer. He just peered at me through the holes of his mask. I was trying to figure out how I could rip the mask off his face. He would see my hand coming before it even reached his face. He was fast, like how he grabbed my phone at lightning speed.

I was able to see his eyes, and they looked familiar. I needed to devise a plan that would get me out of this room.

"Is this some kind of a joke?!" I screamed my heart pounding in my chest.

Silence.

"You scared me. I'm scared okay? You can stop now," I begged.

He straightened up and stepped backwards putting space between us.

I exhaled in relief at his retreating form.

I quickly moved away from the wall and made my way towards the door.

He paused and looked at the lamp. He picked it up and threw it across the room. The bulb shattered and broken glass coated the floor.

I winced at the sound.

My stomach dropped to the floor.

"Come on," I cried. "Please. I'm sorry. I won't even tell anyone about this. Just stop!"

My heart quickened when I noticed he wasn't backing down. He just stood there frozen like a statue.

I looked to see if I could make it to the door in time, but I knew he'd stop me.

I waited for him to make a move, but he didn't. He was still standing there facing me.

I stared at the man, my mouth feeling like cotton. If I screamed nobody would hear me. I was stuck.

The nerve wracking part was I didn't know if he wanted to harm me, or if this was some kind of sick prank.

I glanced at the door again. It was so close—yet so far away.

I took a step back to see if he would follow, but he didn't. I took another step, then another, but he remained planted there. If he wanted to hurt me, he would have done it by now.

I was contemplating running towards the door.

I cursed that Brianna and Matthew's office was locked, and only they had keys to that room.

I clenched my teeth hard and decided the only thing I could do was make a run for it. There was no way I would confront him. There was a good enough distance between him and me, and I wanted to keep it that way.

Without giving it a second thought, I bolted to the door. As soon I made a move, he lunged towards me. I almost hurdled over the oval desk, which was blocking me from freedom. I felt myself get yanked back by my hoodie. He forcefully shoved me, and I landed on a chair the sharp edge stabbing my side knocking the wind out of me. I tried to breathe but cried at the sharp pain that pierced through my body. I slowly gathered myself holding my abdomen and stood up. When I looked up, he was gone. The door was left wide open.

I sprinted out the door not wanting to stay in that room a second longer. I ran down the empty hallway ignoring the sharp pain in my side. Relief washed over me when I saw students swarming the hallway. I never thought I would be happy to see them. I leaned against a wall and sank to the floor my knees too weak to hold me up any longer.

"Aaleyah, are you okay?" someone asked bending down.

I sighed in relief when I saw Matthew and Brianna hovering over me.

I shook my head and put my face in my palms.

"What happened?" Brianna asked.

I lifted my head to look at them. "We need to go to the principal's office."

Matthew held out his hand. I grabbed it and stood up clutching my side as pain shot up my body.

"Ahh," I groaned.

"What's wrong?" Brianna asked looking worried. "Did those guys do something to you?"

"Someone attacked me in the club room," I whispered, my voice shaking.

"Are you hurt? Oh my God!" Brianna yelled.

"Are you okay? Did you see who it was? What happened?" Matthew asked raising his voice.

"Tell us while we walk," he said.

I nodded and told them everything on the way to the principal's office.

Brianna opened the door ushering me to walk in first. I

walked towards the front desk where the Grinch sat.

"I need to see the principal," I told her.

She peered at me through her glasses. "He's eating."

"I need to see him now," I said sternly not giving her any room to object. I didn't have time for her today.

She gave me a long stank face before she huffed and got up. She knocked on his door and went inside his office. A few moments later, they both came out of the room.

"What can I do for you?" principal William asked when he saw us.

I told him what happened. He nodded his head listening carefully, but he didn't seem bothered or concerned there was an intruder in the school. Where I come from this would warrant a lock down and the cops would have been called.

I frowned at his lack of interest and empathy.

"Did you get a look at his face?" he asked when I was done.

"Isn't he supposed to ask if I'm okay first?" I thought in my head.

"No," I said. "He was wearing a mask, and the lights in the room weren't working."

"Are you okay?" He leaned forward to look at me closer. "You don't seem hurt."

"He shoved me, and I fell on a chair."

He nodded. "Let's go look at the room, shall we?"

My stomach churned, already not liking how this was going. I was just assaulted, and he acted like I just told him the girl's washroom ran out of toiletry.

We walked towards the club room, and the three of us trailed behind him and the secretary.

We were silent while we walked to the room. I was so

distracted with my thoughts I didn't even notice when we got there.

The principal stopped in front of the door. I stood next to him and inhaled a deep shaky breath bracing myself. The principal turned to me with his hand on the doorknob. I nodded, signalling him to open it.

He opened the door and stepped in, and I followed slightly hiding behind him.

"You said the light wasn't working?" he asked turning to me.

I nodded.

He walked in more and went towards the light switch and flicked it on. The fluorescent lights on the ceiling illuminated the room.

"Th-that's not possible," I stammered wide-eyed.

The room was spotless, and did not show a single sign of a disturbance. The broken lamp was put back, and the glass was cleaned off the floor. The shade for the lamp was put back on–covering the bulb that was missing. The chair I fell on was placed upright, and the phone he threw across the room was on the coffee table beside my bag.

The principal and the secretary turned to me with accusing eyes.

"I swear to Go—"

"I'm going to stop you right there," he said holding up his hand. "Surely, you see this from my perspective. Everything you claimed was false. I don't know what to think."

"I'm not lying!" I exclaimed. "I was attacked. He was here. He was in this room. I don't know how he cleaned everything so quickly. I-I don't know how he did it, but he was here!"

"Here, look." I walked towards the lamp and took the

shade off to show the missing bulb.

"See." I held up the lamp for them to get a good look.

Their eyes were blank, and I did a double take realizing there was a bulb inside the lamp.

I felt dizzy. "I swear I'm not crazy."

Brianna and Matthew looked at me bewildered, while the principal and the Grinch looked at me like I lost my mind.

"Okay Aaleyah. I know what's going on here. You're angry about your car, and this is how you wanted to get revenge. It's okay. I understand." The principal patted me on the shoulder.

"No! That's not at all what's going on. I'm not making this up. You've got to believe me!" I snapped.

He pursed his lips and shook his head slightly and turned to walk out the room.

"The cameras!" I yelled. "You can check the cameras!"

"Uh, yes. About that, we actually haven't installed cameras in this part of the school yet," the principal said.

I looked at him like he grew a second head. "Why-how, why wouldn't you install cameras?"

"There just didn't seem to be a need for them," he shrugged.

"Then what are those?" I said pointing to the camera hidden in the corner of the room.

I stepped out into the hallway and pointed to the camera that was visibly there. "Then what is that?"

He scratched the corner of his mouth awkwardly. "They're fake. We decided it was better to pretend that there were cameras instead of actually installing real ones."

"You're saying I'm making this up?" I asked.

"I'm not saying you made this up. Maybe you did see

someone. A simple Halloween prank perhaps? But I think you blew it out of proportion," the principal accused.

"A Halloween prank? Are you freaking kidding me? Someone attacked me, and you're saying this was a Halloween prank?!" I shouted.

"I am willing to forget this happened," he said ignoring my outburst. "I won't tell your parents, but don't ever do this again."

"And to think I was about to call the police," he said walking away shaking his head.

I stood open-mouthed as I watched their forms become more distant until they were out of sight.

I leaned against the wall not moving.

"Oh my God," I whispered. "I-I—"

Brianna walked over to me, and wrapped her arms around me. "Come on. Let's go inside."

We sat down on the couch and sat in silence. They were waiting for me to say something, but I couldn't even form the words. Doubt begin to creep in. Maybe I was going crazy, but the ache in my side was a clear indication that everything I said did happen.

I looked around the room examining how spotless it was. Nothing was out of place. Everything was back to normal, and I can't even understand how he did it. He made me look insane. The principal didn't believe me, and I doubted Matthew and Brianna would believe me. I stared at the ceiling blinking back tears.

"Guys," I started.

"We believe you," Matthew interjected.

Brianna nodded and patted my knees reassuring me. "We know you're telling the truth."

"Tell us what happened from the beginning. Start from

class," he said.

"Okay," I breathed. "Everything was normal. The teacher allowed us to sit anywhere we wanted, so I sat in the back. Two of the guys from this morning came in and sat beside me. After a little while they started to itch, and they both ran out of the class. Then the bell rang. I got up, but Mr. Smith held me back."

"Why? I thought he didn't like you?" Matthew asked.

"He doesn't. He always avoids looking at me. He asked me if I was mad at him or something because I sat at the back of the class. He thought I was avoiding him."

Matthew nodded. "Go on."

"I got up to leave, but he stopped me talking about how he understood why I didn't agree with him and that he didn't want this to discourage me. He asked if I was avoiding him, but he didn't give me a chance to answer. Instead, he rushed me out of the room.

Brianna pursed her lips in thought. "That's kind of weird.

"I know," I agreed. "He was distracted by his phone. First time he got a phone call, and he walked out of the room. I waited for like five minutes. Then while I was talking, he got a notification, and thats when he basically kicked me out of the room."

"What else happened?" Matthew asked.

"Um, I walked out of his classroom confused, and I walked towards this room. I tried turning on the lights, but they weren't working. I tried turning on the lamps, but they were unplugged. I thought that was weird, so I went to plug them in. That's when I noticed a guy was behind me. He said nothing. He was just standing there. I thought it was a prank. Maybe one of the guys getting back at me for this morning.

I took a deep breath and continued. "I took out my phone and warned him I was gonna call the police, but he flew towards me, grabbed my phone, and threw it across the room. He cornered me to that wall." I pointed to the wall I was held captive earlier.

"And then he walked away. I thought I was good, but then he picked up the lamp and threw it across the room. He didn't do anything after that, he just stared at me. When I noticed he wasn't making a move towards me, I tried running towards the door, but he grabbed me and shoved me. I landed on the chair badly. By the time I got up, he was gone."

"Did he say anything?" Matthew questioned.

"He told me to watch myself."

"Is there anything else you remember?" he asked.

I paused for a moment thinking. "He seemed familiar."

"How?" Brianna asked.

"His eyes. I've seen them somewhere before, but I don't know where."

I leaned back on the chair wincing in pain because of the movement.

Matthew leaned forward. "Who would want to come after you like this?"

I scoffed. He reached into his backpack and grabbed a notebook and a pen.

"What are you writing?" I asked.

"We have to figure this out because they won't. They don't even believe it happened," he said.

I took a deep breath regretting it immediately as my eyes welled with tears from the pain.

"Are you in pain?" Brianna asked turning to me in worry.

"Yeah it hurts when I breathe," I told them.

"It sounds like you might have injured your ribs. Look at it and tell me how it looks," he said.

"My mom is a doctor, so I know a thing or two about injured ribs." He turned around to give me privacy.

I lifted my sweater up slightly to show Brianna my injury.

Brianna grimaced at the sight of my torso.

"What's wrong?" I asked quickly.

I looked down to get a better look, but I couldn't see properly.

"Can you take a picture?" I asked.

She took out her phone and snapped a photo.

"Here." She held the phone up for me to see.

I stared at the photo in front of me and grimaced.

"It's bruised and swollen," I told him.

"Touch it and tell me your pain level from one to ten," he instructed.

I lightly pressed down on my wound. I held in my breath because of the pain. "Around a six."

"You can turn back around now," I said pulling down my sweater.

"Twist your body from side to side," he told me once he was facing me.

I did as I was told and twisted my torso to the right then to the left.

"How does that feel?" he asked.

"It hurt the same," I said truthfully.

"Do you feel pressure, or a squeezing pain at the centre of your chest?"

I shook my head.

"Good news. I don't think you have broken ribs, but they are definitely bruised. I forgot what you're supposed to do with bruised ribs. Let me search that up quickly—cause you know, I'm not a doctor."

I smiled shaking my head at him.

"It says on here to take pain killers, but forty-eight hours after an injury occurs because it might slow down the healing process."

He frowned. "Hmm, I don't know about that. It sounds a bit sketchy, but let's continue. It says to ice it. That I agree with. Rest and take time off work," Matthew said speeding up.

"Okay. I've read enough." He put down his phone and went to the freezer. He took out cold packs then handed them to me.

"Thanks."

"I'm going to ask my mom about the pain killer thing, but other than that I think I made a damn good diagnosis. I mean, you can go to the doctors to double-check, but why would you want to do that?"

"Right," I said slowly. "It's always good to get a second opinion."

"There's no need. I'm ninety-five per cent sure you have a bruised rib. And if you do, they're going to recommend you rest." He paused.

"Unless I'm wrong and your ribs are actually broken, and you rupture a lung and end up dying because it would be too late to go to the doctor, and then it would be my fault. Oh my God, your mom is going to sue me, and make sure I go to prison for life." He jumped off the couch. "We should go to the hospital."

"Wow, you were so confident a second ago, but that

went south real quick," Brianna laughed.

"I trust your judgment relax. Also I'm not telling my parents," I said.

"Why aren't you going to tell your parents Aaleyah?" Matthew asked concerned.

"I don't want to keep worrying them," I said.

"Okay, okay." Matthew paced back and forth.

He sat down. "We should sign a document saying you agreed with my medical judgment in case something happens."

"Nothing is going to happen," I said hitting him on the back of the head. "*InshaAllah.*"

"You say that when you don't know what's going to happen. You're basically saying you're gonna die," he freaked out.

I burst out laughing ignoring the sharp jab in my side. "It just means God willing. Man, you are so paranoid."

"So you're saying if God wills you'll die?"

"Yeah," I said slowly not knowing how to answer. "I mean death is inevitable right?"

He looked at me like I lost my mind. "Was that supposed to make me feel better?"

"Come on. Take out your notebook. We still have to write those names," I said.

"Yeah, yeah. You're right." He grabbed his pen and notebook. "You know it would take a quick second if you just signed—"

"Matthew!"

"Okay, okay. Let's write those names. Who do we suspect?"

"Half the football team," I started.

He scribbled something in his notebook.

"The entire school administration because of the articles you've been writing. They've been quiet about it, but maybe they were waiting for this day to attack you, and tell you to back off," Brianna chimed in.

"Your English teacher," Matthew continued.

"I seriously doubt a bunch school admins, and a teacher devised a plan to attack and scare me half to death." I shook my head. "All I did was write about my concerns as a student. "

"I bet my money on Garrett and his friends. That's how they probably put the room back together so fast. I wouldn't put it past him. White boy rage. It's a thing you know?" Matthew said.

"They started it. They vandalized my car. All I did was defend myself, and because of that I deserve to be assaulted at school? What the actual hell?" I scoffed.

"What should we do?" he replied.

"I don't know. Nobody believes me. If I try to confront Garrett–he'll just deny it. If I retaliate–they'd kill me and bury my body in the forest, and get away with it. They are definitely capable of it," I said quietly.

"Now what?" Brianna asked.

I shrugged. "I honestly don't know."

We sat quietly for a minute.

"Is this it?" Matthew asked breaking the silence.

I nodded. "Yeah, there's no one else I can think of."

"We'll start here, and solve this case," he announced.

"What's the point?" I asked. "I already know it was probably Garrett and his goons who attacked me. He never confronted me about the articles I've been writing. I thought it was the idiots from earlier, but I doubt they would have been able to plan this that quickly."

"Even if I had proof they wouldn't get in trouble," I continued.

Matthew groaned and closed his notebook. "This sucks."

"I hate Halloween," I mumbled.

"You haven't seen anything yet," Matthew said.

I threw my hands up. "What else can possibly happen?"

Chapter 16

"Man, I spoke too soon," I whispered to myself as I stood beside my parents looking out the window.

"Should we call the police?" I asked.

"No. I guarantee you the police are a part of this," my dad said shaking his head. "I can't believe this."

I took my phone out of my pocket and started recording. My view was partially blocked by the gates in front of the house, but you could still see the group of hooded KKKs standing in front of our house with fire torches. They weren't saying or doing anything, they were just standing there holding the torches. We had just eaten dinner when my mom noticed the light.

Mom sighed and rubbed her face. "What if they try to break in?"

Dad squeezed mom's shoulder trying to console her. "If they were here to do something, they would have done it already. They're trying to intimidate us."

"I don't know," mom whispered. "This is just crazy."

"Come on let's go sit down. It's not doing us any good just standing here staring at them." Dad led my mom out of the kitchen, and I followed.

I plopped down on the single chair beside the couch and watched as my parents tried to keep it together. Their faces were distraught, and I could tell mom was holding back tears. The sight of their faces made me want to cry.

"Are you okay?" I asked mom.

"Yes sweetie." Mom smiled trying to reassure me.

"I'm worried you are too okay Aaleyah," dad said frowning at my lack of reaction to the whole situation.

I closed my eyes. "I don't even know how to begin to explain how I'm feeling. I feel like this is all a dream to be honest."

My dad nodded slowly and put his face in his hands. We all sat quietly letting the moment pass by because none of us knew what to say. How do you explain this situation? I stared at the ceiling, ignoring the pain in my side. I tried to understand everything that was happening.

My heart was heavy, and it felt as though a hand was squeezing it ever so gently. My stomach kept churning. It felt like I had butterflies in my stomach, but butterflies were too soft and subtle. More like bats creating a ruckus in my stomach. It all felt fake like I was stuck in a movie I had no control of.

"I don't want to sleep alone tonight," I confessed to my parents.

I was dreading sleeping alone in my room.

"Should we camp out here?" dad suggested.

"Yes please. That sounds like a good idea," I said feeling relieved.

"Let's get ready for bed and bring some stuff down," mom said.

I went up to my room and brushed my teeth. I stared at

my reflection in the mirror. All the events of today rushing at me at once.

I paced back and forth in the washroom unable to get the pressure off my chest. It was getting worse. The invisible hand was squeezing my heart tighter, and I couldn't relieve the pressure. I gripped the bathroom sink as my vision blurred. I tried to breathe, but it felt like my air supply was being cut off. Like the air was not supplying enough oxygen, like I had forgotten how to breathe. I sunk down to the floor and closed my eyes trying to remember how to breathe. I can't believe I was forgetting how to breathe. The simple act of inhaling and exhaling was a concept I couldn't grasp at this moment. I pulled my knees to my chest and let my tears run freely. I cried silently. I didn't know when the tears started, but now I couldn't stop them.

There were so many emotions attacking me all at once. I didn't know how to handle them. I sat in the corner until I was brought back to reality by my mom's distant voice coming closer.

"Aaleyah are you almost done?" she called from outside my bedroom getting closer.

"Yeah," I called back weakly. "I'm coming."

I prayed that my mom wouldn't come in. I held my breath for a few seconds to hear her footsteps. Thankfully she walked away from my door.

I pulled myself up and stood in front of the mirror staring at my red eyes. I opened the cold water to wash my face. I closed the tap and pulled my hair back into a pineapple bun. I stared at my reflection looking a little better. Hopefully my parents won't notice my red eyes.

I slept between my parents later that night, listening to their breathing. We had watched three movies until we had retired off to sleep. But I couldn't go to sleep. I twisted and turned all night until I was finally pulled into a deep sleep.

I woke up the next morning to the sunlight peeking through the curtains pulling me away from my sleep. I took my phone out and looked at the time.

I jumped up realizing it was noon, and I was late for school.

I ran into the kitchen and saw both of my parents drinking coffee and having what seemed like a very serious conversation.

"Oh, hi honey," mom greeted me. "You kept tossing and turning last night, so we decided to let you sleep in. We decided to stay home. After last night, we were both not feeling like going to work."

I nodded and walked into the kitchen. I poured myself some cereal and coffee and sat down next to my parents.

"Did you want to go to school?" mom asked.

"Oh hell no. Most definitely not."

"Your mom and I were just talking about what we should do."

"About what?" I frowned.

"About what happened yesterday, and what happened to you," dad said.

"What do you mean? What happened to me?" I asked feeling nervous.

I cursed at myself for not being able to lie to my parents. I couldn't get anything past mom, but dad on the other hand, was a little easier. When it was both of them together, it was game over.

"When your dad and I woke up this morning, we couldn't

help but notice the bruise you have on your side."

I opened my mouth to say something, but nothing came out.

"Your shirt lifted up a bit while you were sleeping," my dad explained.

I stared down at my hands silently cursing myself for wearing an oversized shirt. I wiped the sweat forming on my palms on my pyjama pants.

"What happened?" mom asked her voice stern warning me.

She stared at me intensely daring me to lie.

I sighed and bit my lip.

I filled them in on what happened, and watched as their faces became distorted.

Dad looked down and rubbed his hands on his face. "Aaleyah why on God's earth would you not tell us?!" he roared.

"I don't know," I winced. "I didn't want you guys to worry, and telling you guys would have made it more real."

"Oh honey." Mom rubbed my back. "We should tell the school. They need to know what happened. I can't believe a school could be so irresponsible."

"Well," I said sucking in some air. "I told the principal, and they didn't believe me."

"What do you mean they didn't believe you?" dad asked frowning.

I told them about what happened after the attack and what the principal said.

Dad got up and paced back and forth. He stopped and crossed his arms. "Did you show him your bruise."

"They would have said I did it to myself, and that I was making up a story to get attention."

Dad nodded not saying anything.

"Dad say something," I said his silence scaring me.

"The cameras must have captured it. They can deny it, but if we report it to the police, the school will have no choice but to release it to the police since it's evidence."

"About that, he said the cameras in that part of the school are fake. It's meant to scare people into thinking the cameras are real."

"Are you kidding me?!" dad shouted.

"Are they allowed to do that?" he asked mom.

"Yes, they're not obligated to have cameras in school, and there's nothing wrong with installing fake ones. People do it all the time."

Mom leaned forward and bit her nails—a habit of hers when she was thinking hard. "I can't believe this."

"I think we should move back," dad said suddenly.

Mom nodded agreeing with him.

I sighed and leaned back in my chair. I couldn't let my dad throw away everything he worked for because of me.

"Dad, this project is very important to you. If it succeeds, you can take it back home or anywhere you want. Don't throw that away," I said. "I'm fine. I promise I can handle it."

"It's not even a discussion. The safety of my family is way more important than a project."

"Aaleyah," mom started. "We've been here for almost three months, and the number of things that have happened..." she trailed off.

She stopped and shook her head. "I can't possibly imagine what the next ten months will bring us. It's just not worth it."

"I know you guys are worried about me—*wallahi* I'm

worried too. And I know I can be stubborn sometimes, but I can take care of myself, and I know when not to act. I'm not stupid."

"That's not what we're saying honey," mom said.

"I know mom, but we can't leave. That's what they want. They want to run us out of this town."

"Aaleyah, what can we possibly do? It just isn't safe for us." Dad shook his head. "I couldn't live with myself if anything more happened to you."

"We can't run away," I begged.

Mom closed her eyes and sighed. "We're not running away Aaleyah. This place is simply not safe for us."

"I really thought you'd be happy to leave," she continued.

"I do want to leave. I count the days until we finally leave this place, but I don't want it to be like this," I told them.

I looked at dad. "Your job is so important. I don't want you to throw it away because of me."

"Sweetie, this isn't because of you, and a job can't possibly compare to the safety of my family."

"I don't want you guys to make this decision because of me. I'm fine. I can stick it through," I promised.

"We know that, but your mom and I are just afraid that more trouble will come. You got attacked in your school for God's sake. The KKK stood outside our house to terrorize us. Aaleyah, this place is not somewhere people that look like us should be. *Wallahi* it's not safe, and I would never forgive myself if anything happened to you," he said his voice breaking.

I looked down and nodded understanding what my father was saying. "Yeah you're right. It's probably best if we leave."

Dad looked at me with tears in eyes. "Why don't you want to leave Aaleyah? Is it because of your friends?"

"I do want to leave," I said. "But I want you to finish your job. You were so happy that day when you were talking to us about what you do."

Dad leaned over and squeezed my hand. "More opportunities will come. This won't be the end of my career."

"Are you trying to get revenge?" mom asked suddenly furrowing her eyebrows at me.

I shook my head quickly. "No. Absolutely not. I-I don't know. Maybe we should wait a little before making this decision. Let's just see how the next month goes."

"I just don't feel good leaving like this. They'll think they won and when another black family moves here, they'll terrorize them too. They have to know we're not afraid. They need to know they can't chase us away. If we leave, that's going to put them on an even bigger power trip," I explained.

My parents looked at each other communicating silently with their eyes. Dad nodded and turned to me.

"Aaleyah, sometimes your bravery scares me," he confessed. "I understand what you're trying to say, but if another thing happens we're out of here."

I smiled. "Okay deal."

I got up and hugged both of them.

Mom looked up at me unable to hide her worry. "Aaleyah, please be safe. I know you think you can take care of yourself, but please understand this from our perspective. You're our little girl, and we don't want you getting hurt."

She reached out and gently stroked my ribs. "We want to keep you safe."

I smiled at mom blinking back tears. "At least now I

know this world is not all peaches and cream."

Mom shook her head. "You are too strong for your own good."

"I wonder who I get that from." I laughed.

"I'm going to find who did this to you," she said fire shooting out of her eyes with such intensity it could burn down the house. "They're not getting away with this."

"Mother and daughter fight back?" I asked hopefully.

"No, you stay out of this. I don't want you snooping around," mom objected.

"Fine," I retreated.

My mom narrowed her eyes not believing me.

"*Wallahi.* I promise. I'm backing off. I'll keep my head down," I said surrendering, my hands up.

"Will you be able to do that?" she asked not convinced.

"Yes. I just need to distract myself with something," I reassured mom. "Can I post the video from yesterday on Twitter? I think we should speak up about it."

My parents looked at each other.

"Do you think that's a good idea?" mom asked skeptical. "What if you piss them off even more, and this time they come after you for real?"

I paused for a moment thinking about it. "It can go two ways. One, I can post it. It doesn't get too much attraction, and it fizzles out. I delete it and pretend like I never posted it. Or two, it goes viral, and the news gets involved. Black Twitter shreds them to virtual pieces."

"The second option just sounds like trouble," dad said.

I shook my head. "No dad. The second option is good. If it goes viral, then I can say that I don't feel safe, and I'm scared that something is going to happen to me. I'll say that I've already been attacked at school. It will create an even bigger buzz. They'll be swarmed with the press, and they'll be too busy doing damage control. So, if anything happens to me, then people will know who did it."

Both my parents stared at me wide-eyed not saying anything.

"Who does she take after?" dad asked shaking his head.

Mom sighed and looked at me. "You are too smart for your own good."

I stared at mom willing her to go on.

"That's actually a good idea. That is if it goes your way," she continued.

"I think you'd be a really good mastermind. You probably would never get caught because you'd cover up all your tracks," dad interjected.

"Don't give her any ideas," mom said taking a sip from her coffee.

"You should see Matthew," I muttered.

"What?" mom asked.

"Nothing," I said quickly.

"I'm going to my room," I announced before they asked me any more questions.

I sat in the basement with my friends later that night trying to come up with the right words to post on Twitter. We posted pictures of my vandalized car and the costume those idiots were wearing, along with the video I took yesterday of the KKK. They've been blowing up my phone all morning because I didn't show up to school. They thought I died, but I called them back afterwards and filled them in on the KKK drama.

"These people are disgusting," Matthew said.

I told them how close I came to leaving town and they weren't too happy with that. I told them about my plan to take it to Twitter about the racism, and they both agreed it was a smart thing to do. It could go either way, but it was worth a shot.

"Did anything interesting happen at school today?" I asked pressing the tweet button on the last tweet of the thread we crafted.

Matthew and Brianna gave each other a look.

I narrowed my eyes at them. "What?"

"Matthew got into a fight," Brianna blurted.

My eyes widened.

Matthew sighed.

"It wasn't a fight," he explained rolling his eyes at Brianna. "When we walked into school this morning Chad and his minions came up to us. They were covered in rashes, and they couldn't stop itching. It was pretty great. They asked if we did it. I said no. They didn't believe me. They were yelling really loudly, and people started to form around us waiting for a fight. Anyways, I asked them what kind of paint they used. Obviously I knew what paint those idiots used. They said they didn't know. I asked them if it was body paint, and they shrugged. I kind of made a big deal out of that. I was like, 'are you kidding me? How could you not know if you used body paint or not?' People were giggling and laughing at them. They were pissed off that I was embarrassing them. Chad tried to punch me, but he just ended up falling on his face."

He burst out laughing recalling the memory. "Man, I wish you were there. It was hilarious."

I looked at Matthew with concern evident in my eyes. "What if they try to gang up on you?"

He shrugged. "I'm not too worried."

"I don't want you guys to get hurt because of me. I don't want to drag you into my mess."

"You're not," he reassured me. "I have a history with those guys way before you came into the picture."

"What do you mean?" I asked raising my eyebrow. It was the first time hearing about this.

"Where should I start? Fourth grade when Garrett and his friends pushed me into the pavement and shoved sand down my throat?"

"Yeah, they were psychotic since forever," he explained seeing my disturbed face. "In seventh grade, they bullied me severely. I was scrawny and really couldn't defend myself. But the summer before high school, I started hitting the school gym, and I finally grew. I wasn't the small kid they could beat on anymore. Freshman year was crazy because they were always trying to beat me up. I would fight back, and that pissed them off. They never got in trouble, but I did. This one time I got detention for two weeks for defending myself against a fight they started.

"No one bothered to think about the fact that four boys were ganging up on one. Anyways, they backed off because they started playing football, so all their time went there. Until sophomore year when Lewis went missing. They were saying some really messed up things, and I just lost it. I didn't get in trouble because it was a 'sensitive moment' even though they didn't give a crap about Lewis. Honestly, I'm shocked they never got back at me. I think the school made them not do it. Something about their scholarships they want to protect so dearly. That's why Garret hasn't done anything to you Aaleyah. It's because they can't risk losing their scholarships," he finished

"Wow," I said taking a deep breath. "I had no idea. This whole time I was worried about myself that I didn't even think about what kind of history you might have with them."

He shrugged. "A lot has happened. We just never fought back."

"Yeah." Brianna nodded. "And if we did, it would always backfire. Especially when Lewis went missing. We found evidence of Lewis's disappearance, and we published it in the school newspaper. Instead of them investigating it, we ended up getting in trouble. I got suspended for a week, and until this day, I don't know why."

"What kind of evidence?" I asked unable to hide my curiosity.

"It was a dark time for me, and I hacked into the street cameras. They were saying that the night of his disappearance, Lewis was walking down 23rd street where the forest was. They said the last time he was seen was him entering the forest. They believe he might have wandered off, and fell over a cliff or something. It doesn't even make sense. So much was not adding up, so I decided to investigate myself. I searched for him on every camera that I could find. I didn't find him, but I did find the camera footage of 23rd street, and he was not there. Nobody was there. He didn't even enter the forest. They lied. Why would he enter the forest so late at night? There was no reason for him to..." she trailed off.

"What do you mean?" I asked as sorrow filled her voice.

"Hey hey, what's wrong?" I moved closer to Brianna as she put her head in her palms sobbing silently.

"Next week is two years since he disappeared," Matthew explained.

He moved closer to her, and shifted her head on his shoulder letting her cry. I watched as they comforted each other. I had no idea what they were going through, and I couldn't understand. I've been so preoccupied with myself and my problems.

"I'm sorry." Brianna removed herself from Matthew's embrace and wiped her tears.

"It's not your fault," Matthew said.

I sat there silently not wanting to pry.

"What if he was going to the tree house?" she asked Matthew.

"He never went there alone. He knew better than to go into the forest by himself."

"I told him I forgot my bag there that night. Remember? We spent the day there, and when we came back to my house, I kept complaining about it. And when the police said they saw him going into the forest, I just thought..." Brianna sniffled.

"Brianna he loved you. He was smart enough to know not to go into the woods alone late at night a week after Halloween. I guarantee you he didn't go inside the forest, and you saw for yourself the police were lying."

"I know, but still. Did he just vanish? How is it possible he didn't show up in any cameras that night?"

Matthew shrugged. "Maybe there's a blind spot in this town. A place where there are no cameras. Or fake cameras. If the school can put fake cameras in, then maybe the town did too."

Brianna stayed silent for a few moments. "Yeah you're probably right."

"Sorry," she said turning to me. "I don't know why I started crying."

I smiled at her and nodded. "You don't have to apologize."

We sat there and fell silent.

"Can we watch a movie?" Brianna asked breaking the silence trying to distract us from the looming sadness.

"Yeah." I got up from the floor. "Your pick."

We spent the rest of the night in the basement watching a comedy movie to distract us from the harsh reality that is life. The few hours we spent watching the movie was the most peaceful time we've had in a long time. I watched my friends as their faces lit up with laughter every time something funny happened in the movie. I smiled sadly knowing that behind those smiles and laughter was a lot of pain and sadness.

Chapter 17

I stared at my phone the next day in shock. School had finally ended, but to be honest, I don't remember what happened. I spent the entire day on my phone, and the school day finished before I even started. I had to turn my notifications off because my phone was blowing up.

"134k retweets and 325k likes." Matthew stared at his screen in shock at the numbers.

He shook his head. "I can't believe this."

"I know. I really didn't think my tweets would go viral. I have so many messages I don't even know where to start," I said. "Thank God it's Friday. I can spend the weekend reading through them in peace. I don't have to witness the school losing their mind. Hopefully, initial the shock will wear off before Monday."

I spent the entire weekend on social media. I felt bad because I wasn't spending time with my parents, but they seemed to understand. I was getting so much support and love it was crazy. People kept asking me to tweet every hour to update them. Black Twitter did its job. They found Chad, Erin, and Nathen's handles and they've been dragging them.

Thankfully, they posted pictures of what colleges they had gotten accepted to, so black Twitter took it upon themselves to tweet at the schools, and in response they released statements saying they have withdrawn their support and scholarships because they didn't condone these racist acts. And not only Chad and his friends but Garrett as well because they had vandalized my car.

Journalists reached out to me and asked if they could use my tweets, and I told them to go for it. I'm not gonna lie I was a little bit scared. I had no idea what they would do, but with the whole world watching, I felt kind of sad. I'm sad I hadn't done it sooner. I wondered if I should post my essay.

"Go big or go home," I said aloud.

I started another thread about my essay and the mark I got.

I reread my tweet until it was perfect and tweeted it. Minutes later, I was getting hundreds of likes and retweets. People were posting their thoughts about the essay, even some teachers were tweeting at me defending my stance. It was great. I was on a high. I felt like I was finally getting justice after months of being silenced and powerless. I knew that I might regret it, but at the moment, I loved every single minute of it. Having hundreds of thousands of people come to your defence was the best thing anyone could ever experience. However, I knew when I walked into school Monday morning, everything would be different.

I walked down the hall Monday morning, and not to my

surprise everyone was staring at me. They parted the hallway as I walked. I felt like a celebrity—a celebrity that just had a massive scandal. Everyone probably knew what happened. In seventy-two hours, I had put this town and school on the map. This was a small town, and things got around quickly, but I didn't care. At that moment, I felt powerful. Like the device in the palm of my hand was a sword.

They were looking at me with a mix of disbelief and anger, but nobody said or did anything. I was anticipating a push here and a shove there, but nothing. I walked down the hallway with my head high. I was feeling powerful. I had Twitter shred six boys while taking away their future. I had hundreds of thousands of people read my paper all agreeing that my teacher was wrong. They got at him too, but he wasn't on Twitter.

I squeezed the phone in my hand afraid it would disappear. My phone was still blowing up. People kept tweeting at me to keep them updated about school.

"Hey!" someone shouted getting my attention.

I turned around to see Brianna and Matthew running to catch up to me.

Brianna linked arms, and we walked down the hallway together. I smiled and continued walking forward.

Brianna shook her head. "I can't believe the amount of attention this has been getting. I already gained so many new followers."

"I know. This is way more than I was expecting," I agreed.

"I can't believe they all lost their scholarships." Matthew turned to me worried. "That's all they've been working towards for the past four years. Now they have nothing to lose."

"They deserved it. They've lived their whole life not knowing about consequences. I just introduced them to the real world," I said unapologetically.

"You're not scared?" he asked.

I pursed my lips and sighed. "I'm terrified."

"Then why do it?" he wondered.

"Because it's the only thing I could do. They would have continued terrorizing my family until they ran us out of town. Now I have insurance. They can't do anything while so many people are anticipating their next move. They're stuck for now," I explained.

"You're confident about that?" he asked.

I laughed. "Hell no, but I'm hoping that's how things will go, or else man—things will get really bad."

"You have English first?" Brianna asked when we stopped at her locker.

I took a deep breath. "Yeah."

"I mean if he was mad before, he'll probably want to kill you now," Matthew stated.

I looked at Matthew. "Way to make me feel better."

He chuckled. "Sorry. I'm just scared for you."

I sighed. "I know. I am too."

"It was a smart thing to do. I'm just glad it went viral. Imagine if it didn't." He shuddered at the idea.

I nodded and leaned back against the locker and watched all the people watching me. They'd all quickly turn away when we made eye contact.

I rolled my eyes.

"Did you see the article they wrote about Anderton?" Brianna asked changing the subject.

I turned to her. "No. Who wrote it?"

"The New Yorker," she smiled.

"You're kidding me!" I exclaimed.

"Yeah, they wrote an article about Andertons history of missing Africa American people and that racism is nothing new in Anderton. They even included Lewis since his disappearance was the most recent," she sighed. "It's the first time his disappearance is getting any kind of national coverage."

"Wow," I breathed.

Matthew looked down at his shoes. "I wish we could have done this sooner. Maybe then we would have known what happened to him."

"What happened to all of them," Brianna added. "He wasn't the first, and he most definitely won't be the last."

"Come on. We'll walk you to your class," she said changing the subject.

"Okay," I said feeling nervous.

"Are you ready?" Matthew asked when we were in front of my classroom.

"No, but I should go in," I said when the bell rang.

"Bye," I waved.

I walked towards the classroom when I felt a hand on my wrist stopping me.

I looked at Matthew confused.

"Where are you going to go during your spare block?" Matthew asked.

"I think the cafeteria is the best place for me to be."

"Okay I'll meet you at your locker and walk you there."

"You'll be late for class. You don't have to do that."

"Yes I do," he said with a serious tone.

"Fine," I said.

I knew there was no point in arguing with him.

I went inside the classroom and sat down at my regular

desk in the front row. I fiddled with my fingers trying to calm my nerves. I kept taking deep breaths, even though the movement caused me some discomfort. I needed to make sure I didn't seem scared or nervous when Mr. Smith came in through the door. Not just him, but Chad and Erin were also in my class. I doubted they would show up today.

I watched as the classroom filled up with students. They were loud and chatty, but when they entered the room, they would go silent. I felt their eyes burning holes in my face, but I didn't care. Maybe I cared a little bit, but it was being overshadowed by everything else I was feeling.

The teacher entered the classroom with a smile on his face. But his eyes, oh man, if looks could kill. I've never had someone stare at me with such intense hatred while smiling at me. It was very unsettling. He paid little attention to me. In fact, he avoided me all class.

When the bell rang, I packed my stuff quickly and ran out of class before he had the chance to hold me back to talk to me. I didn't want to be alone with him. I walked down the busy hall and went to my locker.

"Hey," I greeted Matthew who was leaning against my locker on his phone.

"How was class?" he asked.

"It was okay. He looked angry, but he kept smiling which was really weird. Chad and Erin didn't come to class."

"They're here," he told me.

"How do you know?" I asked.

"I walked past a classroom earlier when I was going to the washroom, and they were all in there with the principal. I didn't stick around. I didn't want them to see me."

I bit my lip, thinking about the possible things they could have been talking about. One of them probably being how to get rid of me quietly.

"Come on," Matthew urged me. "Don't think about it too much."

"Yeah," I sighed.

We walked down the hallway until we reached the cafeteria. Matthew pushed open the door and walked me inside. There were already a few students there.

"I can take it from here," I joked.

He smiled. "Okay. I'll see you later."

"I'll meet you at Brianna's locker," I told him.

He nodded and said goodbye.

I ignored the wandering eyes following me. I looked at the table I sat at the first day of school. Things were so different back then. I took a deep breath and walked towards it. It hadn't been long since school started, but everything changed so much from back then.

I dropped my bag down and pulled out my books and phone. I spent the first few minutes catching up on Twitter to see what was happening. My brother and friends from back home have been blowing up my phone since they saw my tweets. My brother was petrified with everything that happened. Same with my friends, they all agreed that I should move back, but I told them I was staying for the time being. I put my phone away to start my homework, but I couldn't concentrate. I put my earphones in to play music to drown out my thoughts and began my work.

I didn't know how much time passed, but I was suddenly pulled back to reality when I saw the commotion from the corner of my eyes. I took out my earbuds and looked up to see what was happening. Nathen, Erin and Chad were marching towards me furious. They looked like crap. Like they haven't been sleeping, and their skin was still a little bit red and blotchy.

They stopped in front of my table, and I jumped up just in case they attacked me.

"Why the hell did you do it?" Nathen bellowed.

I winced. Their faces were so red. The anger they were radiating scared me a little.

I didn't say anything. I just shrugged.

Nathen tried to step towards me his fists balled up in anger, but Chad stopped him.

"Remember what the principal said," he said clenching his teeth.

Chad turned around and yelled in anger startling me. His face was red, and it seemed as though he was fighting every nerve in his body not to lunge at me.

Nathen looked at me his eyes hard as stone. "You've ruined our lives."

"I didn't do anything. You guys did this to yourselves," I said nonchalantly.

"YOU POSTED THE PICTURES!" Erin screamed.

"I recall you telling me to post those pictures. You said, and I quote, 'yeah take a picture, people deserve to see how good we look'"

"That's not fair, and you know it," Nathen said stepping towards me.

I laughed in disbelief. "So you guys expected to walk around being blatantly racist laughing and mocking me, and I do nothing about it? Now you have the audacity to come in front of me?" I scoffed and folded my arms in front of my chest. "You brought this all on yourselves."

"It was just a joke," he seethed.

"Really?" I laughed, shaking my head. "You and I both know that's not true. I don't know what you guys want from me. Do you want me to apologize because you know that's never going to happen."

"My whole life, I've dreamed of the moment that I can leave this town. It's all I've ever wanted, to escape my father. This was my only chance for me to leave and make a good life for myself—to not live in fear of my dad. To prove to him that I am worth something, and I deserve a good life. You took that away from me," he said his voice breaking.

I could tell he was fighting back tears, and I felt the tiniest pang of sympathy. But it was so far down I barely felt it.

I walked closer until I was standing in front of him. "I'm sorry about your father, but that does not excuse what you did. You have no regard for anyone that doesn't look like you. You've probably spent your whole life bullying every single kid who wasn't white, and this is the first time you've had someone stand up to you. I'm guessing this is the first time you've had any sort of consequence for your actions. You all deserved what happened to you, and honestly, I wish I could get you suspended from school, but I know that will never happen. This is your own fault. Stop trying to find other people to blame it on."

I turned around and went to sit back down. "Oh and remember, the only person you should try to prove anything to is yourself. Not your father, your coach or your friends."

I shook my head. "Wow. Look at me being nice until the very end."

I put my earbuds in and returned back to my work not caring they were just standing there staring at me. Eventually, they stopped and walked away.

I didn't look up until I heard the cafeteria door open and close.

I knew these three would be easy to deal with, but the

other three—especially Garrett—would be a different story.

I continued to stare ahead of me until the bell rang for lunch. I quickly got up and stuffed my books inside my bag, and walked out of the cafeteria before it was swarmed with students.

Walking down the hallway this time around wasn't bad. People already got over the shock of seeing me, so they weren't staring as hard as before.

"We heard what happened?" Brianna said as soon as I reached her locker.

I narrowed my eyebrows in confusion. "How?"

"News flies in this school," she explained. "Are you okay?"

"Yeah I'm fine." I shrugged to let them know it wasn't a big deal. "They said I ruined their lives, and I let them know they can't blame this on anyone but themselves."

We ate our lunch in the room and talked avoiding serious topics like everything going on at the moment.

"Ugh I'm so nervous about my math SAT," Brianna said leaning back on the couch.

"What are you going to do about your SATs?" she asked me.

"I don't know. I need to sort out this whole SAT thing out. I'll have to do some research."

"Do you know what colleges you're applying to?" she asked.

"Nope. I don't know if I want to go to university in Canada or US. I haven't decided, but I know I'll have to soon."

"By the way," Matthew started. "Do you have your article for this week's paper?"

"Yeah. I wrote it over the weekend, I was so inspired," I said. "I'll email it to you tonight."

Chapter 18

I sat in third period bored out of my mind. I liked biology, but man, this teacher had the most monotone voice ever. I almost dozed off until I heard the phone ring. I rejoiced because that meant we'd get a few moments of liberation from his lecture.

He talked on the phone for a few minutes and turned to me. I frowned a little suddenly feeling uneasy.

"Aaleyah, you're wanted in the office," he said.

Why in the world would I be needed in the principal's office? I never bashed the school. I posted some information about the school, but I did so respectfully.

I packed up my stuff and walked out of the classroom. I walked slowly thinking about all the possible things that might happen. Before I knew it, I was already standing in front of the office. I took a deep breath and pushed open the doors. The Grinch looked up and down at me insidiously.

I rolled my eyes and walked past her.

I took a deep breath and knocked on the principal's office.

He opened it and sitting there, were my parents.

"What are you guys doing here?" I asked confused.

"Have a seat," the principal said.

He walked behind his desk and sat down straightening his tie.

"I wanted to talk to you guys about Aaleyah's Twitter. I'm not sure if you guys are aware of the stuff she has been saying on there."

I scoffed and turned to my parents. Mom put her hands on my knee to keep me calm.

"We are very well aware," she responded. "Quite frankly, I don't see anything wrong with what she said. She did so in a respectful manner, and there is no reason for her to be called into the office. She is exercising her right to speak freely."

"Yes, I agree. That's why we have the school newspaper," the principal said.

"I wanted a bigger audience," I smirked.

He laughed and leaned forward. He put his elbows on the table and rested his chin on his hands.

"You've caused a lot of harm to some of the brightest boys we've ever had the pleasure of educating. They have lost everything because of the stunt you pulled," he remarked.

"I get you might have been feeling angry, but you've hurt some people. That's why I called you here along with your parents. I wanted to ask you to delete your pictures, and to write a statement to the respected schools to ask them to reinstate our boys. You don't even have to write anything. We've done it for you," he said pulling out a sheet of paper from his desk and handed it to my mother.

I bit my lip to keep myself from saying anything. Instead, I leaned forward and read the paper. The statement had me apologizing for everything I posted. It said that the boys were fine young men and didn't deserve to be kicked out and have everything taken from them for a mistake they've committed, and a mistake like this shouldn't define their entire lives.

I chuckled. He was an idiot if he thought I would post that.

Mom ripped up the piece of paper and sprinkled it on his desk and walked out the door.

Dad and I looked at each other shocked, and ran after her quickly, but not after I saw the complete and utter disbelief on the principal's face. That probably didn't go how he was expecting.

We met mom out in the hallway, and she had her hands on her sides pacing back and forth.

"The audacity. Who does he think he is?" she fumed.

"Wow. I mean. You did that," I said to my mom. "You should have seen his face."

"Did anything happen at school today? We tried to text you to warn you we were coming," dad told me.

"My phone was in my backpack. The biology teacher is very strict about phones. I was surprised when he told me I was needed in the principal's office I didn't think about checking my phone."

"Do you want to come home?" mom asked. "We can talk about it there."

I shook my head, "No. I should finish the day."

"Okay," she nodded.

She walked towards me and kissed me on the forehead. "Love you. We'll talk about this later."

"Love you too," I smiled.

I hugged my dad and watched as they exited the school. I walked towards my classroom, but before I reached it, the bell rang for dismissal. I turned back around and went to my locker to drop my biology textbook and to grab my stuff for my next class.

I was zoned out the entire time I was walking. I couldn't stop thinking about how confident that principal was that we would agree with such a ridiculous demand.

I laughed to myself. I was getting a lot of stares from people thinking I was crazy, but I didn't care.

I walked to my next class and sat down not paying attention to anything the teacher was saying. I would have to read the textbook and catch myself up on everything at this point.

I rushed out of class when the bell rang. I was finally being freed from this hell hole.

I walked down the hallway pushing past students to get to my locker.

I suddenly felt myself being pushed so hard I slammed into the lockers the wind being knocked out of me. I coughed choking on air. I was on all fours trying to push myself up.

I was grabbed by the collar and yanked up, and was slammed against the lockers again. I was staring into Garrett's vengeful eyes. He was out to kill, and he wanted my blood.

I quickly interlocked my fingers around the back of his neck, and forcefully pulled his head down introducing his nose to my knee. He crashed on the floor blood gushing out of his nose soaking his shirt.

He cried out and his two minions pulled him off the floor and steadied him as he watched me disoriented. They were holding on to each of his arms, and he was fighting to break free.

"GET OFF OF ME! I'M GOING TO KILL HER! LET ME GO!" he screamed in rage.

I stepped back and watched as he was consumed with fury. Everyone who watched was terrified. They've probably never seen their beloved quarterback like this. They idolized the guy because he's shown them only a good face. That is until today. His hair—usually brushed and neat—looked like a birds nest. His eyes normally clear as day, were bloodshot red. His shirt always ironed and clean, was crinkled—like the lines of frustration and anger on his face. He looked like a mess.

I felt afraid. I felt like I was staring at the devil in the face. Garrett had nothing more to lose, and that made him even more dangerous.

I stared at him as he stared back at me menacingly.

I turned away from Garrett's shouts and screams and went to my locker. I quickly packed up my things up and exited the school. I didn't stop or look back until I was safely inside my car and drove home.

I walked inside the empty house and dropped my bag on the stairs and sat down to catch my breath. My parents went back to work, and I'm glad they did. If they saw me like this, we would be on the next flight back to Canada. I leaned back and closed my eyes trying to calm my nerves. It was only Monday, but today felt like a whole week. I didn't know how I would survive the rest of the week. I was regretting my posts, but I knew it was the smart thing to do. I clutched at my aching side. It's been getting better, but Garret's attack made the pain worse.

My phone suddenly rang. I reached into my pocket and looked at the caller ID.

"Hey," I answered.

Brianna's panicked voice blared through the phone. "Aaleyah where are you?!"

"I'm at home," I explained. "I didn't want to stick around."

"We heard what happened. Are you okay?" she asked.

"Yeah. It was kind of expected."

"Can we come over? I have a plan."

I narrowed my eyes. "What kind of plan?"

"A plan that guarantees that Garrett stays away from us," she explained. "I'll tell you everything when we get to your house," she said before hanging up.

I picked up my bag and went to my room to shower and change before they got to my house. I needed to be comfortable, and I also needed to ice my ribs.

I sat in the dining room with Brianna and Matthew discussing what happened today. They sat there digesting everything I was saying.

Matthew shook his head. "We can't leave you alone anymore. I can't believe you broke Garret's nose and you're still alive.

"He had it coming." I sighed and leaned back in my chair. "I swear today was the longest day of my life. I can't believe I have to do this all over again tomorrow."

I was not looking forward to it.

"I have an idea," Brianna said leaning over.

I sat up interested in what she had to say.

"All we need to do is make sure Garrett stays away from us. I'm not worried about the others since they do everything he tells them. So if they see him backing off, they'll do the same."

"How do we do that?" I asked. "How do we make sure Garrett doesn't go rogue on us? You should have seen him Bri. He looked like he would kill me in a second if he wasn't being held back."

She bit her lip. "We overheard people talking about how violent he was, and it gave me an idea."

She reached into her backpack, and pulled out a worn-out laptop.

"What happened to your other laptop?" I asked.

"It's fine. I use this one for other purposes," she explained. "I'm going to retrieve the footage of Garrett attacking you."

"How?" I asked. "Don't tell me you're going to hack the school cameras Brianna."

"Don't worry. They'll never know. It's not like I'm going to delete it. I'm just going to make a copy, and delete the part you break his nose."

"I'm really good at this. It won't be traced back to us," she said.

"Do you want me to post the video?" I asked

"No," Matthew explained. "We're going to use it as leverage. You'll tell him that you'll post this video if he tries anything else. If he thinks his life is ruined now, he'll know that if you post that video, it would really be over."

"Do you think it'll work?" I hesitated.

"If he knows what's good for him, he'll listen," Brianna said looking up from her keyboard.

"I hope so," I muttered.

"Can we watch the video first before you delete it?" Matthew asked.

Brianna giggled. "It would be my pleasure."

We laughed until we were gasping for air watching my knee smash into Garret's face over and over again.

"Should I make it into GIF for you as a gift?" Brianna asked laughing so hard tears streamed down her face.

We burst out laughing again collapsing on the floor.

"Please do it," I begged wiping my tears.

Chapter 19

I walked into the school the next morning feeling a little more confident. People were still staring at me, but that's all these losers ever did.

I grabbed my things from my locker, and walked over to where Matthew and Brianna were. I ignored all the whispers and stares that were following me everywhere I went. I wanted so badly to confront them about it but decided against it. I didn't need any more attention.

"Hey," Matthew greeted.

"Hey," I smiled.

"Ready?" Brianna asked.

I took a deep breath. "Kinda."

"How are you going to do this?" Matthew wondered.

I bit my lip thinking about the best way to greet the beast. "I was thinking the cafeteria at lunch. I'll be surrounded by people."

"Sounds good. We'll meet here at lunch," Brianna said.

"Okay. I'll see you guys later."

I walked away from my friends and went to my class. I took this time to calm my nerves.

I sat in my second class of the day trying to pay attention to what the teacher was saying. It was hard when my thoughts were overpowering my ability to focus. I needed the distraction. Which was why I was forcing myself to listen to every word coming out of the teacher's mouth. It was counter-productive because while focusing on trying to focus, everything he was saying was going over my head.

I dreaded all the catching up I would have to do when I got home. That's how it's been lately. I go to class, but I can never pay attention. I have to review everything at home or at the bookstore. Despite everything that was happening, I was surprisingly doing well in school–except in English.

"Okay class, that will be all for today. Remember, your exam is on Thursday. Chapter seven to ten. Come prepared."

The bell rang and everyone rushed out of class, but I couldn't get up from my desk. I was too nervous about what I had to do.

"Aaleyah," the teacher called.

I looked up and realized I was just staring at my desk.

I quickly got up.

"Sorry," I murmured running out of the classroom.

I rushed to my locker and dropped my books in there. I walked over to Brianna's locker and saw them waiting for me.

"Are you ready?" Matthew asked. "You don't have to do this if you don't want to."

I took a deep breath. "Now or never, right?"

"Okay. Let's go," Brianna said putting her arms around our shoulders–struggling because Matthew was a full head taller than her.

I pulled open the cafeteria door. I decided the best way

to do this was to not think about it. I had to do it before I talked myself out of it.

Everyone's attention was on us. They stopped what they were doing to stare. This was the first time that we've walked into the cafeteria together during lunch since school started.

I looked around for my target and walked over to him. He was sitting at a table with all of his teammates with a nose splint.

I fought the urge to laugh.

They were watching me anticipating what I was going to do. I stopped at their table and tapped on the kid's shoulder sitting in front of Garrett.

"I need this seat," I told the boy.

He looked at me like I was crazy. He looked at Garrett silently asking for permission and then got up when Garrett gave him a nod.

I sat down in his seat. The nerves were kicking in since I was surrounded by a bunch of football players, but I swallowed them back down.

Garret and I had a stare down.

"You don't look like a raging serial killer anymore," I said breaking the silence.

"The look suits you," I said pointing to his nose.

He didn't reply, but I could see his teeth clench and his jaw move up and down. His hands were also under the table, but I bet everything he was clenching his fists. I knew he wanted to lunge at me again, but the entire school was paying attention to our table. Even the kids in line trying to get their food stopped to watch us.

"What do you want?" he finally asked.

The cafeteria was so quiet you could hear a pin drop.

The rest of the boys were frozen not knowing what to do. I had Brianna videotape everything just in case, and Matthew was standing behind me as support and back up.

I took out my phone, and pulled out the video and handed it to Garrett.

He narrowed his eyes at me but took the phone out of my hand. The two boys sitting beside him leaned in closer to see what was on the phone. I watched as the colour drained from his face.

"How the hell did you get this?" he growled.

I shrugged.

"You can try to delete the video, but I backed it up," I said knowing what he was thinking.

He gripped my phone tightly before giving it back.

I grabbed the phone and put it in my pocket.

"What do you want?" he asked again.

I leaned forward and lowered my voice so no one but the people sitting at the table could hear us. "Stay away from me and my friends. You know what will happen to you if I post this video online."

He shook his head in disbelief. "You conveniently left out the part where you broke my nose. "

"Oh, you want me to include the part where a girl half your size almost knocked your teeth out? I was just doing you a favour."

He glared at me and slowly nodded.

"You better watch yourself," he said lowering his voice. "You're crossing lines you can never come back from."

"Is it a deal or not?" I asked annoyed.

These threats were becoming old.

He narrowed his eyes and studied me. "Why are you so confident I'll listen to you?"

"I know you want to hurt me," I said.

"I don't hit girls."

"Could have fooled me yesterday."

"You're an exception. Terrorists don't count as girls."

The boys snickered.

"The only terrorist here is you," I fired back.

Silence washed over the table

He clenched his jaw but didn't respond.

"I know the only thing you care about at this point is getting out of this town and going to a good school."

"And you ruined that," he growled.

"You still have hundreds of good schools to choose from, but if I post this video, you can say goodbye to whatever spots you have left."

"Screw you," he snapped. "You ruined our lives."

I scoffed and shook my head. "I know you want an apology, but you're not going to get one. In fact, the person that should be apologized to is me."

He clenched his teeth. "You're lucky. People like you don't survive in this town."

"It has nothing to do with luck. Do we have a deal or not?" I asked getting up.

He nodded glaring at me. "This isn't over," he whispered.

I ignored him and walked away with Matthew and Brianna. We stayed silent until we walked out of the cafeteria into the quiet.

"Oh my God," I said my legs feeling weak.

Matthew turned to me. "Damn."

"I don't know what the principal said to them, but it's working," Brianna said.

We were all in our heads preoccupied with our thoughts

that we didn't even notice when we made it to the club
room.

Chapter 2o

The rest of the week went by quiet. Suspiciously quiet. Thankfully, Garrett and his goons did leave us alone. There weren't any more incidents, but I still didn't let my guard down. I felt like things could go wrong at any moment. I was on edge all week, and when the weekend came around, I spent it lounging around not doing anything. I needed a mental break.

I avoided social media the entire weekend, but my tweets were still blowing up, and I didn't have the mental capacity to deal with it. I felt so exhausted. I was able to partially recover from the craziest two weeks of my life. Matthew and Brianna were also dealing with the anniversary of Lewis's disappearance, so we all took a very well-deserved break from everything.

I walked down the hallway on Monday morning feeling better than I did in weeks. Things have calmed down, and people weren't staring at me too much. I kept getting the occasional glances, but I was used to them by now.

"Hey guys," I greeted when I reached their lockers.

"Hey," Matthew smiled.

"How was your weekend?" Brianna asked.

"Quiet."

"You can say that twice," Matthew laughed.

"I'm glad all that is past us," Brianna said. "The past couple of weeks were too much."

I nodded my head in agreement. "I want to finish the rest of the semester peacefully."

Matthew looked at his watch. "We have twenty minutes until the bell rings. Should we go to the room?"

"Yeah let's go," Brianna said, closing her locker.

We walked down the hallway talking about our weekend, and the many followers we've gained on Twitter in the past week. Our story has been featured on several news stations. We've been getting a lot of support from so many people. The school has denied all requests for an interview and have been laying low. They tried to do damage control, but everything blew up before they even had the chance to.

"What the hell?" Matthew fumed as he walked into the room.

"What?" I asked walking in but stopped dead in my tracks at the sight in front of me.

The clean room was now unrecognizable. The computers were on the floor in pieces. The tables were pushed over. The chairs were scattered all over the room. The fridge was knocked over, and all the food inside decorated the floor. The couches were slashed, and the window separating the office from the rest of the room was shattered.

We walked through the mess in horror. I couldn't help but feel responsible. I looked at my friend's distraught faces and blinked back tears. If it weren't for me, none of this would have happened. It was all my fault, and I didn't know what to say to them. They spent the majority of their high school years in this room. It was their escape from the school, and now it was gone because of me.

"Guys I'm so sorry," I started.

"Don't." Brianna stopped me. "This isn't your fault, so don't apologize."

"It kind of is," I said my voice breaking.

Matthew put his arm around me. "I'd rather have them break this room than harm any of us."

I nodded.

"At least we're even now. We can stop worrying," he continued.

Brianna silently kicked around the papers coating the floor. "What are we going to do?"

"Should we go to the office?" she asked.

Matthew checked his watch. "No, let's do it at lunch. I don't have time to deal with the principal right now."

We left the room, and walked our separate ways to our classes.

I sat in my first period class staring out the window. Mr. Smith was talking about our next assignment, but my mind was in a far away place. I felt so bad, and I didn't know what to do. I felt responsible. Their lives were calm and quiet before I came along and flipped everything upside down.

I leaned back in my chair. Mr. Smith knew I wasn't listening, but he would never call me on it. He hasn't interacted with me at all since I posted those tweets. I looked at my phone to see the time.

I bounced my knee up and down impatiently waiting for class to end.

I bolted out of the door when the bell rang.

I needed to find the janitor's office before the bell rang again for class, and I was left wandering alone in the hallway.

I knew there was one close to the cafeteria, so I walked hoping someone was in there. I walked up to the door to see if it was open, and thankfully it was.

The janitor's back was towards me as he was haunched over looking for something. I cleared my throat to get his attention.

The janitor turned around quickly and stared at me.

"What can I help you with?"

"I need some cleaning supplies. Can I get a broom, disinfectant wipes, a dustpan, and some garbage bags please? Oh, and some gloves."

The janitor nodded and grabbed the requested items and handed them to me. I thanked him and made my way to the club room. I walked down the empty hallway trying to calm my rapidly beating heart. I haven't been in this room alone since Halloween. I started spending my spare time in the cafeteria.

I took a deep breath and walked in. I turned on the lights and sighed in relief when I saw the room light up.

I took out my phone and took pictures of the room, but this time I wasn't going to post it. That would end any truce I made with Garrett and his boys. These pictures were for the principal. I wanted to clean up the room a little bit, but I wanted him to see the full extent of the damage. Even though I knew he wouldn't care because this was all in his favour.

I put my phone away and cleaned the room. I flipped back all the tables thrown over, and put all the broken computers back on the table to make it a little more presentable. I couldn't pick up the refrigerator by myself, but I cleaned up all the food off the floor. I gathered all the chairs and put them back, and placed all the papers in the recycling bin.

I groaned when I stood up. I put my hands on my back and stretched.

I looked around the room impressed by how much better it looked. I picked up a broom to clean up all the glass. I swept the entire room and the office dusting off any glass that might have gotten into the keyboards, the couches or anywhere else.

I gathered up all the shards of glass and threw it in the garbage bag. I tied up all the bags and leaned them against the door.

After I was done cleaning I collapsed on the couch, but when I did, the bell rang causing me to jerk up.

I waited in the room for a few minutes until Brianna and Matthew came in.

"Whoa," Brianna said inspecting the room.

The room that was completely trashed earlier was now semi-presentable.

"Wow Aaleyah, you didn't have to clean all of this by yourself. We could have done it together," Matthew said

I shrugged. "I know, but I had a spare block. Might as well put it to use right?"

"Let's go to the office and talk to the principal. Don't worry, I took some pictures of how the room looked before," I told them.

Matthew nodded and walked out of the room. Brianna and I following behind him.

"What do you think he's going to say?" he asked.

I turned to Matthew. "He's probably going to blame it

on us. He's going to say we did it."

We stopped talking when we walked through the office doors.

"Can we speak to the principal?" I asked.

The Grinch looked at me with a glare in her eyes. "He's eating."

"It's an emergency," I urged.

She rolled her eyes but got up from her chair and went to his office.

She was in there for a few minutes before she came back out with the principal trailing behind her.

"What can I help you guys with?" the principal asked not even trying to hide his annoyance.

We looked at each other to see which one of us would speak up.

"The club room was vandalized," Brianna said taking charge.

He frowned. "What do you mean?"

"Someone destroyed the room. All the computers have been broken. We have pictures."

I pulled out my phone and handed it to him, so he could look at the pictures.

He swiped through them quickly not seeming the least bit concerned. I would have expected at least a change in his facial expression. Those computers were very expensive and must have cost the school a lot, but looking at his reaction you would think they weren't worth a penny.

I frowned at his stone cold composure. You would think his school getting vandalized would cause outrage, but no. He didn't care.

He handed back my phone. "I'm sorry. That's terrible."

"Don't you want to come to the room to look around?

Aren't you going to do something? This is damage to school property. That's a serious crime!" Brianna exclaimed.

"I'm sorry," he said. "Due to low funding, we are unable to fix the room and replace the computers. We are going to have to put it on hold for the rest of the school year. Again, I'm really sorry. I know how much this meant to you."

Brianna looked at him appalled. "For the entire year? The school year has barely even begun. There's so much we wanted to write about throughout the year."

"How about we use our own computers? We can still write. We'll just have to access everything on our own. We don't have to worry about printers or any of that," Matthew chimed in.

"No. It's better to stop altogether. I'm sorry," he said shutting down the idea.

He turned around and walked into his office leaving us dazed. We walked out of the office silently until we made it back to the club room.

We sat down on the slashed couches in silence.

"I don't know what we're going to do," Brianna whispered. "This club was going to help us get into university."

Matthew patted her on the shoulder comforting her. I didn't know what to say.

"I can't believe he didn't care," Matthew said.

"That man doesn't care about anything that doesn't have to do with those boys. I'm a hundred per cent sure he's the one who gave them the idea to trash this room in the first place."

Matthew and I looked at Brianna surprised.

"Why do you think that?" I asked her.

"Because it's weird they didn't do anything. You made a deal with them, but the fact that they listened is weird. I don't know. I was sure that Garrett would retaliate. Maybe I'm being crazy," she elaborated.

"I wouldn't put it past him. I think he knew. He didn't look surprised when he was looking at the photos," I said.

"Seriously guys, what are we going to do?" Brianna asked. "The newspaper was the only thing that distracted me from how much I hate everyone and everything in this town."

I bit the inside of my cheek speechless. This was my fault, and no matter how much they want to say it wasn't, I know it was. And she was right. The paper had been a huge distraction. Life in this town was a little more bearable, and I couldn't imagine the rest of the school year without that distraction.

"I wish we could do something outside the school like start a blog or something," Brianna said.

I looked at Brianna cocking my head at the idea. I sat up straight and grabbed my bag. I pulled out my laptop remembering something.

I looked through my bookmarks and clicked the link I was looking for. I've been meaning to talk to them about it, but I kept forgetting.

I turned the laptop towards them to let them read it.

"Annual Journalist of the Future Competition," Matthew read aloud.

"We can expose this town and win $10,000 doing so," I said.

Brianna sighed. "It's a really good opportunity, but writing about this town might not be the best idea. If they found out, it would be the end for us."

"We just have to be really careful," I told them.

"And when the winners get announced, it'd be too late

for them to do anything about it," I continued.

"Don't we need proof that we go to school? We have to ask the administration to print it out for us. Won't that be suspicious?" Matthew asked.

"All we need is a letter from one of the teachers saying that we're a part of the school newspaper, and we can ask Mrs. Anderson for that. She's literally oblivious. We'll tell her it's for college applications. Then we submit our piece before the deadline, and that's it," I explained.

"Come on guys. Let's do it," I urged. "Okay?"

They sat there quietly for a few moments thinking.

"Okay," Matthew said nodding. "What do we have to lose?"

"Okay," Brianna agreed.

"Okay," I smiled.

Chapter 21

We sat in the basement of Brianna's house trying to brainstorm ideas, and so far, it wasn't going well. We spent the entire week trying to come up with something, but every idea we had didn't work.

"What are we going to write about?" Matthew groaned staring at the ceiling while lying on the floor.

"We have concepts we want to talk about. Now we just have to narrow it down," I told them.

"We can write about the influence the KKK has on this town," Matthew suggested.

"It's good, but it's not unique," Brianna replied. "We need to stand out."

I bit the inside of my cheek in deep thought.

"I think I have an idea," I piped up. "But that's only if it's okay with you guys."

They looked at each other confused.

"What?" Matthew asked.

"I know that the disappearance of Lewis has been something that haunted both of you. Maybe we can look into it more. Not through the school this time so you guys don't have to worry about getting in trouble or being shut down," I replied.

I looked at them waiting for a response.

"Okay let's do it," Brianna said surprising me.

"I need to do this. We need to do this. He deserves better than being forgotten. They all deserve better. So, I'm in," Brianna continued.

I looked at Matthew waiting for his response.

"Okay, I'm in too."

I clapped my hands together. "We have about two months to investigate and submit."

"Where do we start?" Matthew asked.

"From the very beginning. We're gonna have to dig up the history of this town. But for now, let's talk about what we know," I said.

I got up from the ground and walked up to the whiteboard that had all of our ideas written out. I erased everything and wrote 'what we know' and underlined it.

"What do we know?" I asked them.

"He was the only black kid at the time of his disappearance," Matthew said.

"It was racially motivated," Brianna added.

They went back and forth throwing out ideas until I had no more space to write anything. I stepped back and looked at the full board. I took out my phone and snapped a picture for future references.

"We have to lay low for the next couple of weeks," I said sitting on the carpet. "We don't want them thinking we're up to something. Besides, once we hit December, everyone is going to be preoccupied with Christmas."

"We shouldn't do anything until then?" Brianna asked.

"No. We can research, but any real investigation is risky. Let's go to the bookstore tomorrow to ask Mr. Moretti if he has any papers or records of the disappearances. We can study too," I suggested.

I entered the bookstore the next day a little nervous. I couldn't help but feel like I was being watched. Plus, I was paranoid. I had to make sure I wasn't doing anything that differed from my regular routine. I had created an uproar, and people were hyper-aware of me now. I had to blend into the background for the next three weeks. Just until people had other things to worry about.

"Hey Mr. Moretti," I greeted.

"Hi Aaleyah. How have you been? Have things calmed down for you?" he asked.

I smiled. "I'm fine. Thankfully things have been quiet."

"No more trouble you hear? I'm too old for this."

"I promise I'm done. I really need to focus on graduating. No more distractions."

"That's good. I'm glad." He nodded. "Your friends are in the back."

"Okay thank you."

I walked to the back where my friends were and sat down next to them.

"Sorry I'm late guys. I slept in."

"How late did you sleep last night," Matthew asked.

"I started a new show on Netflix and lost track of time."

"It was kind of scary too," I confessed. "I had trouble falling asleep."

"You can go up against crazy people in this town, but a

show is what it takes to scare you?" Matthew teased.

"Shut up," I said lightly kicking him under the table.

"What did I miss?" I asked.

"We asked Mr. Moretti for all of the newspapers he has of this town. We told him we're doing a history project, and damn, he has papers dating back to the 1920s. It's crazy," Brianna said filling me in.

I sifted through dozens of newspapers that laid in front of us. Each with boring headlines.

Matthew passed over his newspaper. "I found something."

"What?" I asked looking up.

"The last column of this newspaper talks about some disappearances in a town called Whiyles here in Arkansas. It was happening for months, and nobody was doing anything about it. Until one night, a group of African American kids disappeared at once—like ten of them. They were from fourteen to seventeen years old. After that, the community started protesting demanding answers from the sheriff to find the kids, but they didn't. Instead, the white community started violently beating them up. They also started lynching a lot of people, so the black community retaliated. It became so violent that people started fleeing the town," Matthew explained.

"I've never heard of this," Brianna said in surprise. "Why wouldn't this be in our history textbooks?"

I took out my laptop and searched the town and clicked the only link related to what I was searching.

"It says here that the town was abandoned in 1937 and it's been a ghost town since. Literally no one knows this place exists," I told them.

"How close is this town from here?" Matthew asked.

I googled a map of Arkansas.

"This town is not on the map anymore." I squinted at the screen to figure out how to read a map. "Yeah, I don't know how to read this."

"Should we ask if Mr. Moretti has a map of Arkansas? If he has diaries from the 1600s, he should have a map from the 1930s," Matthew said.

"I'll go ask." I got up from my chair and walked over to the front desk where he was talking closely with a customer.

"Mr. Moretti," I called to get his attention.

"Oh, Aaleyah," He said startled. "What can I do for you?"

"Sorry. I didn't mean to interrupt."

"No, no, that's alright," he smiled.

"I was just wondering if you had a map of Arkansas from the 1930s."

"I think I might." He pursed his lips to think. "That's oddly specific. Why would a young kid want something that old."

"Trust me, this is not something I would like to be doing in my free time. It's for history class," I lied.

The man that Mr. Moretti was talking to didn't turn around. He had his hands on the front desk, and his back towards me. I didn't feel like it was smart disclosing our plan to a stranger.

"Ahh." He nodded. "I'll go check. I'll see what else I can find for you. I want you to ace this."

"Thank you," I smiled feeling a little guilty for lying.

"For a history project, it's odd that you are the only ones here. I mean, this is the only place in this town where you can do research," the man said accusingly turning around once Mr. Moretti was out of sight.

He stared at me with his piercing eyes. He picked up the

baseball cap beside him and fiddled with it.

"Most people use the computer nowadays," I said slowly.

He chuckled and looked at me not saying anything more.

"Hey, did you find it?" Matthew asked coming up behind me.

"He's in the back looking," I told Matthew

"Let's go sit down," I said to him. "He'll bring it to us."

I nudged on Matthews's shirt to get him to walk.

He frowned. Probably wondering why I was acting so weird. Thankfully he didn't question me about it until we sat down.

"You good?" Matthew asked giving me a questioning look.

I nodded and looked behind me feeling like we were being watched.

"I'll tell you guys later," I whispered.

They wanted to question me more but agreed instead.

Mr. Moretti walked to our table a few minutes later. "Here you go."

He dropped a box of stuff on our table.

"Wow," I said surprised. I was only expecting a map.

"I want you guys to do well. Seeing you do research the traditional way makes me happy. Anything I can do to help."

"Thank you," we said in unison.

He smiled and walked away leaving us with more information than we asked for.

Brianna brought the box closer to her and dumped it on the table. "Let's get started."

I took a sip of my coffee and grabbed a handful of papers and started reading. They were interesting, but there was nothing about what I was looking for until I reached a notebook. I opened it curious to see what was written in it. I always found reading people's old diaries very fascinating.

I opened the first page and saw a name written in the bottom corner in small writing.

"Jason," I read aloud.

I flipped through the pages, and there were names written in three columns.

I gasped realizing that I might have been holding a hit list.

"What?" Brianna asked looking up.

I gave her the book to look through it and stopped halfway. She looked up at me understanding.

"We need to look into these names," she said.

She took the notebook and put it in her backpack.

"We can't take that," I whispered.

She shrugged. "He's not gonna notice."

"Here's the map." Matthew moved the papers out of the way, so he could lay the map on the table.

He reached into his backpack and took out a black sharpie.

"We're here." He traced the marker down to the town. "And here is Whiyles."

"It's like 96 miles away."

"How far away is that?" Brianna asked

"Almost two hours," he answered.

I pursed my lips thinking.

"Should we take a road trip one of these weekends and go down there?" Matthew asked.

I narrowed my eyes at him. "Don't be crazy."

Brianna laughed. "Yeah, it doesn't seem like the smartest plan to go to a deserted town."

"Especially a town with that kind of history," I added.

"Yeah, you're right," Matthew agreed. "We should find out as much as we can about this town."

I nodded in agreement.

We all went back to the piles of papers in front of us and went through it for the next hour, and only stopping to talk when something interesting came up.

I tried to pay attention to the papers in front of me, but I couldn't. My mind kept going back to that man who was talking to Mr. Moretti. I shivered just thinking about him.

Matthew must have seen me because he narrowed his eyes at me.

I shook my head and went back to reading, but the only thing on my mind was those cold green eyes.

"Okay I'm done," Brianna said after a while.

"Me too. There's nothing interesting or helpful in here."

They both looked at me waiting for me to say something.

"Sorry guys I was distracted," I said looking at the pile in front of me.

They both reached over to take some papers off of my pile leaving me with nothing.

"I can take some too," I protested.

"I know, but you seem a little distracted."

"Yeah," I said agreeing with Matthew.

I watched them as they skimmed through the papers finishing within a few minutes.

Matthew leaned back and pushed away the pile in front of him. "Nothing here."

"Look at this letter." Brianna leaned in and put it in the middle so we could all see.

She grabbed the notebook she had put in her bag earlier and pulled it out to the first page to look at the name.

"The name signed at the bottom is the same."

I looked at the name to see for myself and picked it up to read it.

"Hmm," I hummed.

I read the letter out loud. "I'm sorry, but I have left with my family, and I advise you all to do the same with yours. This is not something I can do anymore. Don't try to find me."

"Any guesses on what this could mean?" I asked.

They both shook their head looking confused.

"I'm going to take this too," Brianna said putting the letter in her bag.

"What?" she asked at our questioning glances. "This might be useful later on."

"How?" Matthew inquired. "He's probably dead."

"Yes, but we can still try to figure out who he was." She looked at her watch. "We've been here for a while. Should we go home?"

I nodded. "We need to find a place where we can talk freely and leave all this stuff. We can't get caught by our parents."

Matthew and Brianna looked at each other, and silently communicated .

"What?" I asked.

"We might have a place," Brianna said.

"Let's go." I stood up and grabbed my stuff, and crammed them into my bag. I wanted to get out of this store.

We walked to the front of the store with the boxes that Mr. Moretti gave us. We walked through the bookshelves, and the whispers got louder and louder, but not enough for us to hear. They suddenly stopped probably aware of our presence.

I frowned. I've never seen Mr. Moretti act this suspicious. Why would he be talking to this man? Couldn't he see how creepy he was?

"Are you done?" Mr. Moretti asked when he saw us walking towards them.

"Thank you for helping us," I said.

"Of course. Anything I can do to help you get an A." He paused for a moment. "You may borrow these things if it will help you."

"Thank you, but we took pictures," Brianna said holding up her phone.

"Ahh." Mr. Moretti nodded. "Of course. Technology."

I smiled. "See you Mr. Moretti."

"Yes, yes." He waved at us and turned back to the creepy guy when we walked out the door.

I wish I knew what they were talking about. Maybe they were friends. This guy acts nice and polite when he's with Mr. Moretti, so Mr. Moretti probably has never seen the side I've seen of him.

"Where to?" I asked once we were all inside the car.

"Take us to 23rd street. We're going to the forest," Matthew explained.

"Is that the smartest idea? I'm pretty sure going to the forest is asking to get killed and disposed of quietly," I said.

"Don't worry. No one goes there," Matthew replied.

After a while I zoned out Matthew and Brianna's conversation. I was overwhelmed with unending thoughts. I didn't know where to start to untangle them. I gripped the steering wheel tightly, and I kept looking at the rear-view mirror to see if we were being followed. Saying I was paranoid was an understatement.

"Pull in here," Matthew said.

I looked around surprised that I had made it. I didn't even realize I drove that far.

"You good?" Brianna asked eyeing me curiously.

"Yeah," I reassured her. "Let's go."

We piled out of the car and walked into the forest. I stared in awe at the towering trees–the sunlight peeking through the branches casting a soft glow on everything below. I inhaled deeply the smell of nature calming me.

"Nice isn't it?" Matthew asked

"Yeah," I said breathlessly.

"We used to come here a lot," he explained.

"We stopped after Lewis disappeared," Brianna said. "It was kind of our hiding spot."

"It's really nice," I smiled.

We walked silently following the path until Matthew suddenly came to a stop.

"Why did you stop?" I asked.

"This is where the path ends. We're going through the woods now," he warned.

"I'm ready," I said. "This isn't my first time walking through a forest you know?"

"Oh, you have them in Canada too?" he joked.

I rolled my eyes pushing him slightly. He chuckled as he walked in front of me. I followed his footsteps.

"Watch your step," he said as he swiftly jumped over a fallen tree.

I followed landing next to him before he could turn over to lend me a hand.

"Damn your fast."

I shrugged and watched as he helped Brianna jump over the tree.

"We're almost here," Brianna announced.

We walked for a few more minutes until we were in front of an enormous tree with a huge trunk.

Matthew walked around the tree where another tree was closely next to it and called us over.

"Whoa," I said looking wide-eyed at the massive hole at the bottom of the tree trunk. The hole was like an entrance. It was big enough for an adult to walk through it crouching.

Matthew walked in first, and Brianna following closely behind. I stood at the front scared and excited about what might be on the other side of this entrance.

"Are you coming?" I heard Brianna's voice echo through the tree.

I walked in, and a few steps later, there was a ladder. I looked up and gulped. I wasn't afraid of heights, but I wasn't a fan of them either.

I watched Brianna and Matthew climb higher and higher. I took a deep breath and climbed up not looking down.

The ladder ended, and I climbed into the tree-house. I crawled onto the floor and looked around.

I was sure my mouth was gaped open because they both laughed at my reaction. The tree house was huge. There was a small carpet at the back and a coffee table. There were bean bag chairs with patterned blankets covering the floor. I walked over to the opening that overlooked the entire forest. We were nestled safely inside the tree branches. I realized the reason I couldn't see the tree house was because there were so many leaves covering it.

I walked back inside and dropped myself onto one of the bean bag chair.

"Wow! I feel like I'm in Narnia. How did you guys find this place?"

"We don't know who built it, but one day while playing

in the woods, we saw the entry in the tree trunk. So naturally, we went inside, and this is what we found. We furnished it over the years. I forgot how nice this place was," he said softly looking into the distance.

He suddenly sat up straight snapping himself out of the place he was going. "Tell us what happened back at the bookstore."

I bit my lip in thought. My heart was beating hard in my chest. Everything I was feeling rushed back.

"The guy who was with Mr. Moretti." I took a deep breath before I continued, "I think he was the guy who attacked me at school."

"What?!" Matthew asked. "And you mention this now?"

"We could have gotten him," Brianna said.

"And do what? Call the police?" I shook my head. "He knew there was nothing I could do. He had a smug look on his face."

"How did you recognize him?" Brianna asked.

"His eyes, his voice and the way he was acting. I can't believe I hadn't recognized him before," I said trailing off feeling so stupid.

"I was so sure it was Garrett," Matthew whispered.

"So stupid," I muttered.

"You know him?" he asked.

"No," I said. "I met him a couple of times when I first moved here. The first time I saw him was from afar, but the second time he walked into the store to buy notebooks from Mr. Moretti. He was really weird and creepy."

They listened silently to everything I was telling them.

"Wow," Brianna sighed. "What are we going to do?"

I shrugged. "I don't know."

"I don't know if there is anything we can do," I told them

feeling hopeless.

"We can figure out who he is. Do you know his name?" Matthew asked.

I bit my lip thinking. "Um, Larry? No, that doesn't sound right. It starts with an L."

"Lucas?" Brianna asked.

"No," I shook my head.

"Logan?" Matthew continued.

I shook my head again. I bit my nails trying to remember.

"Landon?"

"Leo?"

"Liam?"

I looked up at Brianna. "Yes, yes, Liam. That's what Mr. Moretti called him."

I felt relieved that we at least figured out his name.

"Good teamwork," I laughed leaning back on the bean bag. "But how in the world are we gonna find any information on him? How many Liams are out there?"

"Have some faith." Brianna smiled. "I can do a lot with a name and a face."

I pursed my lips and looked at her.

"Don't worry leave it to me."

"What are you going to do?" I frowned.

"Just a little search on the web." She shrugged.

"Really? Just a little search?" I asked.

"Fine. I'm going to hack into Mr. Moretti's computer to see if he has any transaction history of someone named Liam. It's a small town, and I'm confident there aren't that many. If not, then I'll search the camera in front of the store for his face and run it through the police database to see if I get a match," she explained

"That sounds very illegal," I warned.

"It's only illegal if you get caught," Brianna grinned.

"Um, I'm pretty sure it's illegal either way," I said.

"I know how to cover my tracks, and if I do get caught, I'm pretty sure they wouldn't arrest me. They'd hire me because they'd realize what an amazing asset I'd be to their team. Like Penelope Garcia."

"This isn't a TV show Bri," Matthew said chuckling at her enthusiasm.

"It could happen," she pouted.

"Let's not do anything now. We still need to lay low," I reminded them.

They both nodded.

"What should we do in the meantime?" Matthew asked.

"More research. We can try to figure out what the notebook is, and the letter. We can also do more research about the ghost town. Maybe we'll find something," I told him.

"Alright. I'll try to figure out who the notebook belonged to, and what the letter might have meant. You and Aaleyah try to find out what you can about the ghost town. As soon as people start getting preoccupied with the winter dance and Christmas, then we can start properly investigating. Until then, we don't talk about this unless we're at home or here," Brianna said.

"Sounds good." I nodded.

"We should get going," Matthew said getting up. "We don't want to walk back when it's dark."

Chapter 22

The next few weeks went by slowly, and school was quiet and drama free. Everyone was getting into the holiday spirit. The school was already decorated even though we still had a week and a half left until winter break. The school was also buzzing with excitement because of the winter ball. It was the first school dance of the year.

Our investigation was going quite well considering we couldn't do much. We discovered that most people that fled from the ghost town went to surrounding towns, and since Anderton was the closest in proximity, most of them settled here. Both the black and white community. The black people who fled their town from the disappearances were met with more unexplained disappearances here in Anderton.

We guessed maybe the Jason guy was the leader of the KKK of the ghost town, and we think that he was heavily involved in these disappearances—most of the KKK probably were. When they came to Anderton, the kidnappings continued, but this time at a faster rate than before. We came to the conclusion that it was because the black community retaliated, and they were angry because of it. This time there weren't enough of them to fight back since they were scattered around surrounding towns. We haven't figured out who this Jason guy was, but we do know that he came to Anderton which makes it easier to find out more about him. We decided to go back to the bookstore after school to research more about both towns.

"Guess what," Brianna squealed when I reached her locker.

"What?" I asked curious.

She pointed to my phone. "Look at the group chat."

I opened the message and looked at it wide-eyed. "Is that..?"

She nodded.

"How?" I asked.

"I spent the past few days researching like crazy. I was so close I couldn't stop. He was in an old article from back in the day, and I noticed the name under it."

"Wow," I exclaimed proudly.

"Did you find more information about him in the article?" Matthew asked.

"No, but he seemed pretty important. I don't know why," she said. "Hopefully, we can find something when we go to the bookstore today."

We walked to our class. We were excited because we finally discovered something about this Jason guy. We don't know how it relates to Lewis's disappearance, but maybe it will lead to something. I had a feeling that everything in this town was connected.

"I don't know why everyone is so excited about this stupid dance." I looked around all the chatty students talking about what colour dresses they would buy.

"Where do you even buy a nice dress in this town?" I asked.

"Literally nowhere. People drive up to the city," Brianna explained.

"Makes sense," I said. "I guess what they say about Americans and dances are true."

"What do they say?" Matthew asked.

"Y'all take it way too seriously."

He laughed. "True."

"How many dances do you guys have in a year?" I asked.

"Like 3 or 4. I don't know. I lost count."

"I can't imagine the hassle," I said. "Are you guys going to prom?"

Brianna and Matthew looked at each other and shook their heads.

"No. I can't imagine prom with these people," Brianna said shuddering.

I chuckled.

I looked at my phone and saw that the bell was about to ring.

"See you guys later." I separated from my friends and walked to my class.

I waited for my friends in the parking lot after school. We barely did anything at school since we were nearing the end of the semester. All we were doing now was reviewing our course material which made it a lot easier to focus on our investigation.

"Hey." Matthew opened the passenger door startling me.

He laughed when I jumped up almost dropping my

phone.

I rolled my eyes and greeted Brianna as she came inside the car.

"Let's go." I pulled out of the driveway and pulled into the main road.

"I'm hungry," Brianna announced.

"Me too," Matthew agreed.

"Let's get some food," I said.

I drove down to a local diner and parked.

"We can just order our food and eat in the car," Matthew said sensing my hesitation when we pulled into the diner.

We usually ordered our food ahead of time, so by the time we got there, it would be ready and we could eat elsewhere. The diner was always full, and it was uncomfortable eating when people were grilling you with their eyes.

"No," I shook my head. "Let's go in."

We walked inside the busy diner ignoring all the glares and walked to the farthest booth away from everyone else.

We waited for a few minutes until a young waiter came to take our order. "What can I get for you guys?"

"Can I get the number three with a strawberry milkshake please," I said to the waiter handing him back the menu.

Brianna and Matthew ordered next. We were glad the waiter was nice and didn't make us feel uncomfortable.

"Alright let's talk," I said. "We finally have a lead on this Jason guy, and if we find more information about him, we can figure out exactly how big his role in the disappearances were here in Anderton. We know he was involved in the disappearances in Whiyles because of all the names in the notebook. We need to figure out how it happened and who was responsible. Maybe if we figure that out, we can figure out who's involved here. Like a timeline."

They listened attentively.

"Brianna, exactly what did you find?" I asked.

"Okay," she said leaning over lowering her voice. "I didn't find much, but I do know that this guy was very popular in this town in the late 1930s and early 1940s. They sort of idolized him. The article just talked about all the amazing contributions he made to this town. That makes it easier to find more things about him."

"How?" I asked.

"He was really popular," she repeated.

I stared at her not getting the point.

"This is a small town, and everyone knows everyone. If you're popular and people like you, most likely there are articles about you and pictures hung up all over town. We just need to find out exactly what contributions he made to this town," she explained.

I nodded slowly starting to understand.

"Where should we start?" I asked.

"We can figure out who Jason was. If we actually manage to solve this, it'll be huge. Finding the connections between the ghost town, Jason, the disappearances, and Lewis's case is important. We know that at least half of Whiyles white population fled here.

"The other half fled to surrounding towns, and at least a quarter of the black population moved here. Most black people that moved to Anderton probably didn't have the means to go to other towns since they were further away. At least that's what we think. We think the reason why other people from the community fled to other towns was because Anderton and Whiyles were really close, so they probably didn't want to be close to what they were running away from.

"We know that Whiyles was known for kidnapping black people. Anderton also has a history with these kinds of things, but they were known more for lynching, and if someone went missing, they'd end up being found dead a few days later. When the people from Whiyles came to Anderton, that's when the disappearances picked up, and this time, there were no bodies. It's like people were vanishing into thin air.

"After people from Whiyles came to Anderton, things changed. This is why we couldn't find any information about the disappearances on the internet, because nobody knows about Whiyles. It's like it's been erased from history." Matthew stopped quickly when the waiter plopped the food in front of us.

We thanked him and waited until he was a distance away to continue our conversation.

"I wish there was a way to figure out the names of the people who fled here," I muttered nibbling on a fry.

"There might be since this was a crisis and these people were fleeing their homes. The town must have kept the names of the people who fled here to keep track," Brianna said.

"How would we find that information?" I asked.

"It's probably archived. Finding where it is will be the difficult part."

I bit my lip. "Let's not worry about that for now. We know about Jason, which is a good start. Let's focus on him and his history in this town and how he plays a role in all of this. We still have that notebook of names and the letter he wrote. If we can find out who the people in that notebook were, that could help us a lot. We'll start the article with him since he's our first suspect. Next, we figure out where and when Lewis disappeared. Brianna, you can start researching about Liam."

"About that," Brianna said slowly.

"What?" I asked narrowing my eyes.

"I know you told me to wait, but I couldn't."

"What did you do?" Matthew whispered.

"I did some light hacking, and I found something," she confessed.

"And you're mentioning this now?" I whispered loudly.

"Sorry. I couldn't help myself. Do you want to know who he is or not?" she asked.

"Yes," I whispered.

"I brought my laptop with me. I'll show you guys when we get to the bookstore."

I took a deep breath suddenly getting nervous.

We changed the subject for a while since the diner was starting to fill up again, and people were now sitting around us.

We heard loud voices enter the diner capturing everyone's attention.

I rolled my eyes when I saw who came in.

"Heads up," I warned. "It's the goons."

"Are they coming our way?" Matthew asked since his back was turned to them.

"Yeah, I think they're going to the booth in front of us."

I watched as they walked over to us stopping at the booth I predicted they would sit.

"Are you guys done with your food?" I asked wanting to leave as soon as possible.

"Yeah," Matthew said.

We called over the waiter, and asked for our checks. We paid and got out of there.

"Ugh they ruined my mood," I said as soon as we got inside the car.

Brianna leaned over patting me on the shoulder. "Don't let them."

I drove to the bookstore which took less than five minutes. We piled out of the car and walked inside the bookstore.

"Hey Mr. Moretti," I greeted the old man.

He smiled. "Aaleyah, it's always nice to see you."

"More research?" he asked

"Yeah, I'm writing my History SAT soon, and I need an interesting topic to write about for the written portion."

"The SATs." He nodded. "Anything I can help with?"

"I was thinking of writing about the history of the KKK in this town. Do you have articles or information?" I asked.

I didn't like lying to him, but no one can know what we were doing. Since Mr. Moretti had some sort of a relationship with Liam, I knew I couldn't tell him anything just in case. Not because I didn't trust him, but because I didn't trust Liam.

"Yes, I'm pretty sure if I dig in the back, I'll find something."

"Thank you," I said.

"No problem. You guys take a seat. I'll bring it right over."

We walked through the bookshelves to go to our table but stopped short when we saw who was sitting there with their legs on top of the table reading a book.

He must have sensed our presence because he looked up from his book and turned towards us.

He smirked slightly when he saw us standing there. He

closed his book and got up. "I guess you guys need this table more than I do. More research I gather?"

I stared at him not answering.

"Well good luck," he said glaring intensely.

"Aaleyah, Matthew, Brianna," he said tipping his hat.

I wasn't surprised that he knew who we were, but I knew my friends were because they tensed up when they heard their names.

The way he said our names felt like a threat. Like he was telling us to stay in our lane.

He turned around and walked away until he was no longer in view.

I let go of the breath I was holding in.

"That was intense," Matthew muttered

We sat down at the table a little unnerved of what happened. We couldn't bring ourselves to talk since Mr. Moretti could show up any minute with our stuff.

We talked superficially about school until Mr. Moretti showed up with a small box full of articles, and put it in the middle of the table.

"Thank you." I smiled.

"No problem," he said, patting my shoulder.

"Mr. Moretti," I called before he walked away.

"Yes?"

"Who is that guy exactly?" I asked curiously.

He pursed his lips for a second. "I don't know much about him. He comes in once in a while to buy notebooks from me. He also spends time here to read sometimes."

"Why?" he asked.

"He's...weird," I mumbled

Mr. Moretti laughed. "He's just a little shy. Not really a people's person, but he means well."

I thanked him again.

We didn't talk about anything since the very person we wanted to discuss was in the bookstore. He probably was creeping around the bookshelves listening to our conversation. Whatever Brianna wanted to tell us would have to wait.

Matthew grabbed the box and dumped everything on the table. It was filled with old articles and pictures. I took out my notebook to take notes. There were many things I needed to keep track of.

We split everything three ways and got to work. Most articles I read weren't that interesting. I read more articles until I came across one dedicated to "The hero of Anderton". I leaned back in my chair and read the article. There was a picture of a man wearing a white KKK gown with a little boy on his lap. He was sitting behind a large frame of another man wearing the same gown, sitting on the same chair. I flipped the page, and sat up when I saw the subtitle, "The Legacy Continues, Gordan Levi-Pedleford takes over".

"Hmm," I hummed. The name sounded familiar.

Matthew and Brianna looked up at me.

"You find something?" Brianna asked

"I think so," I told them. "Let me keep reading."

They nodded and went back to their piles.

I continued reading and quickly realized that this Gordan guy in the picture was Jason's son, and the man in the frame behind him must have been Jason. I read the article carefully, it talked mostly about how they transformed this town making it community and family-oriented. It mentioned all the contributions they made to the town. Especially helping out those who fled from Whiyles.

"Oh my God!" I said, bewildered when I read the last

line. It finally clicked.

I stared at the article frozen. "I can't believe this."

"What?" Matthew asked at my sudden outburst.

Brianna was also looking up.

"Listen to this," I told them. "The family legacy will live on through Gordan L.P and his son William, and hopefully they can follow in the footsteps of the man who started it all, Jason L.P."

Matthew shook his head in confusion. "I don't get it."

"William L.P," I said. "Doesn't that name ring a bell?"

They had a blank look on their face for a few seconds until they figured out what that meant.

"Principal William?" Brianna asked in low voice covering her mouth.

"There's no way!" Matthew shouted.

"Shhh!" Brianna scolded him.

"Sorry," he whispered. "But oh my God."

Brianna shook her head. "I can't believe it, but at the same time, I can."

"The rumours were true," Matthew said dazed.

"We still don't know if he's recruiting students, but we do know he's directly related to all of it," I said.

"So, our principal is the grandson of the man we're investigating." He laughed hysterically. "Wow."

"I never trusted him," Brianna muttered.

"What does this mean?" Matthew asked.

"We have to be careful," I told them. "But it also makes it easier for us because we know that Jason was responsible for all the disappearances between 1930 to 1950s. His son took over in 1957 until he got too old. Now the principal is continuing this sick family operation," I assumed.

"Damn he's old," Matthew said.

"Yeah, which means he also has a long history. If the principal did take over the sick family tradition, then he probably is responsible for Lewis's disappearance," I noted.

"You think so?" Brianna asked chewing on her bottom lip.

I nodded. "We have to figure out how the principal is related to all of this, and if he does end up being the leader of the KKK, then yes, he probably is."

"What if he's just the leader of the KKK, but not involved in the disappearances?" Matthew asked.

"I highly doubt that," I said. "It's a family legacy. Also, the disappearances didn't stop, and I don't think he passed it down to someone else."

"I wish there was a way we could attend one of their meetings," I confessed.

They both rolled their eyes.

"You want to walk into the lion's den?" Brianna asked.

"They won't know we're there. We'd hide," I explained.

Matthew scratched the back of his neck looking conflicted. He turned to Brianna giving her a knowing look.

"No. No way," she said shaking her head.

"What?" I asked.

"A long time ago, we fell asleep while we were in the tree house, and when we woke up it was night time. While we were walking, we might have stumbled across one of their meetings, and we hid behind the bushes and watched," Matthew explained.

"That was risky and dangerous, and we can't just go looking for a KKK meeting. That's literally the stupidest thing I've ever heard," Brianna warned.

"We'll be careful," I promised. "Come on Brianna."

"It's way too dangerous," she said shaking her head.

"We got lucky because we came when it was over, and there were like three people still around. We had to wait twenty minutes after they left to leave, and that was in the summer. It's almost winter, and the leaves are crunchy. They would be able to hear our footsteps from a mile away."

She sighed. "But there might be another way to do this without putting ourselves in danger."

"How?" Matthew asked.

"Cameras."

I frowned. "Where in the world would we put cameras in the middle of the forest."

"In the tree," she explained. "I have a small black surveillance camera that we can use."

Matthew furrowed his eyebrows. "I'm pretty sure they'd see it. And why do you have a surveillance camera?" he asked.

"Don't worry about it," Brianna shot back.

He rolled his eyes and leaned back in his chair crossing his arms.

"Anyways, we're going to try to put it in the trees. Hopefully, the leaves will hide it, and since it's going to be dark, I doubt they'd see it. We'd just have to set up a day before."

"How would it hang in the tree? How is the quality in the dark?" I asked not convinced.

"I'll show you when we get back to my house," she said.

"Did you guys find anything in the articles?" I asked changing the subject.

"Nothing interesting. Just events that were happening, and this Jason guy seemed to be involved in all of them," Matthew said.

"Let's finish the rest, and we can go to my house to plan," Brianna suggested.

We agreed and got back to our piles.

After the big revelation we made, reading everything else that came after wasn't relevant.

I flipped through the articles skimming through the pages.

"This can't be all of it," I said when I was done.

"There must have been an underground newspaper because this ain't it," I continued. "How can there be no information about all the people that went missing?"

"Maybe there was, and we don't know," Brianna said.

I sighed. "Are you guys done?"

"Yeah." Matthew stuffed his pile back inside the box.

Brianna and I ended up putting a few pictures and articles in our backpacks. We both agreed Mr. Moretti probably wouldn't notice.

We walked up to the front desk to drop off the box.

I tensed up a little when I saw Liam sitting in Mr. Moretti's chair. I always felt nauseous and unnerved whenever I was around that man. Especially knowing he was the one who attacked me on Halloween.

"Where is Mr. Moretti?" I asked slowly.

He pointed to the back.

I walked up to the front desk dropping off the box.

"He's such a freak," I said once we were inside the car.

"You don't even know the half of it," Brianna muttered.

We sat in Brianna's basement, and she scribbled on the white board.

"Okay," Brianna said the marker pressed up against her chin in deep thought. "We know that it starts with Jason."

She taped a picture of Jason we took from Mr. Moretti

and wrote "Criminal #1", she took a picture of the principal and put it next to Jason's picture, "Our main suspect".

"What else do we know?" she asked.

"The disappearance of Lewis is related to this twisted family history, and the principal might have been directly involved," I said

"Probably is," Matthew threw out. "Wouldn't put it past him, and nobody would ever suspect a high school principal."

"Perfect disguise," Brianna agreed.

"Okay, we need to figure out if the principal is the leader of the KKK. Once we confirm, we can safely assume he took over," I said.

"What do we know about Liam?" I asked Brianna.

"His name is Liam Morris. He's twenty-five years old, and has quite a history. He's been to juvie and prison."

I bit my nails nervous for what she might say next. "For what?"

"Theft, and a few aggravated assaults. He also has a restraining order against him. After he was released, he moved here. He's been here for quite a bit."

"Any history here?" Matthew asked.

"No, he's been clean ever since."

"So, he's a violent criminal." I shook my head.

"Do you know where he works?" I asked.

"No. There's no job listed here. But there is an address."

"He lives on the other side of town," she continued.

I looked over at Matthew who was zoned out. "What are you thinking about?"

He jumped up suddenly and started pacing. "Okay, so we think our principal is evil right?"

We both nodded wondering where he was going with

this.

"When you got attacked at school, it was right after you pissed off Mr. Smith, and you've already had your altercations with half the football team. You've also been writing in the school newspaper for a few weeks."

"So?" I asked.

"Think about it. You pissed off some people, and you get attacked in school. Not only that, he covered everything up to make you look crazy. I've been thinking about how he made the room go back to normal. You were gone for what five—maybe ten minutes? It's impossible he did that all by himself. He had help, and I'm positive that it was probably Garrett and them. Which means that they orchestrated the whole thing with the principal's knowledge. They were all in on it."

He paused to gather his thoughts. "Which makes Liam a hitman."

"What?!" I exclaimed. "Come on, this isn't a movie."

"They hired Liam to scare you. He also told you to watch yourself which was insinuating that if you didn't back off, you'd be..." he made a throat-slitting gesture. "Which is the exact definition of a hitman."

He took the marker from Brianna and wrote Liam's name and the word hitman next to it.

"We have to be careful around him," Matthew warned.

"Yeah," I agreed. "I kind of feel like he's on to us. I can't explain how, but I think he is."

"We could set up cameras inside his house," Brianna suggested.

I stared at her wide-eyed. "And why on God's earth would we do that."

"To see what he's up to. If he's a hitman, we have to be

careful."

"You don't think we should watch a KKK meeting, but you think it's okay sneaking into a criminal's house and installing cameras." Matthew shook his head at her.

"He's just one person, and they're a group of people," she defended herself.

"Yeah, and where would we even get cameras?" I asked.

"Online," she said. "They have everything."

Matthew and I looked at each other stunned that she would even suggest this.

"We are not sneaking into his house," Matthew said.

"Why not? It'd be really easy. I'll just observe the cameras in front of his apartment to figure out when he comes and goes. When we learn his schedule, we go in and install them."

"We're not cops," I told her.

"You don't have to be a cop," she said.

"I'm pretty sure you do because then it would be illegal," Matthew stated.

"Whatever. We're investigative journalists. Same thing," Brianna pointed out.

"Pretty sure it's not, but whatever," Matthew said giving up.

"We don't have to do it now, but we should consider it."

"What would watching him do for us?" I asked her.

"Well, for one, we'll know what he's all about. Why doesn't he have a job? Second, if we think he's onto us, we'll be a step ahead of him. And if we catch him doing anything illegal, we'll turn him in. He's also on his 2nd strike, so the next time he commits a crime, he's going to jail for life."

I considered what she said.

"Can we see your camera?" Matthew asked changing the

subject.

"Yeah," she said jumping up.

She walked over to a closet and took out a box.

"It's small," I said holding the camera in my hand. "I doubt they'd see this at night hidden by a bunch of leaves."

"How does it do at night?" Matthew held up the camera and inspected it.

"It has night vision with audio, and it's 4k," she replied.

"How are we going to put it on the tree branch?" I asked.

She got up and walked back to the closet. "We have two options."

She held up the first device. "This one is a clamp, so you would just clamp it on the tree branch. But the branch would have to be a certain size for it to be sturdy, so this might not be the best option."

"This is a flexible tripod twist mount that you wrap around the tree branch," she said holding up the second device. "Which is the better option in my opinion."

Matthew nodded impressed. "So when do we do this?"

"When do they meet?" I asked.

"It was on a Friday last time," Brianna said. "I think that's their day. Tomorrow we go and hide the camera."

"Wait does that mean we have to have it recording for a whole day. Can it last?" I asked.

"Yeah, the battery life is amazing on this thing, and it uploads to the cloud immediately," she answered.

"Tomorrow?" I asked.

They both nodded.

"If the principal is actually a part of this, then we know where to start. We should also try to find all the names of the people who went missing and exactly where they went missing assuming the police were telling the truth about it. Maybe we can find a link between their disappearances, and it might lead us to something about Lewis," I suggested.

"Brianna, do you think you can find the names?" I asked.

"Yeah, but I will have to hack into the police database. They probably only have recent names. Everything else would be archived non-digitally."

"That's okay for now. We only need recent names."

"I'm also going to look back at the footage from Lewis's disappearance. I'm going to look through the cameras again to see if I missed anything," Brianna said.

"Sounds good." I looked at my watch realizing it was getting late.

"We should get going," I said to Matthew.

We walked upstairs saying goodbye to Brianna and her parents.

"Do you think we're in over our heads?" Matthew asked once we got inside the car.

"A hundred per cent," I said. " But we've made it this far, and we're so close. Just imagine how powerful our article will be? This is major, and to think that a bunch of high school kids are the ones to write about this is huge. We can expose this town, and everyone involved."

"You're right. This could be huge," Matthew agreed.

"We just have to be extremely careful," I stressed.

"Thank you for the ride," he said when I pulled up to his driveway. "See you tomorrow."

I waved at him and made my way home enjoying the silence. The lack of noise helped me untangle the mess in my head. The next few days were going to be crazy, and I needed to prepare myself.

Chapter 23

We walked through the forest the next day to start our mission.

"Do you guys know where we're going?" I asked.

We've been walking for some time, and I couldn't help but feel like we were lost.

"Yeah!" Matthew yelled from upfront. "Just a little longer."

I walked behind them looking behind me occasionally. I felt like we were being watched which did not help with my paranoia.

We walked through the silent forest a bit longer until we were standing in an empty spot with a fire pit in the middle and trees surrounding it. It was hidden and a perfect place to have a meeting. It wasn't huge, but it was big enough to hold a small group of people.

"Damn," I said thinking of all the messed up things that probably happened here.

"We should hurry up," Brianna said.

I walked around the space looking up at all the trees,

and walked up to the only climbable tree. "This tree is perfect. It's right in front of the pit too."

"Who's going to climb?" Brianna asked, looking between Matthew and me.

"Matthew, I think you should climb," I said.

"Why me?" he asked narrowing his eyes.

"Because you're tall which means you can reach further."

"Fine," he said taking the camera and tripod from Brianna and putting it in his pocket.

"If I fall to my death it's your fault," he threatened.

Brianna giggled and I rolled my eyes at how dramatic he was being.

We watched him as he climbed up the tree effortlessly. He placed the small camera on the tree branch using the twist stick mount to secure it. He carefully twisted the stick mount around the tree branch and slowly let go.

"Look it works," he laughed.

He climbed down and walked over to us and looked up at the tree to see if he could see it.

"Perfect," Brianna smiled.

She took out her iPad from her bag and her portable WIFI she takes with her everywhere.

She was silent for a few minutes in deep focus.

"Okay, it looks like we're good." She turned the iPad towards us so we could see what the camera was capturing.

"Aaleyah stand in the middle. I want to see how much I need to zoom in to see your face."

I nodded and walked to the middle beside the fire pit and waited.

"It's good now," she said.

She put everything in her backpack. "We should head

back now."

"Yeah let's go," I agreed

I laid in my bed staring at the ceiling thinking about everything we were doing. It's safe to say I was having second thoughts about the investigation. I don't even know how we came to this point, but I felt like we were in too deep to stop. What we were doing was undeniably dangerous, and if my parents ever found out, I would be shipped back on the next flight to Canada—no doubt.

"Better not get caught," I said to myself.

I looked at my clock and saw it was one in the morning.

"Crap," I muttered not realizing that it was late.

I turned off the lamp beside my night table and sunk into the bed. I felt my eyes get heavy when my head hit the pillow.

I woke up the next morning with butterflies in my stomach. Today would be the day we discovered if our principal was involved in the disappearances.

I took a deep breath and got out of bed. I walked to the bathroom and turned on the faucet to wash my face letting the cold water shock my system. Then I brushed my teeth and did the rest of my morning routine.

When I was done, I walked into my closet and picked out a hoodie and jeans, not feeling like dressing up. I took out a hijab and ran down the stairs to the kitchen, and greeted my parents. I sat down at the island to eat the breakfast my parents were making.

"You have one week until winter break," dad said putting a cup of coffee in front of me. "You excited?"

"You have no idea. Almost three weeks of not seeing anybody from school? Sounds like heaven."

Mom laughed "I can't believe how quickly time went flying. You're going to finish this year before you know it."

"Six more months. Easy peasy," I muttered taking a bite of my eggs.

"I should get going," I told my parents after I finished my food. "I'm taking Brianna and Matthew to school today."

"Love you guys," I waved.

I walked to my car and drove to pick up my friends.

"You guys ready for today?" I asked once everyone was inside the car.

"No. I feel like puking," Brianna said. "I couldn't sleep last night."

Matthew turned around to look at Brianna. "It'll be fine. Don't worry."

She shook her head. "That's not why I wasn't able to fall asleep. I stayed awake all night looking through the disappearances, and surprisingly I was able to go back quite a bit. I mapped out all of the places it said they disappeared. I also read the statements the families gave."

"Did you find anything?" I asked.

"No I stopped, because it was getting too much," she said.

"We can look through it today when we go to your house," I suggested.

"Sounds good," she agreed.

I pulled up to the school and parked.

"I need more coffee," Brianna muttered once we entered the loud school.

"Come on." I took her arm and dragged her to her locker.

We talked in front of their lockers until it was time for us to get to class.

I walked down the hallway pushing through the crowd to get to the class I hated the most.

I hope today goes by quickly I thought to myself.

We sat in Brianna's basement after school reading all the statements that were given. It was all random, and there were no patterns which had us frustrated.

Brianna ran down the stairs with a map of Anderton and thumbtacks.

She put the map on the wall. "We can use this map to mark where the victims were last seen."

"How far should we go?" I asked.

"We should keep it recent. Ten years?" she replied.

We read through the statements from the past ten years and marked the last locations of the victims before they were kidnapped on the map.

We stepped back and looked at all the markings we've made.

"It looks random to me," I said.

"Same," Brianna agreed.

We quietly stared at it until Matthew spoke up.

"I don't think it's random," he whispered.

We looked at him confused.

He picked up the laptop we were using and took a sharpie and wrote something on the map.

He stepped back after a few minutes to let us observe.

My eyes widened as I inspected the map carefully.

"It looks random, but it's not. I wrote all the ages of the victims and what time they disappeared. All the people who were the age of thirty to forty-five years old are over here." He drew a circle around four pins. "That's these people, and they disappeared somewhere in this area early mornings of the day."

Brianna walked over to the map and looked closely. "When they were headed to work?"

Matthew nodded. "The next group is high school students."

He drew a circle around the high school students who were kidnapped. "They disappeared during the night in this area. Which is where the movie theatre, bowling alley and the diner are. It's where teenagers hang out."

He circled a bunch of random pins. "These are people in their twenties coming home from university for breaks. These people disappeared during specific months like Thanksgiving break, winter break or summer."

"And this pin is an oddball." He paused and circled a specific pin.

"Lewis," Brianna whispered.

"Lewis didn't stay late at school, nor did he go to where all of the other kids went, but he wasn't in the forest and we know that because we've checked the footage. So, we actually don't know where Lewis went missing," Matthew said.

Brianna sighed. "This is good for our article, but sucks for us because we still don't know where Lewis went missing. I wish we could talk to his parents one more time."

"Why don't you?" I asked.

"They moved to Washington a year after Lewis was kidnapped," Matthew explained.

"And I don't want to ask them over the phone. It seems

kind of rude," she said.

"What if we drove up there?" I suggested.

"Like a road trip?" Matthew asked.

"Yeah, school ends in like a week. It can be like a four day trip," I proposed.

They both paused.

"What about your brother? Don't you want to spend time with him?" Brianna asked.

"We don't have to go right when school ends. We can go the second week, and he can come with us. Besides, he's coming on Sunday, so it's okay. On second thought, he has to come with us. I don't think I can convince my parents to let me go alone."

"I'm down. I just have to ask my parents," Matthew said.

"Me too," Brianna agreed.

"Maybe we can go to Whiyles too?" Matthew suggested.

"No," Brianna and I said in unison.

"Fine. You guys are no fun."

I laughed. "No. We're just not trying to die Matthew."

"Are you going to tell your brother?" Matthew asked becoming serious.

I shook my head. "No way. He'll need to think that it's just a road trip."

"What are you going to tell him when we talk to Lewis's parents?" Brianna questioned.

"You guys can say you're going to visit a friend that moved there, and I'll distract him."

"Sounds good," she said.

"What time is it by the way?" I asked.

"Almost ten," Brianna replied. "They should be done by now. The footage should upload itself to the cloud soon."

"Aaleyah," Matthew called my name after a few moments of silence.

"Yeah?" I answered.

"Have you thought of college yet?" he asked.

I nodded. "I picked out a few universities that I want to attend. They're a mix of Canadian and American schools, so I don't know."

"What program?" Brianna asked.

"I was thinking journalism. I was confused about what I wanted to do for a while. But after joining the school club and investigating for this contest, I realized that I like doing it."

Brianna smiled. "I'm happy you figured out what you want to do."

"I think you should come to Boston with us," Matthew said. "Brianna wants to go to MIT, and I'm thinking of Boston university."

Brianna nodded. "Yeah apply with us. It would be crazy if we all went to school in the same city."

"I'll apply. I guess I'll decide where I want to go if I get accepted to any of the schools I applied to."

I smiled to myself thinking.

"What?" Matthew asked.

I looked up at Matthew. "I was so sure that I was going to go back to Canada for university. The thought of staying here didn't even cross my mind, but now I'm really thinking about it."

He smiled. "We have that effect on people."

I laughed. "You're so ugly."

He chuckled.

"We really hope that you stay Aaleyah," he said.

"Me too," I smiled.

Brianna waved us over. "It's ready."

We rushed over to Brianna and tuned into the KKK meeting.

There was a man in a white gown lighting up the fire pit.

"Damn. It's serious serious," I whispered not believing what I was witnessing.

A few moments passed until a group of people entered the open space from all sides of the forest. They were wearing gowns and hoods, so we couldn't see anyone's faces. Two people brought tables. They laid out food and drinks on the table which shocked me.

Their meeting started after they filled the space. We listened as they recited something at the same time.

"Bible," Brianna explained.

After they finished, the man who had started the fire stood in front and welcomed them—calling them his brothers and sisters.

He made a speech about white supremacy, and how white people were the superior race and how every other race were inferior blah blah blah. He talked about how they were placed on this earth to set things right blah blah blah.

I scratched my head disturbed.

The rest of the meeting went on like this. Different people would stand in the front and say something racist. After the first three speeches, the shock was wearing off.

The man who started the meeting came back to the front and closed the meeting with another bible recital.

People took off their hoods. They shook hands and socialized with one another.

Matthew squinted at the screen. "I think that's Garrett."

I looked at what Matthew was staring at. "Probably is."

"Damn," Brianna said shaking her head. "A few of the football players are handing out food."

"I'm not shocked, but I kinda am," I said. "I don't see anyone else from school."

We watched carefully looking for anyone we can make out.

The man who led the meeting finally took off his hood revealing who he was.

"I kind of hate that we were right," I muttered staring at the principal.

After everyone got their food and drinks, they went back to the front.

"I am glad that there are more people at this week's meeting than last week. However, the younger population are still not as involved as we would like them to be. That's our goal for next week. I would like to see more younger people." He took a drink. "We'll end the night here. Please feel free to stick around to eat."

"He really is trying to recruit high school students," Matthew whispered in disbelief.

We watched until every person was gone, and the fire was put out.

Brianna closed her laptop. "Now we know I guess."

"I can't believe we go to a school where the principal is responsible for the disappearance of our best friend," she said blinking back tears.

Matthew pulled Brianna into a hug. "If we do this right, we can expose him."

"Damn right we are," she said. "And we're also going to that dance."

I frowned. "Why?"

"To snoop. He's using his job as a front, and we need to see if we can find anything that can help us. If he's using the school as a disguise, then he might be hiding something there," she explained.

I thought about it. "Do you really think that's a good idea? If we get caught, it's over for us."

"This is the only time we have to do this, and I want to know what's behind the construction area at the school," she said.

"What do you mean? I thought they just ran out of money," I asked.

"I've been thinking recently." She paused and bit her lip. "Ever since discovering all of this, I've been feeling suspicious about it. It doesn't make sense. You say you run out of funding but don't raise money? If they wanted to raise the money, they could have done it in a heartbeat."

"You think something is there?" Matthew asked.

"Think about it. It's a perfect cover. I can't think of the number of times I've walked by and haven't given it a second thought," she said

I thought about it for a moment and nodded.

"Okay," I agreed. "We go to the dance."

"What's the plan?" I asked.

Chapter 24

I hugged my brother tightly.

"I can't believe you're finally here," I said finally letting go.

He smiled. "I know. I missed you guys so much."

We walked to the car chatting with excitement to each other. We were so preoccupied with our reunion we didn't notice all the glares and stares we were getting.

Aamir looked out the window while we drove back home. "Man, this place is so ugly."

"I told you, and you thought I was being dramatic."

He chuckled. "This place is actually worse than you described.

"We're here," dad announced pulling into the house.

"Whoa," Aamir stared wide-eyed at the gated mansion.

I opened the front door and walked inside the house.

I threw my hands up. "Welcome to our crib."

He looked around the house in awe. "The ceilings are so high."

I laughed. "It looks better in real life eh?"

He nodded.

"Come on. I'll show you to your room. You can freshen up and then I can give you the grand tour."

We walked up the spiral stairs dragging his suitcases behind us.

"Here's your room," I pushed the door open and let him inside first.

"Wow it's huge." He walked inside and jumped on the bed.

"I'll be downstairs," I told him.

I walked to my room and changed to more comfortable clothes, and ran downstairs to the lounge room where my parents were sitting.

"I'm so happy we're all together again," mom smiled.

"Me too," I said. "He's going to be so shocked."

Dad laughed. "I can't wait to see his reaction when he goes around town."

Aamir came downstairs a few minutes later. "I'm ready for the tour."

"Okay." I jumped up. "Let's start in the basement."

I ran to the stairs.

"This is the home theatre," I walked further in the basement and let him inspect the space.

"A whole theatre?" he shook his head. "Damn. You were really living large."

"We don't go to the theatre here. I'd rather not be in a dark space with a bunch of crazy white people."

He laughed. "Would they actually do anything?"

"These people are crazy and racist. Not a good combination."

I walked further into the basement and over to the other side. "This is just the chilling area. We have a pool table, a couch, TV and a kitchen.”

“Wow, this is so lit,” he said. “You’re lucky you can chill here with your friends all the time.”

We went back upstairs. I took him to the first living room. “This is the living room, but we don’t really come in here.”

I took him back to where my parents were sitting.

“We normally spend all of our time here,” I said referring to the lounge room.

I showed him mom and dad’s office, the gym, the kitchen and the dining room.

We sat around the dining table after giving him the tour.

“I really missed your cooking mom,” Aamir said stuffing his face.

“Slow down,” mom laughed.

We ate our food, talked and laughed, and caught up on the time we missed with Aamir.

After dinner, we sat in the lounge room with ice cream and talked some more.

“How’s university?” I asked him curious.

“Hard. There’s a lot of course work. It’s so stressful, but a thousand times better than high school.”

“Did you apply to universities yet?” he asked.

“No. Not yet. Soon though,” I answered.

“Have you figured out what you want to do?” mom asked.

“I think I want to do journalism,” I told them.

Dad smiled. “I told you. I knew you’d find something.”

“How’s your work dad?” Aamir asked.

“Good. We’ve made lots of progress. We’re actually moving faster than we were expecting–which I’m happy about.”

"What's been happening here?" my brother asked. "So much happened to you Aaleyah."

"You don't even know the half of it," I said, shaking my head. "What did I last tell you?"

"You posted those tweets that went viral. Did anything happen after that?"

"Well they were pissed. They called mom and dad to the office to get me to delete my tweets and release a statement recanting it."

"What did you guys do?" he asked looking at my parents.

Dad and I looked at each other and laughed.

"Your mom ripped up the paper and sprinkled it all over the principals desk," dad said between chuckles.

Aamir looked at mom impressed. "Wow mom."

"He really tried it that man." She shook her head annoyed. "He's truly something else."

"They also destroyed our newspaper room," I continued. "They knew they couldn't do anything else, and the principal refused to fix it. He said they don't have enough funding to fix it, but I don't believe him."

"Wait what?" mom looked at me wide-eyed.

"Did I not tell you guys?" I asked sheepishly.

Mom glared at me. "Uh, no, you did not."

I chuckled nervously. "Sorry, it didn't seem like that big of a deal compared to everything else."

"Aaleyah, it doesn't matter if it doesn't seem like a big deal to you. We still want to know everything that happens in that school. Don't keep anything from us," dad said giving me a stern look.

"Okay I promise I'm not hiding anything else about school," I told them.

Technically I wasn't lying. It's true that nothing else

happened at school other than Garrett attacking me, but they did not need to know that. Outside of school, on the other hand, was a whole different story.

"That sucks Leyah," my brother said.

"It's okay." I smiled. "I've learned a lot. I guess you could say I've matured."

"So, they haven't bothered you after that?" he asked.

"No. they give me dirty looks in the hallway, but they haven't approached me and my friends."

"That's good, but I still don't trust them," mom said. "Be careful around them."

"Aren't I always?"

Mom rolled her eyes. "No. Not really."

I changed the subject since we were crossing over to dangerous territories. I didn't want my parents to ask me any more questions.

"How come you don't talk to Iman anymore?" My brother asked after my parents had gone to sleep.

"We still talk. Just not as much," I told him truthfully. "I don't know. It's just not the same anymore?"

"How come?" he asked.

I paused and sighed. "It's not their fault. It's me. I'm not the same person I was back then. And that's saying a lot since it's only been four months. I just can't vibe with them the way I used to, you know? I'm not interested in the things they talk about, and truthfully I'm pretty sure they're not interested in the things I have to say either."

I shrugged. "People grow apart I guess."

I frowned. "How do you know I don't talk to Iman anymore?" I eyed him curiously.

"Relax. It's not what you think. She DM'd me on IG to ask what's up with you."

"Nothing is going on with me," I said

"Really? Because it seemed like you were hiding something from mom and dad earlier."

I chewed on my lip nervously.

"Come on. You can tell me. I promise I won't tell them," he nudged.

"Aamir, if you open your mouth, I'll rip you apart limb by limb," I threatened him.

"Did you kill someone?"

"Shut up," I said rolling my eyes.

I took a deep breath. "Okay. So I might have omitted a few things from our dear parents."

He stared at me waiting for me to continue.

"After I posted those tweets, one of the guys tried to attack me."

I watched as my brother's eyes widened.

"He didn't though. He only pushed me into the locker, and I broke his nose," I said quickly before he could make a big deal out of it.

"That is attacking you," he said loudly.

"Shh!" I whispered.

"Sorry," he said this time quieter.

"It's okay. We used that against him," I continued.

"What do you mean?" he asked.

"My friend Brianna is a tech nerd. She hacked into the school cameras and got the footage of him attacking me. I confronted him about it at school, saying that if he didn't leave us alone, we'd post it on Twitter, and he'd end up losing the rest of his school admissions and whatever other scholarships he had left."

"Hang on," I continued pulling out my phone. "Brianna made me a gif of me breaking his nose."

My brother looked at me wide-eyed. "Damn, it seems like you've made some interesting friends."

He watched the video wincing when my knee smashed into Garrett's nose.

My brother cracked up almost waking our parents up.

"I was worried for nothing," he said calming down.

"Yeah I got this handled," I shrugged.

"What else are you hiding?" he asked

I frowned. "What makes you think I'm hiding anything else?"

He rolled his eyes. "Come on Aaleyah. You might be able to fool them, but you can't fool me."

I stayed quiet not knowing what to say

"Don't start keeping secrets from me now," he whispered.

I looked at my brother feeling conflicted.

"I—" I sighed not knowing how to continue. "Aamir, you can't tell a soul no matter how crazy what I'm about to tell you is."

"I won't *wallahi*," he swore holding his hands up.

I took a deep breath.

I looked around the room making sure my parents weren't hiding in a corner listening to us.

I moved closer to my brother. "I don't know where to start."

I paused for a few moments trying to collect my thoughts.

"Alright. So, this town is sketchy. Like really sketchy. Remember how I was telling you there's a high number of black people that have disappeared in this town?"

He nodded.

"My friend's friend was one of the victims that got kidnapped," I told him.

"Damn," he whispered. "When?"

"Two years ago. After the club room was destroyed, we decided to enter a competition where high school students submit a story, and they win the chance for their story to be featured on national news and a grand prize of $10,000."

He scratched the back of his head. "That's a lot of money."

"I know. We decided that we'd investigate the disappearances in this town—focusing more on Lewis' kidnapping."

"Okay," he said ushering me to continue.

"At first we didn't do anything. We just read lots of articles and did research. We wanted to lay low because people were still focused on us after everything that happened at school."

"What did you guys find?" he asked curious.

"A lot."

I told him about Whiyles and what happened there. I told him about the people who fled that town and came here to Anderton, and the disappearances still continued. But this time at a faster rate than ever. I let him know about the mysterious man Jason and that it turned out he was the grandfather of the principal at school.

I also told him what we did on Friday night, and he chuckled overwhelmed with all the information I was telling him.

"We want to take a road trip to Washington to talk to Lewis' parents. I need you to come," I finished.

"I—wha—I," he stuttered.

I waited for him to say something. I gave him a few minutes to get over everything I told him.

"Is there anything else?" he asked.

I told him about our plans for next Friday at the dance.

"Is that it?"

"For now," I told him.

He laughed in disbelief. "You're insane."

"So you'll come with us?" I asked

He sighed. "Can I talk you out of it?"

I shook my head.

He sighed again. "Then I have to go. Mom and dad won't let you go alone."

I clapped my hands happily. "Thank you Aamir."

"You guys are seriously out of your minds. I can't believe you set up cameras. What if they found it?" he asked.

"Matthew and Brianna got it back yesterday," I told him.

"What about the dance? What if you get caught?"

"We won't. We'll be very careful. Brianna will take care of the cameras," I told him.

"And this Brianna girl, what's wrong with her? Does she know that hacking into police database is like a felony."

"Yeah," I scratched my head. "She's really good though. She knows how to cover up her tracks."

"Man this is wild," he said processing the information I dumped on him.

"What are you thinking?" I asked wanting to know his thoughts.

"How crazy this is," he replied. "This is extremely messed up, and what you're doing is taking crazy to a whole new level."

I lowered my head.

"But," he continued. "But what you guys uncovered is huge. If you do publish this, the FBI will probably get involved and investigate. Aaleyah, I'm proud of you."

I smiled at my brother. "Thank you."

"But be careful, you're not invincible. This is seriously dangerous. This is real life and not some Nancy Drew book. You guys can get seriously hurt. These people are literal criminals."

"Yeah, but Nancy Drew could never–"

"I'm serious Aaleyah." My brother cut me off. "I won't tell anyone. You don't have to worry, but you have to tell me everything you do from now on."

I nodded.

"I need to know that you're safe in case anything goes wrong. Share your location with me," he suddenly said. "This way, I know where you are in case something goes wrong."

"Okay that's fair," I agreed.

He stayed silent for a few seconds. "This is so much more exciting than what I'm doing back home. I'm kind of jealous."

"I know right," I said excited. "I never thought that we'd end up finding out all of this stuff."

"Who do you think from your school is involved? You said the football players were at the meeting. Did you see any of your teachers there?"

We spent the rest of the night talking about theories and different potential outcomes of the case. It was 3 am by the time we went to sleep. We would have kept talking, but I had school the next morning.

Chapter 25

My friends stared at me in shock.

"I thought you weren't going to tell him?" Matthew asked.

"I wasn't, but he got it out of me. He's very persistent," I muttered.

"What did he say?" Brianna asked.

"Don't worry he won't tell. He's pretty cool," I told her.

"Okay," she said relieved.

"He was really shocked," I laughed thinking about his facial expressions when I was telling him everything.

"By the way, we moved everything from my basement to the tree house. I was scared that my parents would find it. We didn't tell you because you were with your family and we didn't want to worry you," Brianna said

I nodded. "That's smart, thank you."

"Are you guys sure nobody is going to find it in the tree house?" I asked.

Matthew nodded. "Nobody knows that place exists except us, and hopefully it stays that way."

"What do you guys want to do after school?" Brianna asked.

"Y'all want to meet my brother?" I suggested.

Brianna and Matthew looked at each other.

"Sounds good," Brianna said.

"What should we do?" Matthew asked.

"We can show him around town and just hang out. He's going to be really disappointed," I laughed. "He thinks I'm exaggerating when I say there's literally nothing to do in this town."

"Is your brother hot?" Brianna asked suddenly.

I looked at her disgusted. "Ew Brianna that's my brother."

"I'm just asking if he's hot," she said.

"That's weird," I told her.

Matthew chuckled shaking his head.

"I'm going to class," I said walking away before she could say anything else.

We picked up my brother after school.

"Where are we going?" Aamir asked putting on his shoes.

"We're showing you around town," I told him.

"Matthew, Brianna, this is Aamir. Aamir these are my friends Matthew and Brianna," I introduced them once we got inside the car.

They shook hands and greeted each other.

"I've heard a lot about you guys," Aamir said with a big smile.

"You too. You guys look so much alike," Brianna responded.

"People always think we're twins," I told them.

"But I'm better looking, so we don't look that much alike," Aamir shrugged.

My friends laughed and I glared at my brother.

"We're going to start from one end of the town and make our way down the other end," I announced.

Aamir and my friends talked while I drove. I was happy that they were getting along with no awkwardness. I listened as they talked about school and living in this town. Matthew and Brianna kept asking him about university and what it was like. I would join in sometimes, but I spent most of the time watching them interact.

"We're here," I told him.

Aamir looked around. "There's nothing here."

"Yes there is." I pointed to one building. "There's the post office, that's the police station, and that's the law firm."

"Back in the car," I said to them.

"You brought me here for that?" my brother asked annoyed.

"I said I was showing you around town," I shrugged.

Once they piled back in, I drove back showing him everything we saw. He was stunned and couldn't believe how small the town was.

"And now we're at the most fun part of this town," I parked the car in front of the diner and got out.

"This is where people hang out," Matthew said.

"There's the theatre, diner, bar, and bowling alley," he continued.

"You were right Aaleyah. This place sucks," Aamir said shaking his head.

"And you thought I was being dramatic," I laughed.

"I couldn't imagine it being this bad." He turned to my

friends. "How do you guys live here."

"You guys come from a big city so this must be a shock, but we've lived here all our lives. It doesn't seem too bad to us," Brianna replied.

My brother nodded understanding.

"Is it me, or are people staring?" Aamir asked looking around.

"Are they?" I asked genuinely not noticing. "After a while, you get used to it."

"Just ignore it," I said pushing him towards the diner. "Let's go eat."

We walked towards the diner ignoring all the stares we were getting. It didn't bother us too much, but I knew that it bothered Aamir.

We walked inside the diner.

"Let's go sit in the back." Matthew pointed to an empty booth.

We sat down in our booth and waited for a waiter to come to us.

Aamir skimmed the menu on the table. "Is this place good?"

"It's pretty amazing. The milkshakes are so delicious," I told him.

"I still can't believe how small this town is," Aamir said after our waiter came and took our orders. "People here seem like they really suck."

"Welcome to Anderton," I sighed.

"How did you get used to the stares?" Aamir asked. "I didn't imagine it would be this bad."

I thought about it for a bit. "It was really hard at first. I felt uncomfortable and hated going to places. I didn't really explore the town that much, and at school, I was being gawked at like I was some freak."

I paused staring into space remembering how hard it was those first few weeks.

"Did you ever consider taking your hijab off?" my brother asked breaking me away from those memories.

"Um," I said taking a deep breath.

"Yes I did," I told him truthfully. "I thought maybe if I did take off my hijab, things would get better."

"And?" Matthew asked.

"I can take off my hijab and hide my faith, but I can't hide my skin colour. So, I kept it on. I knew nothing would get better if I did, and besides, I didn't want them thinking they won. I just felt like if I took it off, they'd think that they had gotten to me."

My brother and friends stared at me not saying anything.

"What?" I asked.

"You're strong," Brianna answered smiling at me.

"I have a great support system," I said truthfully.

"I wish I could've been there for you," Aamir said after a while. "It sucks you had to go through this alone."

I nudged him. "You were there for me Aamir. You would listen to me complain for hours."

We got distracted by our food being plopped down on our table.

We thanked the waiter and dug into our food.

I looked over at Aamir who was inhaling his food. "How is it?"

He gave a thumbs-up unable to speak with his mouth full.

"What are you going to do with the money you guys win?" Aamir asked when his mouth was no longer full.

"If we win," Matthew corrected.

"Come on man," Aamir said. "There's no way you guys won't win with that story. And if you don't, then it's definitely a conspiracy."

"I haven't thought about it," Brianna told him. "It really isn't about the money for me. It's about finding the truth."

Matthew nodded in agreement. "Exposing this town and finding justice for our friend is more than enough."

"Aren't you guys scared knowing what you're dealing with?" Aamir wondered.

"Yeah, it's risky, but we've been careful so far. We just have to make sure that we don't get caught," Brianna said.

"And this road trip?" Aamir asked.

"Well," Matthew started. "We wanted to go visit our friend's parents in Washington."

"We thought that it would be rude if we called them suddenly out of nowhere," Brianna added.

Aamir nodded. "How long were you guys thinking?"

"Driving there takes around two days," Matthew answered. "For about five days?"

"Are there any other options other than driving?" Aamir asked. "My parents won't allow us to take a road trip by ourselves. Is there like a bus we can take? That'll make them feel better."

"I'm sure there is," Matthew said.

"Bus it is. We should book our tickets soon. It's the holiday season, so people are starting to travel," Brianna added.

"We should ask our parents first," she continued.

"When?" Matthew asked.

"I think we should do it on the same day," I said. "Maybe tomorrow?"

Matthew nodded. "What if they say no?"

"That is not an option. Be as convincing as you can be," Brianna said. "We have to talk to Lewis's parents."

"Brianna, you do know who my parents are, right? When they say no, it's a no."

"Well then, make sure they don't say no. Do you want me to go with you?" Brianna asked.

Matthew shook his head. "No, they'll think it's only us two, and that would be a definite no."

"True, true," she said thinking. "Call us if you need back up."

Matthew nodded. "Wish me luck."

"What about you two? Are you worried?" Brianna asked.

"Yeah, they are very hard people to convince," Aamir said.

"And if they ask you why Washington in particular?" Matthew asked.

Aamir thought for a moment. "Because it's pretty close, and it's a nice destination."

"You think they'll believe that?" Matthew asked.

"It's not a lie. I've always wanted to see the White House," Aamir said truthfully.

Matthew sighed. "Let's pray that it goes well."

We stood outside of the diner trying to figure out our next destination.

"Where to next?" Aamir asked leaning against the car.

"I don't know. I feel like we've shown you everything worth showing," I said.

"What about that old guy who owns the bookstore you're always talking about," he asked.

"Mr. Moretti?" I smiled. "You want to go to the bookstore?"

"I can't believe I'm about to say this, but that sounds exciting," he said.

I laughed. "Bookstores are exciting."

"For who exactly?" Aamir asked.

I crossed my arms. "For smart people. How am I even related to you?"

He rolled his eyes. "I can't believe you think going to a bookstore is fun, that's just sad."

I walked over to the driver's seat. "Whatever, just get in the car."

"You guys are so similar but different," Brianna said once we were inside.

"I'm the better sibling. I'm sorry you guys had to deal with her for this long." He shook his head. "Must have been hard."

Brianna and Matthew both laughed while I gave them the death stare.

"I know where you sleep Aamir," I warned.

"Joking, joking," he chuckled.

"She's really scary," he told them.

I rolled my eyes. "Only when you annoy me."

He held up his hands in surrender. "I'm trying to make it back to school alive."

"Is this Mr. Morteni guy as cool as you say?" Aamir asked.

"Moretti," I corrected. "And yeah, he's really chill."

"I'll make sure to remember that," he said.

"You better. I don't want you to embarrass me," I warned.

"We're here," I announced.

"That was quick." Aamir looked around the plaza not

believing we made it here already.

"Everything is within walking distance," Matthew said.

"Then why do you drive?" my brother asked.

"Because mom and dad don't want me walking around. They said it's safer for me to drive."

"Smart," he agreed.

"Let's go in," I said getting out of the car.

I silently prayed that Liam was not there as we walked towards the store.

I opened the front door taking a deep breath and walked in.

My brother didn't know who Liam was. He didn't know that he attacked me at school. I omitted that information knowing that my brother would react as soon as he saw him.

"There's nobody here," Aamir said as we walked into the empty store.

"He's probably in the back," I told him.

"I thought I heard someone come in." Mr. Moretti walked towards us holding a box of books.

Trailing close behind him was Liam who was also carrying a few boxes.

I clenched my jaw at the sight of him. I also felt a pang of jealousy. He allowed Liam in the back room and not me. He made it seem like no one but him could enter.

"Hey Mr. Moretti," I greeted him hiding my envy.

He smiled. "It's always a delight seeing you and your friends."

He paused and looked at my brother. "You must be Aamir. I've heard a lot about you."

He put down the box and stuck his hand out for a handshake. "It's nice to finally meet you."

Aamir shook his hand. "I've heard a lot about you as well. It's nice to meet you too."

"Your sister says you're on the soccer team at your school."

Aamir nodded. "Yes I am."

"Is it hard balancing your school work and sports?" Mr. Moretti asked.

"At first yes, but after a while it became manageable," Aamir answered.

"That's good to hear and what about your grades?"

Aamir smiled. "I'm doing well this semester. I have a 3.7 GPA. Hopefully, it doesn't go down with my final marks."

"Damn your brother is smart," Brianna whispered in my ear. "And hot."

I coughed loudly surprised by her comment.

Brianna giggled at my reaction while everyone else looked at me concerned.

"You okay?" my brother asked.

I nodded.

I glared at Brianna when everyone returned to their conversations.

"You two look a lot alike."

We all looked at Liam surprised that he even said any-thing.

"We get that a lot," Aamir answered.

Liam nodded slowly. "You're a year older?"

"Yes I am."

"You guys must be pretty close." He looked between me and Aamir intensely.

"We are," Aamir answered.

"How long you here for?" Liam asked

"Three weeks. I leave early January."

"You have a nice amount of time to spend with your family."

"Yeah, I wish it was a little longer. Three weeks is not enough to get over the mess of last semester."

Liam chuckled which caused me to narrow my eyes at him.

"I hope you enjoy your stay here. Though this town is a little boring."

"A little?" Aamir scoffed. "This place is like a punishment."

Liam laughed, and not a fake laugh. But a hearty laugh that lit up his hardened eyes and melted his cold face into a more inviting one.

I frowned confused about how quickly he switched up. I looked at my friends, and by their expressions, they looked as confused as I was.

"How's your social project coming along?" Liam suddenly asked me.

"It's going really well. Found more things than we were expecting," I replied, not breaking eye contact.

I watched his eyes hardened while he stared at me. "I bet."

I nodded not knowing how to reply to that. Liam silently continued to stare at me sending uncomfortable shivers down my spine.

"I'm going to show Aamir around the bookstore," I said breaking eye contact first.

I walked with my brother and my friends followed close behind.

My brother opened his mouth to say something once we were out of earshot to probably ask why I was being weird.

"Not here," I whispered.

He narrowed his eyes but nodded anyway.

I gave Aamir a tour of the bookstore. I showed him all the cool things that Mr. Moretti carried. Including the diaries dating back hundreds of years—which seemed to impress him. We even sat down at the table and talked for a bit. Although I was feeling uneasy about Liam, I still managed to have fun. Mr. Moretti even joined us after a while to tell us stories about how and when he built the book store, and that it was a surprise for his late wife. We listened in awe as Mr. Moretti took us on a journey of his life.

"You guys should get going," Mr. Moretti said to us after a while.

I looked at the clock to see what time it was, and gasped when I saw the time read 9 pm.

We got up to leave and walked to the front.

"It was really nice meeting you Mr. Moretti." Aamir smiled and stuck out his hand.

"It was a pleasure meeting you as well young man." Mr. Moretti shook Aamir's hands firmly.

"Bye," I waved before we exited the store.

"I hope to see you again before you leave Aamir," Mr. Moretti called out.

"I will definitely stop by again," Aamir said.

We exited the bookstore, and the cold air of December welcomed us.

"That was fun," Aamir said once we were inside the car.

I raised my eyebrows at him.

"I thought going to a book store wasn't fun," I mocked.

"Don't misunderstand me. It was only fun because there is literally nothing else to do here, but Mr. Moretti is chill."

Aamir chuckled. "Never thought I would be calling an old white guy chill."

We laughed.

"Hey, why were you acting so weird earlier. Was it because of that guy?" Aamir asked.

I fought the urge to look at the rear-view mirror to look at my friends, but if I did, my brother would know something was up.

"That guy gives me the creeps that's all," I told him.

I didn't lie. That guy really did creep me out.

Aamir frowned. "He seemed nice to me."

I shrugged. "I guess."

I zoned out of the conversation my brother and friends were having after that. I couldn't get Liam out of my head. That was the first time I've seen him display any emotion other than the stone-cold one he has on his face all the time. I looked over to my brother momentarily. If this was the first time I met him, I would have thought he was nice too. I knew the truth. He was dangerous, but I couldn't tell my brother that. If they met again and my brother acted differently around him, Liam would know something was up.

I sighed, ignoring the questioning look my brother gave me.

"You okay?" he asked.

"I just can't stop thinking about the sad story that Mr. Moretti told us about his wife," I lied.

"Yeah, poor man," he said.

I pulled up to Brianna's driveway and looked at her from the rear-view mirror. "See you tomorrow."

"See ya, it was really nice meeting you Aamir," she smiled.

"You too," my brother replied. "I heard you're good with computers. Maybe you can teach me how to hack into my school and change my grade for one of my classes. Uh oh, I think you guys are starting to rub off on me," he joked.

"Just a grade? What's the fun in that. I can create an entire fake transcript."

Aamir stared at her wide-eyed.

She burst out laughing at his expression. "Joking. I'm joking."

"Okay," Aamir nervously laughed.

"The offer stands if you change your mind." She waved at us, closing the car door not giving Aamir time to answer.

"I-I thought she was joking." Aamir scratched his head.

Matthew chuckled. "I guarantee you she's not."

I pulled out of the driveway and made my way to Matthew's house.

I listened as my brother and Matthew talked about sports and other things I really didn't care about. I would join the conversation once in a while, but I mostly zoned them out and focused on driving.

"It was nice meeting you dude," Matthew said once I pulled into his driveway.

"You too," Aamir said fist-pumping him.

"We should shoot some hoops," he said to Matthew. "We have a basketball hoop in our backyard that I don't think has been used yet."

"I've been meaning to use it, but there never seemed to be enough time in the day," I confessed.

"I'm down. I can come by tomorrow after school," Matthew said.

"Sounds good," Aamir replied.

"See you guys tomorrow," Matthew said getting out of the car.

I smiled and waved at him.

"I like your friends," my brother said once we were alone.

I smiled. "They're pretty cool."

"Did you have fun today?" I asked him.

"I did. But this town seriously sucks."

I laughed. "I told you, man. You didn't listen."

"It's not totally a bad thing though," he said.

I frowned. "What do you mean?"

"You rely more on the people than the place. You get to know them better. There literally is nothing to do here other than get to know those around you and interact with them. There are no distractions."

"Did you read that in your sociology textbook?" I asked.

My brother laughed. "Shut up."

"But you're right," I said seriously.

"At least there are a few cool people here," he confessed. "I was worried about you when you first got here."

"I was worried too," I said. "But I'm happy with the way things turned out. Don't get me wrong this place still sucks, but it sucks a little less now."

My brother leaned back in the chair and closed his eyes.

"Aaleyah," he said once I pulled into our house.

"Hm?" I hummed parking the car.

"Be careful."

I turned my head to look at Aamir. "I will. I promise."

"Okay," he sighed.

I studied my Aamir's face. "You okay?"

"Yeah, I'm just worried."

"Why?" I asked.

"Because I saw the people in this town. I know you already told me this is how people are here, but experiencing it first hand was different."

I nodded. "Don't worry, most of these people wouldn't do anything other than stare, and they occasionally throw some racist slurs. Other than that, it's all sunshine and rainbows."

"Aaleyah," he said. "I'm serious."

"I promise I'll be careful. We'll be careful. We won't do anything stupid."

"Everything you guys have done so far has been stupid."

"True, but it's been reasonably stupid. Our stupid is calculated and planned perfectly. It's not stupid stupid."

He rolled his eyes. "That doesn't make any sense,"

"Yes, it does. You're just too stupid to understand," I shrugged opening the car door.

"But don't worry," I continued. "We won't do anything—"

"Stupid?" he finished.

"Yeah," I smiled. "We'll be careful."

"I hope so or else I'm screwed. I can't imagine how mom and dad would react if they found out about all of this. They would kill me," he shuddered.

"Ahhh. " I nodded slowly. "You're not actually worried about me, but yourself?"

"Shut up Aaleyah. I'm obviously worried about your safety," he said. "Because if anything happens to you, then I'll be the one getting in trouble. I need to protect myself."

I shoved my brother playfully.

He laughed.

"I thought I heard voices," dad said once we entered the front door. "You guys have been gone for a while. Did you have fun?"

"Yeah," my brother replied, taking off his shoes. "We spent most of our time in the bookstore."

"The bookstore huh?" dad chuckled. "You guys went to the bookstore for fun. Never thought I'd see the day. Maybe coming here wasn't a bad idea after all."

"Why are you laughing?" mom asked dad.

"Guess where they were?"

"Where?"

"The bookstore," dad said laughing. "I don't know why I find it so funny."

"What's wrong with the bookstore?" I asked offended.

"Nothing," dad said calming down.

He walked over to me and put his arms around my shoulder. "Bless your heart."

"The bookstore is a fun place to be—for intellectuals." I flipped my hijab across my shoulders and went to the living room.

Dad followed me into the living room. "Are you saying we're not intellectuals?"

"You said it, not me."

Dad chuckled.

"Did you meet the owner?" dad asked Aamir.

"Yeah, he was cool. Unlike everyone else in this town," Aamir answered.

"Did you guys eat?" mom asked.

"A while ago," I said realizing that I was hungry.

"There's food in the oven," she said getting up. "I'm going to head to bed. I have a lot of marking to do tomorrow. Love you kids."

"Love you too," Aamir and I called out.

Dad got up and stretched his arms. "I should probably get some sleep too. It's been a long day."

I yawned fatigued by the long day.

"You tired?" my brother asked.

I nodded. "Today was a long day."

"Get some sleep. You have school tomorrow."

I groaned thinking about going to school.

"Come on," my brother laughed. "You only have three more days."

"I know, but I hate that place," I said getting up. "I'll see you tomorrow."

"Goodnight," my brother called out.

"Goodnight," I replied.

Chapter 26

Friday rolled around before our eyes. Time was flying by so quickly it was hard to get used to it. School had been calm the past few days. The teachers let us slack off, and there wasn't much teaching going on. I contemplated skipping so many times but I knew if I did, my parents would have my head. I had to be on my best behaviour since they let us go to Washington.

If I did anything wrong, I knew they would change their minds. We were surprised that our parents agreed—with the condition we would be flying instead of taking the bus. They didn't answer right away but took two whole days of thinking plus a meet up between the parents for them to let us go. They wouldn't tell us what they talked about in their meeting. It hasn't set in that we were actually leaving. I knew it wasn't a vacation, but I couldn't help but feel excited.

"I think we're ready for today," Brianna said looking up from her laptop momentarily.

I wiped my sweaty hands on my knees. "I'm nervous."

"If we get caught we're dead," Matthew said.

Brianna closed her laptop. "Well, better not get caught then."

"Can't we do this after we come back? If we get caught, we won't be able to visit Lewis's parents," Matthew pointed out.

Brianna sighed. "I know, but if we don't do this today, we won't have another chance. Don't worry. I got you guys. I won't let you get caught."

I took a deep breath. "I guess we're doing this today."

"How was your brother's hangout yesterday?" Brianna asked.

I leaned back on the couch and sighed. Since taking my brother to the bookstore, he's been spending lots of time there. I don't blame him since there was nothing to do in this town. He had nobody to hang out with while I was at school, and my parents were at work. Aamir seemed to have gotten closer to Liam, and my brother wouldn't stop raving about how cool he was. I felt uneasy because I knew he had an ulterior motive. They even hung out yesterday outside the bookstore which worried me a lot, but I knew I couldn't say anything.

"My brother thinks Liam is cool. They played video games in his apartment."

Brianna leaned forward. "Aamir went to his apartment?"

I nodded.

"This is perfect. We don't need to sneak into his apartment anymore. Aamir can plant the cameras for us."

"We said we weren't doing that unless absolutely necessary," I told her.

"I know that, but this is a perfect opportunity, and we shouldn't let it pass," she urged.

"My brother doesn't know who Liam is, and if I tell Aamir what he did to me, he'll lose it. It will only get us in trouble."

"I know, but we can't miss this chance. You should think about it," she said seriously.

I stood in front of the mirror inspecting my dress. I smoothed it down with my hands and took a deep breath.

I jumped when my brother rushed into my room. "Be careful Aaleyah."

"Close the door," I whispered.

I watched as he closed the door and made his way over to my bed sitting on the edge.

"We'll be careful. Hopefully everything goes as planned."

"And if it doesn't?" he asked.

"Hopefully everything goes according to plan," I repeated.

He threw his hands up in frustration. "You don't even have a plan B?"

"The plan is to not get caught no matter how many letters we assign to it."

"We have to make sure we don't get caught," I repeated. This time to myself.

"Okay but—,"

My brother stopped talking when he heard the doorbell.

He looked over to me his eyes widened. "You're really doing this?"

"Yeah," I nodded. "It's too late to back out now."

"Come on let's go," I ushered my brother out of my bedroom and made my way downstairs.

I smiled when I saw my friends.

"You guys look amazing," I said once I reached the bottom of the stairs.

"You look amazing too," Brianna smiled.

"Yeah, red suits you," Matthew agreed.

I smiled. "Thank you."

"Should we get going?" Brianna asked.

"Wait, wait," mom said running into the foyer.

She held up her phone. "We need to take pictures."

"Okay just a few though. We don't want to be late," I said.

I put my arms around Brianna, and Matthew was on the other side of her.

"Okay, say cheese."

We did as we were told and smiled as brightly as we could.

"Okay one more."

We stayed in position until the camera flash went off again.

"Okay now—"

"That's enough," dad laughed cutting mom off.

"You kids better get going before she holds you hostage all night."

"Love you guys," I waved opening the front door.

"Have fun!" mom called out before I closed the door.

I let out a deep breath once I got inside the car.

"You guys ready?" I asked.

Matthew shook his head. "Nope, this is probably the stupidest thing we could do."

"I am," Brianna said. "I think we got this."

"At least one of us is confident. Last chance to abort mission," I said.

I looked at my friends, waiting for any objections.

I bit my lip nervously.

"Okay then," I said pulling out of the driveway.

We drove silently to the school. Each of us preoccupied with our own worries. However, there wasn't enough time in the ride to worry for too long.

We sat in the car for a few moments. Nobody wanted to get out first, and I didn't blame them.

I opened the car door signalling to my friends it was time.

They got out of the car and came to stand beside me.

Brianna turned to us looking nervous. "Everyone remember the plan?"

Matthew and I nodded.

"Then let's go." She walked and Matthew and I followed behind her.

We walked to the front doors noticing the group of excited students posing in front of the school snapping pictures with their friends.

The often sunken vibe of the school was replaced with a more vibrant one. Their laughs echoed off the walls, and their smiles were radiant. An odd sight to see since usually all I ever saw were their glares.

We walked up the front steps of the school. The students must have noticed our presence since the laughs suddenly stopped. I could hear the faint sound of music coming from the gym.

We ignored the glares and questioning stares we were getting from everyone and made our way inside of the school.

"Why are they staring at us so much?" Matthew asked annoyed.

"They never thought we'd come to this dance in a billion

years, and they're right," I told him. "Let's go and take pictures, we need to blend in."

I ushered my friends in front of the photo booth.

We waited in line and watched as the students ahead of us posed in front of the camera laughing and smiling.

When it was our turn, we picked up some props placed out and posed with them making funny faces at the camera.

We thanked the photographer as he handed us our photos, and we laughed at how silly we looked.

"That was fun," Brianna giggled.

"Should we go to the gym?" I asked

"Yeah," Matthew said.

We walked down the hallway admiring the decorations hanging from the wall. They took this entire winter wonderland to a whole other level. The school looked unrecognizable. Fairy lights draped the walls, and fake snowflakes hung from the ceiling.

Brianna shook her head. "I can't imagine how prom is going to look. I would come only to see what theme they picked," she confessed.

I laughed. "Same."

We walked down the hallway, and the sound of the music was getting louder as we got closer.

Matthew reached for the door handle. "Ready?"

Brianna and I nodded.

He opened the door.

"Wow," I said. I looked around in awe at how beautiful the gym looked.

"This is so pretty," Brianna squealed.

I took out my phone to capture the moment.

"I really wasn't expecting this," I admitted.

"Me too," Matthew agreed.

I scanned the room for an empty table and stopped when I saw one in the back.

"Let's go there." I pointed to the table.

"How long should we wait?" Matthew asked once we sat down at the empty table.

"An hour. We can't disappear too early," I told them.

"What should we do for that hour?" he asked.

"Have fun," I said.

They looked at me and frowned.

"Come on guys. We came all the way here. Let's actually have fun," I told them.

"This sucks," I said forty minutes later.

I watched as the rhythm challenged students tried to dance along to whatever song was playing now.

"This is hilarious," Matthew laughed. "They're so bad it's painful."

"I can't with this music." Brianna shook her head in irritation. "Whoever made this playlist is cancelled."

"We've been here for almost an hour, and they haven't played one song that wasn't country. One or two, I can tolerate, but for forty minutes straight?" I closed my eyes irritated.

"Should we just go?" Brianna asked. "We've been sitting here for almost an hour, and I don't think anybody would think anything if we left."

"Okay," I agreed. "Let's just wait for ten more minutes and then we can go."

"Never mind," I said a minute later. "I don't think I can listen to one more country song."

"The only dance they know is throwing their hands up,"

Matthew said once we walked out of the gym.

I laughed. "Did you see Chad? He really thought he was good."

I shuddered. "I almost died of second-hand embarrassment watching him."

We walked down the nearly empty hallway and walked out of the school. The entrance was empty this time compared to the many students that were there earlier.

We walked over to my car and got inside.

I started the car and drove away from the school. I parked a few blocks away where there were a bunch of trees blocking us from people's view.

I took off my seatbelt and twisted my body so I could see my friends better.

"Alright," Brianna said getting her laptop out of her bag. "Now that the cameras captured us leaving, we're good. Since we're entering through the back of the school we don't have to worry about the camera's capturing us coming back. When you two go inside the school, I'm going to scramble the feed, so they don't see us wandering around. It's going to be tricky since I'll have to put each camera on pause, basically playing back the previous footage. Once you guys are no longer in the view of that camera, it'll go back to real-time. Which will be even harder if there are any major movements because they'd notice. You guys need to avoid it at all cost, but we don't have to worry about that since everyone is in the main hallway."

I listened carefully as if I was hearing every detail for the first time even though we've talked about this plan every day for the past week. I appreciated Brianna for repeating everything to us helping us calm our nerves.

"Once we get to the school, I'll put us on a three-way

call, and you guys will be able to communicate through these headphones," she instructed holding up her ear buds.

I let out a breath and nodded.

"Let's change," I told Matthew.

He took his bag and went behind the trees.

I opened the car door and let my legs out, so I could put my running shoes on comfortably.

I took off my heels ignoring the cold painful breeze of the winter air.

I got up and went to the back to get out the backpack my clothes were in.

I took out my black turtleneck and my black sweatpants and put it on top of my dress praying that it didn't crease it.

I took off my hijab, leaving the black under piece on and threw it in the backpack.

I put on my black cap and pulled the hood of my sweater up.

I took out black gloves and put it in my pocket and went back inside the car.

"You're fast," Brianna said impressed.

"I didn't need to change," I told her.

"Aren't you uncomfortable with the dress underneath?"

"Yeah, it's annoying, but it would take too long if I took it off and put it back on."

She nodded and went back to her laptop.

We waited for a few more minutes until Matthew came back inside wearing black attire similar to mine.

"What took you so long?" I asked.

"I can't put my sweats on top of my suit unlike you," he said. "It's so damn cold. Next time you're going behind the trees. I call dibs to change inside the car."

"Okay fine," I rolled my eyes.

"Are you ready?" I asked Brianna.

"We're good," she said.

I started the car and made my way back to school–this time parking behind a dumpster.

I took out my phone and put the ear buds on.

I answered Brianna's call, and put the phone inside the deep pockets of my sweats.

I watched as Matthew did the same. Once we were both ready, we got out of the car and put our gloves on.

We ran towards the school using the key that Matthew had to the science lab. He was supposed to give it back at the end of the school day, but he kept it for this and thankfully, the teacher hadn't noticed.

We went inside the dark room, and turned on the flashlights on our phones.

We went to the front door and waited for Brianna to give us the go.

"You guys are good," Brianna's voice blared through our ear buds.

"Let's go," I said.

I opened the door and peered into the hallway, and it was empty.

We decided to split up. It would mean more work for Brianna, but we needed to do this fast.

"Brianna," I whispered. "Matthew is going to the principal's office, and I'm going to Mr. Smith's classroom, is that okay?"

"Yeah," she said. "Those parts of the school are empty. There shouldn't be a problem."

"We'll meet at the club room when we're done so we can go to the construction area together," I said

"Good luck," I told Matthew.

"You too. Be careful."

I walked away from him.

I walked in the dark empty hallway towards Mr. Smith's room. Since this was the last day of school until January, they had turned off most of the lights.

I contemplated turning on my flashlight but decided against it in case it attracted attention.

I clenched my jaw and bit my lip hard almost drawing blood.

I let out a shaky breath and urged myself to continue on. The last time I walked down an empty hallway and entered a dark room by myself, things didn't go well for me. I kept reminding myself that it was different this time, but my heart wouldn't stop racing.

I walked quickly and checked my surroundings constantly to make sure that I was actually alone.

I walked up to the classroom and took out the pin I put in my pocket earlier. I wasn't a master at picking locks, but after watching many YouTube tutorials and practicing, I became good at it.

I inserted the pin into the lock and wiggled until I heard a click.

I opened the classroom door and closed it quietly behind me.

I took out my phone and turned on the flashlight, and scanned the room to make sure no one else was here except me.

I walked over to Mr. Smiths desk and sat on his chair pushing myself towards his computer.

I turned on the computer praying that he didn't have a password on his desktop, and he didn't.

I highly doubted I would find anything. I don't think

anyone would be stupid enough to not put a password on their desktop if they were hiding something.

I looked through his files and emails trying to find anything interesting, but there wasn't anything.

"Nothing on his computer," I updated.

"Same," Matthew said.

I opened his drawers and shined my flashlight inside.

I reached for the last drawer, but I couldn't open it. I frowned and got out of the chair to kneel on the floor, so I could tug at it better. I took out my pin again and opened the drawer.

I grabbed my flashlight from the floor and shined the light.

I scoffed when I saw what was inside.

"What?" Brianna asked.

"There was a locked drawer, and I opened it. There's alcohol inside it. Anyways there isn't anything here. I'm going to head to the club room."

"Same. I'll meet you there," Matthew said.

I closed the drawer and made sure I left everything the way I found it.

"You're clear," Brianna said.

I opened the door and stepped into the dark hallway once again.

This time the walk wasn't bad since it wasn't far from the club room.

"Hey," I greeted Matthew once I got to the room.

"You ready?" he asked.

I chewed my lip nervously and turned towards the wing under construction.

"Not really," I said. "How do we know if there aren't any cameras in there?"

"I highly doubt it," Brianna chimed in.

"Alright," I let out a deep breath. "Let's go."

I walked towards the construction area with Matthew close beside me.

I looked at Matthew. "You ready?"

"Yeah."

"Let's go." I stepped inside.

"What do you see?" Brianna asked.

"Construction," I told her.

We kept walking until we reached the end of the hall.

I looked around not seeing anything. "There isn't anything here."

"What's behind those panels?" Matthew asked.

I shrugged.

Matthew walked towards the panels of wood that blocked off whatever was on the other side.

"What?" I asked.

He inspected the wall running his hands over it.

He walked tracing his hands on the wall until he suddenly stopped.

I watched intensely wondering what he was seeing that I wasn't.

He pushed on a panel opening it like a door.

I gasped. "How did you know?"

"It looked like a door," he said stunned.

"Come on." He stepped inside.

I quickly followed him and saw there was another door.

We looked at each other puzzled and opened it.

I took out my flashlight and shined the light on the wall to see if there was a light switch.

I walked over to it and turned it on.

We watched as the fluorescent lights lit up the room. We

froze and held our breaths.

"What?" Brianna's voice snapped us out of our trance.

"I'll FaceTime you." I took out my phone and called her.

I walked around the room my phone capturing every detail so Brianna could see it.

I inspected every inch of the small room. There wasn't much in it. It was very minimal. I was expecting a room with dead deers heads hung on the wall and KKK flags surrounding it, but that wasn't the case. There wasn't a single flag in sight. You wouldn't know what kind of people this room belonged to. There was a round table on one side of the room with five chairs around it. On the other side of the room, there were two tables with computers on them.

"I don't know what I was expecting, but this wasn't it," Brianna said.

"What could they be possibly doing here?" I asked aloud.

"Check the computers," Brianna said.

I walked over to the computer and sat down on the chair. I handed the phone to Matthew so he could continue FaceTiming with Brianna.

I turned on the computer and waited for it to start up.

I stared at the black screen puzzled. There were a bunch of numbers and letters. I had no idea what it meant.

"It's encrypted," Brianna said sensing our confusion. "We won't find out whatever is on that computer. You guys should get out of there."

"Yeah," I agreed.

I hung up the phone and turned to Matthew. "Did you take pictures of everything?"

He nodded. "We're good."

"Let's get out of here."

I exhaled sharply once we got inside the car. "This just keeps getting bigger and bigger. I don't even know anymore."

"Thank God we didn't get caught." Matthew leaned back in his seat.

I drove back to the area we were earlier.

"At least we know there is something at the school," I said.

Brianna closed her eyes. "Yes, but we don't know what, and there is no way we're doing this again. We can't include this."

"Why?" Matthew asked.

"Because once we publish what we saw inside the school, they would destroy all the evidence. We can't risk that," she said.

I rubbed my temples. "What do we do?"

"I don't know." She threw her hands up frustrated. "I don't know, but what I do know is that whatever is in there is important, and we need to figure out what we're going to do with it."

She paused. "Matthew, send me those pictures and delete them from your phone. I'll print them out. We can leave it in the tree house."

"Sending it now."

Chapter 27

I walked inside the house later that night exhausted. I entered the living room and saw my brother with his feet kicked up watching something on TV.

"You're back." He sat up quickly taking his feet off the coffee table. "What happened?"

I closed my eyes and collapsed on the couch beside Aamir.

"Are you okay? Did something happen?"

"No, nothing happened. Everything went as planned," I told him with my eyes closed.

"Then why are you like that?" he asked.

I sighed and opened my eyes.

"We found something," I whispered.

He narrowed his eyes. "What?"

I replayed everything in my head and told him how the night unfolded and what we found.

My brother shook his head in disbelief and laughed. "I can't believe this."

"Neither can I."

He looked at me amused. "You are literally the black Muslim version of Nancy Drew."

"Nancy Drew wishes," I joked.

My brother chuckled.

"What are you going to do?" he asked seriously.

"We don't know," I told him. "This has to be our secret for now."

"At least you guys were right," he said

I yawned. "This was the longest night of my life."

"Oh my God," I laughed remembering the actual dance. "You should have seen how they were dancing. It was so bad you don't even understand."

"I know I saw your Snapchat. I would have left right after the first song. I can't believe you stayed for that long," he laughed.

"Go to bed. We have to pack tomorrow."

"Oh my God," I said remembering. "We're leaving on Sunday."

Aamir nodded. "Did you forget?"

"I was so worried about this that I completely forgot."

"Okay," I said getting up. "I'll see you tomorrow *inshaAllah*."

I woke up the next day late into the afternoon.

"I can't believe you guys didn't wake me up," I said walking into the living room.

Dad snorted. "We tried three times. You were completely out."

"Really?" I laughed. "I didn't hear anything. I was so tired."

"Did you have fun last night?" mom asked.

"No." I sat down on the couch with a bowl of cereal. "It was horrible. I'm never going to another school event."

Dad laughed. "You're dramatic."

"I'm really not," I told him. "They couldn't dance, and the only music they were playing was country music. It was the worst."

"No prom then?" mom asked.

"Nope. I would never put myself through that torture again, but the decorations were so pretty. I'm kind of curious about what they would do for prom."

"It was pretty nice," my brother agreed.

Dad looked at my brother. "How do you know?"

Aamir held up his phone. "Snapchat old man."

"Hey!"

"Joking, joking," my brother laughed holding his hands up in surrender.

Are you guys excited about tomorrow?" dad asked.

I nodded. "I think it's going to be fun."

"You guys need to start packing. I don't know why you waited this long," mom said.

"We're only gone for three days," I told mom. "That's a backpack."

"Doesn't matter. It's better to pack slowly instead of rushing last minute," mom said.

"I'll go pack after I eat." I held up my bowl of cereal.

Aamir got up. "You can eat it upstairs. Let's get it over with."

"Watch," I said turning to mom. "It won't take us more than twenty minutes."

"With your indecisiveness?" mom scoffed.

I pouted. "You'll see."

I stared at my closet forty minutes later with my travel bag wide open.

"Three days," I said out loud to myself. "I need clothes for the flight."

Easy. I just need sweatpants and a sweatshirt.

Check.

Now I need three outfits.

"I wonder what the weather is like over there?"

I packed one sweater just in case.

I decided to wear a sweater dress one day since it's an easy outfit.

Now two more to go I thought in my head.

I went for jeans and a grey shirt with a long black overcoat for another outfit. It matched the vibe of Washington.

I finished packing and closed the bag. I walked out of my closet and dropped the bag on the floor.

"Twenty minutes huh?" mom said once I walked into the lounge room.

"It's hard to decide what to wear," I said defensively. "There are so many factors to consider."

"It's not that serious," Aamir remarked.

"You probably packed one outfit to wear for all three days."

"I have my airport outfit, three pairs of jeans and three shirts. Plus, the one I'm wearing to the airport," he replied.

I rolled my eyes. "Whatever."

Dad chuckled. "Should we watch a movie?"

We landed the next day, and to say I was exhausted was an understatement. I couldn't sleep the night before because of the nerves, and now I was feeling the repercussions of that.

"I'm going to call mom and dad and tell them we land-ed," Aamir said.

"We should call our parents too," Brianna agreed.

I walked over to an empty seat and plopped down.

Saying goodbye to our parents was easier than we thought. We were expecting a bunch of rules and sadness since this was the first time I was flying without my parents but no. They gave us hugs and told us to be safe. I guess they weren't as worried since we were flying to a place we could reach in a few hours.

"Let's grab a taxi," Matthew said once everyone was off the phone.

We grabbed our bags off the floor and went towards the exit of the airport hoping we'd find a taxi. We walked outside the cold winter breeze shocking our bodies.

We inched past people to find a taxi. Thankfully there were many, and we found one quickly.

"Where to?" the driver asked once we were all inside.

Matthew took out his phone and showed the address to the cab driver and he entered it into the GPS system.

"We'll arrive in about twenty minutes. Get comfortable," he told us.

I put my head back against the seat not needing to be told twice and closed my eyes.

By the time everyone woke up from their naps at the hotel, it was night time. We decided that it was too late to go anywhere far and decided to explore the area our hotel was in.

"First, let's grab some food," Brianna said once we were in the plaza beside our hotel.

"Let's get Chipotle," I suggested.

"I'm down. I've never had Chipotle," Matthew said. "Let's go inside before we freeze to death."

We walked inside the restaurant and got seated and we ordered our food.

Since the restaurant was empty, our food came quicker than we expected.

"What should we do next?" Matthew asked once we finished eating our food.

He checked his watch. "It's too early to go back."

"Let's go figure skating," Brianna suggested. "I'm pretty sure we passed a skating rink earlier."

Aamir nodded. "I'm down."

"Me too," I said.

Matthew got up. "Alright."

We followed him and walked down the nicely lit plaza until we reached the skating rink that was buzzing with families and friends. People were sitting down drinking hot chocolate watching their loved ones skate up and down the ice.

I smiled. "This is nice."

"Let's go," Brianna grabbed my arm and led me to the register to pay for our skates.

The man kindly gave us our skates and directed us to the ice rink.

"I'm scared," I said wobbling trying to skate on the ice. "It's been a while since I've done this."

Brianna grabbed my arms trying to steady me. "It's like riding a bike. Even if you haven't done it in a while, your body will still remember."

She let go of my arms. "Watch me."

I watched as she glided one foot in front of the other.

"Now it's your turn," she said skating back to me.

"Okay." I took a deep breath.

I tried mimicking what she did wobbling at first, but after ten minutes of skating around, I was slowly getting the hang of it again.

I practiced until I got my rhythm back.

"Let's have a race," I told my brother.

He laughed.

"Scared?" I challenged.

"No. You literally couldn't skate twenty minutes ago."

"It's not that I couldn't skate. My body momentarily forgot." I skated around him to prove my point. "I remembered."

"Fine," he turned to Matthew. "You be the judge."

"I'll stand over there, and whoever touches my hand first wins," Matthew said.

We nodded and watched as he skated to the opposite end of the rink and stood with his hands wide open.

"Get ready," he yelled out.

We both got into position.

"GO!"

I charged down the ice going as fast as my legs could go–Aamir right beside me. I bent my knees even further and dug my skates even deeper into the ice to give me more momentum.

I skated faster and faster until I was an arm's reach away from Matthew.

I gave myself one last push and touched his extended arm. I skated towards the skating rink wall to stop myself.

I turned back around and skated towards my friends.

"Who won?" I asked trying to catch my breath.

"Tied," Matthew said. "You both touched my hand at

the same time."

I laughed. "That was fun."

Aamir nodded heaving.

"Let's go sit down," I said. "I want some hot chocolate."

We skated towards the exit of the rink and stepped outside. We grabbed our shoes and returned the skates.

"You guys grab that bench, and we'll grab the hot chocolate," Aamir said motioning to Matthew.

Brianna and I walked towards the empty bench.

"You ready for tomorrow?" I asked her.

She looked up at me. "I'm really nervous."

"I called Lewis's mom and told her that Matthew and I took a vacation down here and remembered they moved here. We asked if we could visit, and she said yes, but I'm still nervous." She scratched her head. "I don't know."

"What don't you know?" Matthew asked from behind us.

He sat down and handed her the hot drink, and Aamir handed me mine.

"Just talking about tomorrow," she said taking a sip of her hot chocolate.

"I'm worried," Matthew confessed. "I don't want to open old wounds for them."

"Same," Brianna agreed.

"I think they'll be happy to see you guys. Yes, it might be opening old wounds, but seeing you two might also bring back good memories. It might remind them of the life he lived and that he had good friends who haven't forgotten about him. Friends that are trying to find the truth," I told them.

"You guys are coming with us, right?" Brianna asked.

Aamir and I exchanged a glance. "I thought you two

would go since they don't know us. We don't want to intrude," I said.

"I already told them about you guys," she said. "They're cool with it."

I bit my lip thinking. "Okay sure."

"Now I'm nervous," I chuckled. "What time are we meeting with them?"

"They said tomorrow when they get back from work. Which gives us the first half of the day to go explore the city," Matthew said.

"That's good. We have an early flight the day after, so we don't have to worry about staying out too late," I yawned.

"You still tired?" Matthew asked.

"That race took a lot out of me," I said.

"We should get back. It's getting colder." Matthew got up.

I got up too. "We should rest. We have a long day ahead of us tomorrow."

Chapter 28

We walked around the Washington Monument the next day and took pictures. It was the last stop in our itinerary for the day. It had been a long day, but we had so much fun. We visited the White House and the Lincoln Memorial.

It was crazy seeing something I had seen on TV so often in real life. It was mesmerizing. We also visited the National Air and Space Museum and the National Museum of African American History and Culture. There were so many other places we wanted to visit, but we knew we didn't come here for a vacation.

"Let's start heading back," Brianna said. "I checked and there's a restaurant close to Lewis' parents house we can eat at."

We walked inside the small restaurant, and I took a deep breath inhaling the delicious aroma of food floating around.

"I hope their food tastes as good as it smells," Matthew said.

"Hello," the restaurant host greeted us at the door. "For

four?"

"Yes please," I answered.

"Follow me," she smiled.

We walked behind the restaurant host and sat down at the booth she placed the menus on.

"Your waiter will be with you in a moment."

We smiled and thanked her.

I flipped through my menu liking everything I saw. "Everything sounds so good, but their pastas are really speaking to me."

"Same," Matthew agreed.

I closed my menu finally deciding. "I'm ready."

"Me too," Matthew said. "Are you guys ready? The waiter is coming."

"Yeah," Aamir and Brianna said passing their menus to the front.

"How are you guys feeling?" I asked once the waiter had taken our orders.

"I couldn't sleep properly last night," Matthew admitted. "I was tossing and turning all night."

"Me too," Brianna said. "I fell asleep a few hours before we had to get up. I'm exhausted. I can't wait to go back home," she confessed.

She picked up a napkin and ripped it into small strips.

"We'll be home around 3 pm tomorrow, so we'll have the entire day to sleep when we get home. We just need to suck it up," she said distracted by her napkin.

"How's the article coming along?" Aamir asked changing the subject.

"Pretty good actually. We divided up everything we'll be talking about. We laid out the articles and pictures we're using in the tree house," Matthew said. "After we gather all of our evidence, all we need to do is write."

"What else are you guys looking for?" Aamir wondered.

"Concrete proof. All we have are speculations of what happened to these people. We need to figure out exactly what happened to them," Matthew answered. "Hopefully, we'll find out something today we didn't know before."

Aamir nodded. "You guys came a long way already. I'm really impressed."

"Here you go." The waiter placed our food on the table with the help of another waiter.

We thanked them and dug into our food.

I twirled the delicious creamy pasta with my fork and took a huge bite.

"Oh my God," I said between mouth fulls. "This is really good."

We stopped talking for a few minutes while everyone got accustomed to their food.

"I really needed this," Brianna said.

"Me too," I agreed. "But I'm kind of sad."

"Why?" Matthew said .

"Because we won't be able to come to this restaurant ever again," I explained.

"Unless we come back," he said.

"I don't know how I'll be able to eat food anywhere else when I know this place exists. Food will never taste the same to me again," I pouted.

Matthew chuckled.

"We have twenty minutes left," Brianna said.

I returned to my food and wolfed it down.

I dropped the fork on the plate and leaned back in my seat. "The itis is hitting me."

"Me too," Aamir said.

Brianna got up. "We don't have much time left. Let's go."

We walked to the front to pay.

"Come back again," the host at the front said smiling.

"How close is their house from here?" Matthew asked Brianna.

"Five minute walk," she said.

"Lead the way," Matthew replied.

We arrived exactly five minutes later.

Brianna took a deep breath and knocked on the front door.

A few moments later, a beautiful middle-aged woman opened the front door greeting us with a warm smile. "Please come in."

"Oh my," Mrs. Wiremen said. "You guys have grown up so fast. Just look how tall you are Matthew."

"Come here," she said opening her arms. "Give me a hug."

Brianna and Matthew walked over to the lady accepting her embrace.

"It's nice to see you again Mrs. Wiremen," Brianna said letting go.

"Yes," Matthew agreed. "It's been a while."

Mrs. Wiremen smiled sadly. "It has, hasn't it?"

She turned over to us. "These must be your friends."

Brianna introduced us to Lewis' mom.

I held out my hand out for a handshake but was greeted with a hug instead.

"I'm a hugger," Mrs. Wiremen said.

I laughed and hugged her back.

A tall man entered the entryway. "Are they here?"

He greeted us warmly and shook our hands. "It's really nice to see you again. You have grown up so much. Makes me wonder how our boy would have looked if he were here."

He smiled his eyes going somewhere momentarily–probably exploring a memory of his son.

"Should we head to the living room?" he asked pulling himself back.

We nodded and followed them into the living room. It was decorated with many photos of their family. Even though their son was gone from their home, it still felt warm and welcoming.

"How have you two been?" Mrs. Wiremen asked.

"Good," Brianna replied.

They filled Lewis' parents in about what they have been up to for the past two years and what universities they've applied too. Aamir and I told them where we came from and what brought us to Anderton.

"How has the town been treating you?" Mr. Wiremen asked looking at me and Aamir.

"Man," I sighed.

"You don't have to say anymore," he chuckled. "If it's like anything I remember, you must have had a hard time."

"At first," I admitted.

"But as time went on, things didn't get better," I said truthfully. "But I got used to it."

"What about you young man?"

"I've only been here for a week, and I haven't gotten used to it," he shook his head. "It's very different from what I'm used to."

Mr. Wiremen nodded. "I bet."

"How have you been Mrs. and Mr. Wiremen?" Brianna

asked.

The couple looked at each other communicating silently. Mrs. Wiremen put her hands on top of her husband's and squeezed it.

"We've been alright." She smiled. "We just miss our baby boy so much. You had questions you wanted to ask us?"

"Yes." Brianna took her notebook out of her bag.

She briefly explained everything we were up to without giving away too much information.

"We just wanted to know everything about his disappearance. Where he told you he'd be. Do you remember anything else that stood out to you?" Brianna asked.

Mrs. Wiremen took a shaky breath. "Well, he didn't go inside the forest. That's for sure. We never really understood why they said that."

Mr. Wiremen nodded agreeing with his wife. "That day, he came back from hanging out with you two. He said that he was going to that old man's bookstore quickly to grab a book and that he'd be right back, but he never returned."

I frowned and looked at my friends, and by the look on their faces, this must have been news to them as well.

"I knew he went there a lot, but I didn't know he went that night," Matthew said quietly.

"He went there a lot?" I asked.

Brianna nodded. "He was close to Mr. Moretti. Lewis loved books."

I cocked my head to the side and leaned in closer. Mr. Moretti had never mentioned him, and Brianna and Matthew never mentioned it either.

"If that was the last place, then why didn't they mention that in their police report?" I asked.

"We don't know. After we told them about his last known location, the police insisted that the last place he was seen was the forest," Mrs. Wiremen said.

We talked for a little while longer, but the only thing I could think about was Mr. Moretti and Lewis. This was the first time I was learning he was also close with the old man. Maybe it's a wound for him too.

"Thank you for meeting with us," Brianna said putting her pen and book in her bag.

"No problem. It was truly a pleasure seeing you kids again," Mrs. Wiremen smiled.

We got up and walked over to the door. We put on our shoes and said our goodbyes to Lewis' parents.

"I already got us an Uber," Matthew said pointing to the car waiting outside their house.

We went inside the car. Nobody said anything about what just happened. We were all preoccupied with our own thoughts. We didn't even notice when the car pulled up in front of our hotel.

"We're here," the driver announced.

We thanked the man and got out of the car.

"Should we change and talk?" Matthew asked.

"Yeah, I think we should. Let's meet in our room. We'll call you guys when we're done," I said.

Brianna and I headed up to the room we shared and collapsed on our beds.

"I am so exhausted," Brianna yawned.

I closed my eyes. "Me too."

"Wanna take a shower first?" Brianna asked.

"Yeah." I got up. "If I don't get out in fifteen minutes, I fell asleep."

"Okay," she laughed tiredly.

We sat on the floor of our room with the pizza we ordered in the middle.

"Where should we start," Matthew asked grabbing a slice of pizza.

"Well," I started. "There's something that's been bothering me. I didn't know that Lewis was close with Mr. Moretti."

"He used to go there a lot." Brianna shook her head. "I never thought of it as important, but if that was the last place he was seen, it's something we need to look into."

Matthew clenched his teeth and put down his pizza. "I don't want to say this." He closed his eyes looking defeated. "Brianna, when you were searching for Lewis in the cameras, did you check the cameras beside the bookstore?"

She closed her eyes. "No. It never crossed my mind."

"I think maybe you should check," he said quietly.

She hesitantly got up to retrieve her laptop.

She sat down and let out a deep breath, and typed away at her computer for a little while until she stopped.

"Here it is," she said looking up at us.

We moved closer to her so we could see the laptop.

We watched closely as the security footage from that night played.

It was dark outside, but the streets were well lit from the street lamps.

She fast-forwarded until a silhouette of a person came into view.

"Oh my God." Brianna leaned in closer to get a better look at the screen.

I looked over to my friend who now had tears in her eyes.

I squeezed her shoulder to try to comfort her and turned

my attention back to the screen.

Just like Lewis' parents said, he did go into the bookstore that night. But that wasn't the shocking part. It was that Lewis never came back out.

We watched for what felt like hours waiting for him to leave the bookstore, but he didn't. The sun had risen, and we had given up.

We sat quietly not knowing what to say.

I blinked back the tears that were forming.

"I—" I was stunned.

"I know," Matthew said reading my mind. "I know."

When Lewis' parents said the last place he went was to the bookstore, something in my gut had awoken. I ignored it not wanting to believe the man who I have grown so close to, the man who I confided in when I had nobody, the first person who had become my friend when I was having such a hard time settling in, was a part of all of this.

I remember how I went there every day the first few weeks of school. I would tell him about my day and the hard time I was having because of the people who went to my school.

He would always give me advice and tell me stories to make me feel better. He was someone I thought I could always trust to tell me the truth—someone who challenged my intellect and always pushed me to do better.

"I just don't understand. Why?" I rubbed my face. "It doesn't make sense to me."

"He would give me these lectures about how I needed to do better, and he would give me advice. Why would he tell me these things? Why would he try to help me?" I asked my voice breaking.

"To gain your trust probably," Matthew said.

"It was all a lie?" I couldn't believe it. "But he's so different. He was the first person in this town who made me feel welcome. I just can't believe he's a part of all of this."

"I know," Brianna said. "But Aaleyah, if you stop going to the bookstore or start acting differently, he'll know something is up—which might put you in danger."

My brother shook his head quickly. "No way are you going back to that bookstore."

"He won't do anything to her. She has hundreds of thousands of people who know of her existence because of her viral tweets," Matthew said. "But I'm actually more worried about you. You're an easier target than your sister. They're known for kidnapping students who are visiting their families on holidays."

"Yeah," I agreed. "You definitely can't go back there. He was so interested in you that first day he met you, and now I think it's because he's found his new target."

"I wonder what he gets out of it?" Matthew asked.

Brianna pursed her lips thinking. "Money probably. Nobody does these kinds of things for fun."

"Money makes sense," Matthew said. "I've always wondered how he kept that book store running when not that many people buy from him."

"I can't believe this is happening," Aamir said finally speaking up.

"Same," I sighed.

"Do you really think I'm his new target?" Aamir asked.

"Yeah." I clenched my jaw. "Until we know for sure what's going on, I don't think you should go back there."

"What about Liam?" my brother asked. "Do you think he's involved?"

"Um," I said taken aback by the question. "Since he's

close with Mr. Moretti, I don't think he can be fully trusted."

My brother nodded. "That sucks. He was pretty cool."

"So was Mr. Moretti," I said.

"True," Aamir said.

"If Lewis entered that store, he must have exited somewhere," Matthew said suddenly.

Brianna looked up. "What do you mean?"

"What business does this old man have in all of this?" he asked.

He stood up and started pacing. Something he often does when he gets an idea. "Think about it. We know our principal is the leader, and that they're using the school for something. We just don't know what. Where does Mr. Moretti fit in all of this?"

I paused to think. "Maybe that's where they keep them? He could have a hidden room like the school."

"Maybe," he agreed. "But for what? I don't think they're serial killers. There would have been bodies found. Maybe they use the people for sacrifice for their KKK meetings, but I also don't think that's it. What are they up to, and why haven't we seen Lewis exit the building or at least see people carrying him out?"

"What are you thinking?" I asked Brianna who was staring into space.

She stopped biting her nails and looked up at us. "This might sound far-fetched."

"Nothing is far-fetched at this point," I told her.

"I've been thinking a lot about those computers," she started. "It doesn't make sense to me why a computer would be so heavily encrypted. I mean, we're dealing with a school principal here. Yes he's a criminal, but he's not some spy. It just doesn't make sense. But then it got me thinking. We've had so many disappearances in this town and not once has a body been found. These people have disappeared without a trace."

"Yeah?" Matthew said, urging her to continue.

"Encrypted computers? People vanishing into thin air?" she asked.

"I'm not following what you're getting at," I told her.

"Human trafficking," she said.

I opened my mouth but then closed it when I realized I couldn't make a sound.

"Human trafficking?" Matthew asked disturbed. "Are you serious?"

"Think about it. Those encrypted computers probably access the black market. It makes the most sense," Brianna explained.

"Wow," Aamir said. "You guys are some serious detectives. But in all seriousness, I think it's time for you guys to contact the police. The real authorities. Not those cops. I'm talking FBI."

Brianna scratched her forehead. "I agree. When we send in our article, I think we should also tell the authorities so they can start investigating."

"Okay," Matthew agreed. "We still haven't figured out how Lewis left the building."

"There's a back door probably," I said. "I've never seen it. He's been so suspicious about it. He's never let me help him even though he always complained about how messy it was, but he let Liam help."

Brianna chewed on her lip. "If he let Liam go to the back and not you, wouldn't that mean they're working together. There's clearly something he doesn't want you to see."

"It's bothered me for a while," I said.

"Don't even think about sneaking in there," Aamir warned.

"Even I know that's way too dangerous," Brianna said.

She looked at her watch. "We should get some sleep. Information overload."

"Yeah it's getting late." Aamir stood up. "See you guys tomorrow."

Chapter 29

I stared at my parents in shock.

I couldn't believing what I was hearing. "What do you mean it burned down?"

My mom looked at me confused not understanding my reaction. "I mean it burned down. They think it was some stupid kids who left a candle in there or something."

"That's crazy," I whispered biting my nails.

"I have to go. I just remembered I forgot something in Brianna's suitcase," I told my parents.

"You just got back," mom said. "Can't you get it tomorrow?"

I shook my head. "No, it's really important."

"Fine. Don't be gone for too long."

I grabbed Aamir's arm and dragged him outside.

"I can't believe this," I told him. "Everything was in that tree house Aamir! Everything!"

He put his hands on my shoulder. "Hey, look at me. We'll figure this out."

He grabbed the keys from my hand and went to the

driver's seat.

"Call Brianna and Matthew. Tell them we're on our way," he said.

I called Matthew first since he lived closer.

"We're five minutes out," I said once he answered.

"It wasn't an accident," Matthew said as soon as he entered the car.

"What are we going to do?" I asked distraught. "Those pictures and articles were all the proof we had."

Matthew pinched the bridge of his nose. "I know. I know."

We drove in silence until Aamir pulled into Brianna's driveway.

I took out my phone to dial her number, but she was outside her house before I did.

"We need to go somewhere to talk." Brianna entered the car.

"Let's go to the coffee shop," I suggested.

"Where is that?" my brother asked.

I directed him where to go and sat back in my seat.

Silence filled the car. I could not believe everything we've worked so hard to uncover was gone.

It was the day before Christmas Eve, so the shop was empty since people were probably busy scrambling for last minute gifts.

We ordered our drinks and walked to the back of the shop so nobody could hear our conversation.

"What now?" Brianna asked.

I sighed. "I don't even know how this could have happened."

"It's not an accident. I know that much for sure," Matthew said. "Nobody but us knows about that place, and since the tree burned down yesterday, that rules out the chance of us accidentally leaving the space heater on. Someone did this."

Brianna closed her eyes defeated. "Who could have possibly known where we were keeping everything?"

"I can think of only one person," Matthew said.

"Liam?" Brianna asked.

He nodded. "He's the only person that we suspect who suspects what we're doing."

"How did he know where the tree house was?" Brianna asked.

"I knew it," I whispered to myself.

They all turned to me.

"I always felt like someone was following us. Watching us. I thought I was being paranoid, but now I know I wasn't," I explained.

My brother frowned. "I know that we think that he's somehow involved with Mr. Moretti, but why else do you think he would've done this?"

"Because he's a hitman," Matthew said.

"What?" Aamir leaned forward. "What are you talking about?"

"Crap," Matthew said. "I forgot you didn't tell him."

My brother looked at me. "Tell me what?"

"There's something I didn't tell you about Liam," I said.

He waited for me to continue.

I was nervous not knowing where to start, but I knew I needed to tell him everything. So I did.

"Why the hell didn't you tell me?!" Aamir yelled gaining the attention of the other people in the shop.

"Shh," I quieted him down.

"Why didn't you tell me Aaleyah?" he asked again this time quieter.

"Because I knew you'd act like this. I was scared if you saw him you'd do something, and that would have given everything away," I told him.

He shook his head in frustration. "You're damn right I would have. I would have beaten the crap out of him for laying a hand on you."

"You let me hang out with that psychopath. I went to his house!" he whisper-yelled.

"I know, I know. But we knew he wouldn't do anything to you. Especially since he knew that it'd be traced back to him. If he wanted to hurt you, he would've already. Besides, he seemed cool with you," I said.

"The guy is normally really mean and cold, but he was actually having a conversation with you, and it seemed like you guys got along—it seemed genuine."

"Aaleyah that man attacked you in your school. He's crazy!" Aamir exclaimed.

"I know. I'm sorry," I apologized.

"You better not be hiding anything else from me," he warned.

I held my hands up. "I promise that's it *Wallahi*."

"Do you guys know for sure it was him?" my brother asked. "What about the principal and those football play-ers?"

Matthew shook his head. "They don't suspect that we're on to them. They don't really pay attention to us at school anymore."

"What are we going to do about the article?" I asked.

"I don't know," Brianna sighed. "We're going to have to

review everything we have and see if we can still write it."

"It's not fair," Matthew said.

"He's always getting in our way," Brianna agreed.

"What are you thinking," I asked Brianna. "I know that look in your eyes."

"I might or might not have a plan, but you won't like it," she said.

"What?" I frowned.

"Has Liam contacted you?" she asked Aamir.

"Yeah. He asked how the trip was."

"No," I said shaking my head knowing what she was getting at.

"Come on," she begged. "This is the only choice we have."

"It's too dangerous. What if he gets caught?" I asked her.

"Can I know what you guys are talking about?" Aamir asked.

I turned to my brother and told him what Brianna was suggesting.

"I'm down," he said.

I blinked at him. "What do you mean you're down?"

"I'll do it if it'll help you guys."

"It's too dangerous," I warned.

"It'll be fine. I'm pretty sure it's the least dangerous compared to what y'all have done," he said.

"What are we looking for?" I asked. "What will we gain from this?"

"We might find something that can help us. We should investigate the fire and see if we can prove that it was arson. If we can prove that he did it, then that's strike three. We can put him away for good," Brianna said.

"Fine," I said scratching my eyebrow. "But where are we

going to find a camera small enough that he won't notice."

"I'm pretty sure my dad has one. He has all these gadgets. I'll look through his things and see if I can find something," she replied.

I nodded. "Does he have an audio recorder too?"

"I have one. It's a pen," she said.

"Do I even want to know?" I asked her.

She shook her head. "Probably not."

"You can put it in your pocket and drop it somewhere he won't be able to find it," she told Aamir.

"When?" I asked.

"Soon," Matthew said. "I think you should respond now and see what he says. The downside is that he'd have to retrieve it."

"I can go back before I leave. He'd think that I'm saying goodbye to him," Aamir suggested.

"I don't know. It's too risky. If he finds it, it's over. He's intuitive. He knew we were lying about the research project. If he finds a random pen lying around in his house, he'll inspect it, and I'm pretty sure he'll be able to tell what it is," I cautioned. "Brianna you should research more into him. Maybe you missed something that can help us. Maybe he's wanted for a crime, but nobody knows he's here. We can tip the police off or something. We never know. If you can't find anything, then let's explore this option again before Aamir leaves."

She thought about it. "Okay, I'll look him up in the larger databases. I'll start with the FBI."

"Pause," Aamir said. "That's like a proper crime, you can go to jail for that—for a long time."

"I know how to cover my tracks I promise. They won't be able to trace my IP address back to me. To them, I'm a hacker from Germany," Brianna assured him.

My brother looked at her skeptical. "You sure?

She nodded. "Like ninety-five per cent."

"What about the other five per cent?" he asked.

"There will always be a hacker better than me. Let's just hope they're not working with the FBI because that would suck," she said. "Don't worry, they won't care about me looking into a lowlife criminal. I think it would be a major problem if I were looking into something more serious."

"I mean, if you're confident," he agreed.

"I am," Brianna said. "I'll get back to you guys after Christmas. I'll be spending the remainder of today sleeping, and I'm going to be spending the next two days with my family. If they see me on my computer once, I'm scared they'll break it."

"I think we can all use a few days where we are not focused on this," I said. "Let's meet in four days."

"Hey, I know we said four days, but I've been reading over our notes to see what we can do with the article," Brianna said over the phone later that night. "We can still write it. Thankfully we've planned everything, so we know what we'll be talking about. It sucks we don't have the articles to reference. We'll just add that someone didn't want us finding the truth, and they burned the tree house, and we can include articles about that."

"You couldn't stay away, could you?" I laughed. "But that's good news. I'm glad."

"That's it. I promise. Next time it'll really be four days. I mean three days now," Brianna said.

I said goodbye and hung up the phone.

I jumped on my bed exhausted. I felt relieved we could still write our article, but I still couldn't shake the frustration I felt about our things being burned down. I knew we needed to take a break from this. We've been investigating for the past few weeks non-stop.

I closed my eyes that night happy that I was finally in the comfort of my own bed, because God only knows how much I needed it.

Chapter 30

"I can't believe this."

Brianna leaned back in her chair and looked at me. "I know. I didn't believe it either when I saw it, but it's real."

"Are you okay?" I asked my brother.

He shook his head. "I don't even know anymore."

"What does this mean?" Matthew asked. "Because this changes everything we thought we knew."

I closed my eyes. "I think we need to pay our friend a visit."

I waited for objections.

"Okay then," I said when I didn't hear any. "Tonight we'll pull one final mission."

We watched nervously as Matthew wiggled at the door handle trying to get it open. He jiggled the pin in the keyhole moving it up and down until the door unlocked.

"We're in," he whispered.

We walked into the dark room careful not to make any

sounds.

I turned on the light switch and walked into the room examining everything.

"Let's split up," I told them.

"Aamir and I will look in the living room, and you guys check the bedroom," Matthew said.

I nodded and walked towards the hallway that led to the bedroom.

"I'll check the closet," Brianna said.

I went towards his bed.

I lifted his pillows and checked under the mattress but found nothing.

I looked through his drawers lifting each item of clothing to make sure I didn't miss anything.

"Nothing," I called out.

"Same," Brianna said.

We walked out of the room and made our way back into the living room.

"What the hell are you doing in my house?" We heard a voice say from the living room.

I stopped dead in my tracks and looked at Brianna wide-eyed. "I thought he wasn't supposed to come until later?" I whispered.

"He wasn't!" she hissed.

"I won't ask you again," he said this time a little louder.

"Crap," I whispered under my breath.

I took a deep breath and walked into the living room.

"We know your secret," I said hoping I didn't seem scared.

Liam narrowed his green eyes at me and scoffed. "What the hell are you talking about?"

I walked over to where Aamir and Matthew where

standing. "Why don't you tell us."

His eyes pierced through me. He clenched his fists and walked towards me.

Aamir was about to intercept, but I held him back.

"You don't know who you're messing with little girl," he said his voice low and threatening.

"I'm pretty sure I do." I looked up at the man. "Brian. That is your name, isn't it?"

He stepped back, and his eyes widened. "How the hell...?"

I shrugged.

I saw his face twist in horror.

"Don't worry," I told him. "Nobody knows except us."

The man put his hands on his waist and paced back and forth.

He suddenly stopped and looked at us. "Okay then. I'll just have to kill all of you."

My friends stepped back terrified.

"You can't do that," I said.

"I have to call this in," he whispered to himself.

"Wait," I said walking closer to him. "You don't need to do that either."

"Yes I do," he said firmly. "You have absolutely no idea who or what we're dealing with, and I'll be damned if I let a bunch of kids ruin this."

"Listen, if anybody is ruining anything for anyone, it's you," I stated matter-of-factly.

"I—wow—" he huffed in disbelief. "I can't believe I'm listening to this."

He looked at me. "You have no idea what you're getting yourself into."

"I do," I said before he could walk away. "I do. I think

we might be able to help you, but we have a few requests."

He turned back around—this time somewhat amused. "What can a bunch of high school kids do for me?"

I shrugged. "I don't know, but you've got nothing to lose."

He thought about it for a moment.

"I think I'll take my chances." He turned around and walked towards his bedroom.

"Wait!" I pleaded.

He stopped walking and turned around.

"I think you should hear us out," I told him. "We might have information that can help you."

"I'm good," he said not budging.

"Are you the one who burned down our tree house?" Brianna asked suddenly.

He nodded. "I couldn't risk you guys leaking this to the media. I've been working on this investigation for two years."

"That was months of investigation you criminal," Brianna hissed.

"I didn't burn your stuff. I stole it. I just burned the tree house to make you think it burned," he confessed.

"Is that supposed to be better?" I asked.

"Listen, I admit you kids are impressive, but there's nothing you can offer me. I'm sorry. I'm calling this in," he said.

"You sure?" I questioned. "I remember you saying you've been working on this for two years. We probably uncovered more in two months than you've been able to do in those two years. So I say you do need our help, but your ego is too big to accept it from us."

"This has nothing to do with my ego," he said narrowing

his eyes.

"Listen," I told him. "Let's work with each other, huh?"

I stuck out my hand for a handshake.

He stared at my extended arm and laughed.

He shook his head. "I can't believe this is happening,"

"Come on," I said dropping my hands. "You have information we need. We have information you need. I think together we can make the pieces fit."

I held my hand out to him again.

He stared at my hand again–this time shaking it.

He closed his eyes. "I'm going to regret this."

"Or this might be the best decision you've made, and you might finally solve this case," I said.

He sighed. "God, I hope so, or I'm dead. You've got balls kid, but you're reckless."

"I've never understood why people use balls to refer to bravery. I mean, it's really weak. I can kick you now, and that would send you out." I shook my head. "Doesn't make sense."

Brian scratched his head. "I guess you're right."

"You better not be thinking about screwing us over, or we'll expose you," I lied.

He stared at me like I was crazy. "You wouldn't dare. This is a federal police investigation."

I shrugged. "I'll just say it was an accident."

He scoffed running his hand through his hair in frustration. "Are you threatening a police officer?"

I shook my head. "No. I'm just informing you of what would happen if you do happen to cross us. I wouldn't call it a threat but a promise."

He didn't respond but just stared at me as if I had grown another head.

He took a deep breath. "How did you find out about me anyway?"

"I..." I laughed nervously. "It's a long story."

"I have time," he insisted.

"It's also really boring," I said.

"I've got nothing to do," he persisted.

"I hacked into the FBI database and ran your photo through it, and here we are today," Brianna said.

I stared at her wide-eyed.

"You what?" he gawked at her.

"You guys are crazier than I thought," he whispered to himself.

"I can arrest you for that," he told her. "That's easily twenty years in prison."

She shrugged. "You wouldn't risk your cover. But look at the bright side, you've now got eyes inside the high school."

"A lot of shady things are happening in there," Matthew added.

He thought about it for a moment. "But what about your contest?" he asked.

I frowned. "How did you...?

"You're not the only one who's been keeping an eye," Brian said

"We're not going to be submitting," Brianna answered. "This is more important."

Brian nodded. "Okay."

"What are the conditions?" I asked once we sat down.

"You guys are not going to be pulling any more of your reckless stunts or else I'll tell your parents," he threatened.

"Fair," Matthew agreed.

"Everything gets run past me," he added.

We nodded.

"I also want updates of what goes inside that school."

"Fine," I said. "Anything else?"

He got up suddenly and walked over to a closet and pulled out a box. "I want to know everything you know."

He sat back down and took out the things he stole from us.

He passed us the pictures we took the night we snuck into the school.

"Where and what is that?" Brian asked.

"We don't know what it is," Brianna answered. "But we know where it is."

"The school," I told him.

He nodded. "I'm guessing this is where it goes down."

"What goes down?" Aamir asked.

He pondered for a moment wondering if he should tell us.

"We've been trying to investigate these disappearances for a while, but it has been virtually impossible. No bodies, no witnesses, nothing. Every time we thought we had a trail, it would go cold. Back to square one. Until a few years ago, we received an anonymous tip. We've suspected human trafficking, but we didn't have any evidence. However, this tip helped us trace one of the transactions. We found out that they hold auctions through the dark web, and the highest bidder would get the victim. These auctions are untraceable, and we haven't been able to trace the buyers either. But it did lead us here," Brian revealed.

"We were right," Brianna whispered. "Oh my God."

I grimaced. "I can't believe it."

"Now that you guys have found this place, we can raid it." He exhaled. "But we have to find who the suspects are first."

"We know," Matthew said.

We filled him in about the principal and the recent discovery that Mr. Moretti is involved in this, which didn't surprise him at all.

"You're not surprised about Mr. Moretti?" I asked.

He shook his head. "Why do you think I spent so much time with him? The old man is a suspect."

I stared down at my lap and bit my lip.

"I'm sorry," Brian said suddenly. "I know how much you liked him."

I nodded.

"When are you headed back?" Brian suddenly asked my brother.

"On the 5th," Aamir answered

"I have a reason to believe that you might be the next target," he revealed.

"Why do you think that?" I asked.

"I couldn't help but notice the interest that Mr. Moretti took in you the first day he met you. You're tall, athletic and smart. Probably the perfect victim in their eyes," Brian disclosed.

"You need to be cautious," he told my brother.

Aamir nodded.

"What do they do to the people?" I asked.

He paused. "Well, human trafficking is the 3rd largest crime industry in the world behind drugs and arms trafficking. It generates about $150 billion every year worldwide. People think that it's not something that happens in countries like the United States, but that's a misconception. There's sex trafficking, labour exploitation, organ trafficking, but we haven't been able to pinpoint what kind of trafficking this is."

We sat there silently not knowing what to say. It made me sick that something so disturbing existed in this world.

"What now?" Aamir asked a few moments later.

"We need to raid the school and make arrests. We can't do that without any solid proof," Brian said.

"The picture," I said.

He shook his head. "That's not how all of this works. If I turn this into my superiors, they'll ask how I got a hold of this, and if I tell them about you, then they'll say this investigation is compromised. They're already threatening to pull me out. We can't raid that school without a warrant, and we can't get a warrant unless we have proof. In most cases, we can get away with raiding the school if we have reasonable suspicion, but all we have are speculations, and that's not going to work."

"What do we do?" Matthew asked.

"I have a plan," he said.

"Are you going to tell us that plan?" I asked when he didn't continue.

"No. I need to speak to my superiors."

"Ugh," I groaned. "I thought we were going to be honest with each other?"

"You're very persistent aren't you?"

Brian looked at us contemplating whether he should tell us or not.

"Fine," he said finally, and filled us in on his plan.

Chapter 31

"Absolutely not," I protested.

"This is the only choice we have," Brian tried to convince me.

"We are not using my brother as bait," I said firmly. "Find another plan."

"We'll have a surveillance crew and SWAT on standby. We won't let anything happen to him," Brian said.

I closed my eyes. "This is a small town, how do you think you're going to get a team of agents here without raising suspicion?"

"Why don't you let me worry about that," he remarked.

"How do we even know this is going to work. What if Aamir isn't even their next target?" I asked.

"He is, and this is going to work," he said confidently.

"Aaleyah." My brother put his hands on my shoulder so I could face him. "I think I need to do this."

"Aamir, this is life or death," I trembled.

"I know, but at least we'll have back up this time, and thinking about all of the reckless crap you've pulled, I don't even think this tops the list," he said.

"I'm serious Aamir."

"I'll be fine. I think we can trust Liam. I mean Brian," Aamir assured me.

I turned to look at Brian. "What's the plan?"

"I've been working to get close to Mr. Moretti for the past two years to gain his trust, and I think he trusts me now. I just need to figure out if he trusts me enough to include me in his plans. We have until Aamir heads back, so we need to make this happen as soon as possible. We can't proceed with the plan unless I can be in that room," he replied.

"How are you going to do that?" I asked.

He stared off into the distance thinking and then turned back to me. "Let me worry about that, but I need you guys to be on standby. When I'm ready, I'll let you guys know how we'll proceed."

"How long do we have to wait?" Brianna asked.

"Hopefully, not long. We need to get this done before Aamir returns. When I know for sure I can be in that room, we'll discuss the plan," Brian said.

Four days. That's how long it took for Brian to contact us. We almost gave up on him until he told us we were on the go.

"What took so long?" I asked Brian.

"Why are we meeting here? What is this place?" I asked looking around the abandoned building.

"Because," someone said behind me.

I quickly turned around and saw a tall man with a badge hanging off his neck.

There were a bunch of men setting up equipment in the building.

"This is my boss. You guys can call him Agent Nordon," Brian said introducing us to the man. "This is why it took me so long. I had to notify them about the plan."

"I still don't like this Brian," Agent Nordon said. "We should get their parent's approval. This can come back to bite us. We don't have time for a lawsuit. Her mom's a lawyer," he said pointing at me.

"How?" I asked confused.

They just looked at me not answering.

"He's over eighteen," Brian said pointing to Aamir. "He said he wants to go through with this."

Agent Nordon sighed. "Fine. But if anything goes wrong, this is on you."

"Yes sir," Brian nodded.

The man looked over at me and shook his head.

"What a miserable man," I said when he walked away.

Brian laughed. "You can say that twice."

"Get ready for briefing," a voice called.

"I need to go," Brian said. "You guys wait over here."

"Why can't we come?" Matthew frowned.

"Because this is official police business," Brian answered.

"I don't care. That's her brother, and this is all happening because of us. Get us in that room, or I'll hack into one of those computers and watch," Brianna threatened.

Brian scoffed. "You're begging to get arrested, aren't you?"

"You and I both know that's not going to happen." Brianna crossed her arms.

Brian put his hands on his hips and sighed. "How did I get caught up in this. I don't know if you guys are brave or just plain stupid."

"Just get us in that room Brian." I crossed my arms too.

He narrowed his eyes. "That's agent Brian to you."

"You said you wouldn't go behind our backs, and that's what you're doing." Matthew clenched his fist.

Brian shrugged. "My hands are tied."

"I don't think they are. You're just not trying hard enough," I told him.

Brian pinched the bridge of his nose in frustration. "I can arrest you for all the stupid stunts you guys pulled. You committed a bunch of crimes. Take your pick of which one I should arrest you for."

I narrowed my eyes at him. "You attacked me at my school."

"Listen," he started. "I'm really sorry about that, but I had to do it to keep my cover."

"I don't give a crap about what you had to do. You traumatized me and really hurt me. You almost broke my ribs. So the least you can do is get us in that room," I expressed.

He looked at me deciding what to say.

"Fine," he agreed. "But then after that we're even."

I rolled my eyes. "After that, I won't need anything else from you."

"Let me go talk to my boss," Brian said. "Wait here."

We watched as he talked to his boss who seemed to be against what Brian was suggesting.

"I don't think they're going to let us watch," Matthew said.

"Aamir come here," I called over to him.

He walked away from whoever he was talking to and walked over to us.

"What's up?" he asked.

"They're trying to have a briefing without including us,"

I told him.

He frowned. "That's not cool. They said I could be there."

"Wow," I scoffed.

"Do you want me to talk to them?" Aamir asked.

I shook my head. "I have a better idea."

"What?" he asked.

"I think we should say that you won't do it unless they include us in the briefing and their plans. It's not fair they take all of our investigation and hard work just to shut us out."

"You think that'll work?" he wondered.

"They spent all this time, money and resources to make this arrest. They won't risk anything going wrong," I told him.

"You're right," he agreed.

"He's coming back," Brianna said.

"Sorry, he won't budge," Brian announced.

"Fine," I said. "Then we won't be a part of this."

"And I won't go through with this," Aamir added.

"You already agreed," Brian scolded.

"Well I changed my mind," Aamir smirked.

"I…" he sighed.

He walked away and went to talk to his boss again. This time his boss looked over at us and closed his eyes shaking his head.

He walked over to us. His strides powerful and demanding.

"You kids don't know what you're getting yourselves into," Agent Nordon said angrily.

His voice was deep and firm making me a bit scared, but I didn't back down.

I shrugged.

"I can arrest you right now for interfering with police investigation," he threatened.

"We're not interfering with anything. You're the ones who brought us here," I said not backing down.

He clenched his jaws. His adam's apple bobbing up and down.

"Fine," he agreed. "But when this is all over, I'll be having a very long conversation with your parents."

I smiled feeling satisfied.

"What if he tells our parents?" Matthew asked, concerned when he walked away.

"I don't think he will. He's just trying to scare us," I told him

"Come on," Brianna said. "They're starting."

We walked into the room and sat down in the chairs at the back they set up for us. The room was buzzing with police officers.

"This is really cool," Matthew said his eyes lighting up with excitement. "I can't believe this is happening."

"Way better than writing an article," Brianna agreed.

"Let's get started," Agent Nordon said his authoritative voice stopping all conversations happening in the room.

He motioned to Brian. "Agent Callahan will brief us."

Brian stepped up to the front. He told the rest of the officers in the room about his two-year undercover mission and the recent breakthroughs he's made or rather us four made.

"However, I could not have done it alone," he said just when I was zoning him out. "If it weren't for those meddling kids," he added gaining laughter from all of us.

"Seriously,' he said once everyone had calmed down.

"Those kids sitting at the back helped me significantly in this investigation. Granted, they were extremely reckless and almost exposed this entire operation."

Some people chuckled looking back at us.

"But," he continued. "They found the room in the school, they uncovered their principal's identity and found proof about the bookstore owner's role in all of this."

The people in the room clapped for us throwing us off guard.

"Just when I thought he was about to take all the credit for our hard work," Brianna whispered.

I smiled happy that we were being recognized, and not dismissed as the kids sitting at the back.

"In terms of the plan," he continued getting everyone's attention back.

"Aamir has agreed to be our bait," Brian said. "I notified Mr. Moretti that I called Aamir to the bookstore tonight, so this is going down folks."

I took a deep breath feeling nervous.

"Tonight at 20:00 we'll move out. I'll already be inside with the suspects. Aamir will come afterwards. Mr. Moretti arranged transportation for him, and they'll be coming through the alleyway to take him. The principal will be there overseeing the operation. We'll have two tactical teams stationed outside the bookstore," he disclosed.

He drew on the whiteboard demonstrating. "Team A will be stationed out here. It's hidden away from the main road, so you won't be seen by any oncoming cars. Team B will be behind the alleyway in this corner. We'll also have a standby team at the school, so when the arrest is made, we can move in before they try to destroy any evidence."

"Aaleyah you'll be with the team outside the bookstore

to be near your brother. We need one of you to lead us to the room in the school," he said looking at Matthew and Brianna

"I'll go," Brianna volunteered.

He nodded. "We only move in on my signal. Let's not mess this up."

Chapter 32

I sat inside the van waiting for the operation to begin. Aamir was walking to the bookstore and about to enter the building.

"We don't have visuals, but we're monitoring the situation by audio," one officer explained sensing my nerves.

I nodded.

"He'll be fine," Matthew reassured me.

"Yeah, if he's not, it's my head our parents will be having," I joked trying to keep my anxiety under control.

"The boy is now entering the building," someone updated.

The van suddenly got quiet, and everyone was listening through their headphones.

"Aamir," Mr. Moretti greeted my brother like he was genuinely excited to see him. "We've missed you around here. How was your trip?"

I clenched my jaw listening to him talk.

"It was amazing," Aamir told him. "We had a lot of fun."

The agent in charge lifted his headphones from one ear and turned to me. "He's doing really well."

I sighed in relief and nodded.

"Ahh, yes," Mr. Moretti agreed. "Washington is truly a place with a diverse history. You would need a month to properly explore."

"How is your sister doing?" he asked. "I haven't seen her around here in a while. I've missed her."

I rolled my eyes.

"She's good. She's not really doing anything. She says she wants to spend her break not leaving her bed, and catching up on the shows she's missed."

Mr. Moretti chuckled. "I guess she really is a teenager after all. I often forget she's so young,"

"You're meeting with Liam aren't you?" Mr. Moretti asked.

"Yes, is he not here yet?"

"Yes, he is. He's in the back helping me move a few things," Mr. Moretti replied.

"Actually," he continued. "I don't want to be a bother, but I could use all the help I can get. It would get the job done much faster."

"Of course," Aamir said politely.

"This way," Mr. Moretti said.

"Forgive me. I'm not as strong as I used to be. I'm afraid old age is wearing me down."

"I'm happy to help," Aamir insisted.

"Such a polite young boy you are. Your parents have raised you exceptionally well. Both of you," Mr. Moretti complimented.

"Thank you," Aamir replied.

They talked for a bit until they reached wherever they were headed.

"What is this place?" my brother asked suddenly.

"Forgive me," Mr. Moretti said.

I heard a loud thud and a groan from my brother which caused me to jump up.

"Hey, hey," the agent said. "They just knocked him out. They need him alive. He'll wake up soon."

"That doesn't make me feel any better," I croaked. "He's hurt."

"If something was wrong, Agent Callahan would send a signal," the agent insisted.

I nodded sitting down again. "I don't like this."

"Your brother is brave," the agent said. "Trust that he'll do well."

I took a deep breath and put the headphones back on.

"When are the buyers getting here?" Brian asked.

"Soon," another voice which sounded like the principal said.

"I guess we missed his entrance," the agent said.

I nodded and continued listening.

"He's waking up," a voice announced.

"Do you recognize that voice?" the agent asked.

I shook my head and turned to Matthew.

"Sounds familiar," Matthew said. "But I don't know who exactly."

"What the hell," my brother groaned. "What the hell is going on? Why the hell am I tied up. What is going on?!" he yelled when he didn't get an answer.

"Should we knock him out again," the mysterious voice spoke again.

Matthew scoffed shaking his head. "That's Garrett."

"He goes to school with us," I told the agent.

"Why would a high school kid be involved in this," he whispered to himself.

"We need him in good condition," the principal said.

"You're a part of this?" my brother asked someone.

"Sorry kid," Brian said his voice low and cold–transforming into Liam.

"Are you going to kill me?" my brother asked.

Our principal laughed. "Oh God no. What good would that serve us. We're going to sell you."

Aamir remained quiet.

The phone suddenly rang.

"It's the buyer," the principal said.

He answered the phone. "Hello? Uh-huh."

He stayed quiet listening to whatever was being said at the other end of the line. "I see. I'll take care of it."

"Whoa, whoa, whoa," Mr. Moretti yelled. "What in the hell are you doing William?"

I frowned wishing I could see what the hell was going on.

"There's a van outside!" the principal yelled

"Put down the gun first and let's talk about this," Mr. Moretti pleaded.

"Why is there a van outside?" he shouted. "You really expect me to believe that it's not suspicious hiding in the alleyway like that?"

"We've been made," the agent said in his earpiece.

"Oh my God," I whispered my voice breaking.

"How do you know if anyone is even in there? Someone could have left it there." Mr. Moretti tried to reason with him.

"This happened because you brought him in this!" the principal shouted. "This has never happened before, and suddenly someone new shows up, and everything goes to shit? Just because we hired him to scare that girl didn't mean it was an invitation. He didn't even do a good job. It just made her braver."

"Oh my God," I whispered trembling.

"I had nothing to do with this," Brian said his voice not wavering. "Why don't you go check outside and see if anyone is in there before you jump to conclusions?"

He stopped. "Fine but you're coming with me."

"What is he doing?" I asked the agent frantically.

"He's taking him outside where he's outnumbered."

"All teams on standby," the agent said to his earpiece.

I continued listening bouncing my knees up and down.

"What the hell is going on?" Aamir asked.

"Be quiet," Garrett snarled.

I felt faint. "Oh my God."

I sat there numb and frozen until I heard a gunshot.

I jumped from my chair and tried to run outside of the van until someone grabbed me from behind and pulled me back.

Matthew gripped my arms tightly. "You can't go out there."

"What if that was my brother?" I said, trying to squeeze out of his grasp.

"Suspect is in custody and the brother is safe," I heard someone say through my headphones.

I lost all strength in my legs and leaned against my friend for support. "*Alhamdulilah*."

I sat back down in my chair and listened to the commotion going on outside.

I bounced my knee up and down nervous until my brother came inside the van.

I leaped up hugging him almost knocking us both back.

"I was so worried," I cried. "Are you okay?" I asked inspecting his head.

He rubbed the back of his head. "It hurts."

"I'm glad you're okay man," Matthew said hugging him.

"Thank you," Aamir said.

"Man, that was scary." Aamir's voice trembled.

"What happened after Brian left?" I asked. "You guys stopped talking and then boom a gunshot."

"The gunshot came from outside," he said. "I think your principal tried to shoot Brian,"

I gasped. "Oh my God. Is he okay?"

"Yeah he's fine. He said it was just a bullet graze. He'll need some stitches."

"What happened after that?" Matthew asked.

"We were all frozen from the sound and then suddenly there were cops kicking down the door, and they arrested them, and they escorted me to the truck. It's a mess outside. They said they won't let us leave until the situation has been contained," he said.

"I think we should call our parents," I whispered.

They both nodded understanding it needed to be done.

"But first let's wait for Brianna," I said.

What were you guys thinking?!" Mom's face was twisted in fury.

I have never seen her so angry in my life.

"It's not his fault," I said. "I brought him into this."

"I don't care!" she yelled causing me to flinch.

She sighed and put her face in her palms not saying anything more.

My dad paced back and forth silent.

"Dad say something," Aamir begged.

"Never in my entire life did I expect you two to do something so utterly stupid. I am extremely disappointed," he said his voice stern.

Both Aamir and I lowered our heads too scared to look at our parents.

He sighed. "But at the same time, you guys took down human traffickers. I don't know if I should ground you for the rest of your lives or congratulate you."

Mom shook her head. "I can't believe this. Who can we talk to?"

She looked around and walked over to a nearby officer.

"Who's in charge here?" she demanded.

"This way ma'am." The officer led the way to where Agent Nordon and Brian where.

They followed the officer, and Aamir and I trailed behind.

He led us inside the bookstore and pointed to where Brian and Agent Nordon were standing.

"Which one of you is in charge?" mom asked fuming.

Agent Nordon stepped forward. "That would be me ma'am."

My mother glared at the man in front of her. "You have endangered my children. I could sue you for that."

"We had no intention of having your kids here, but your daughter is very persistent. If I can take the time and explain the situation to you," Agent Nordon explained.

My mom thought about it and nodded.

They walked off into a corner and talked.

"What's going on?" I asked Brian once my parents had walked off.

"The buyers got away. We're trying to track their location now." Brian filled us in.

"You don't seem worried," Aamir said.

"It's a small town. They can't get too far," Brian replied.

"What about the computers?" I asked.

"Our team is working on them now. Don't worry. We'll find something soon."

"Keep us updated," I told him.

"You guys did good. Thank you for your hard work. We truly wouldn't be here without you guys," he said changing the subject.

I smiled. "I'm glad it turned out well in the end, even if it means we're dead."

He laughed and then looked at my brother. "You're a brave kid. You never once lost your cool."

"Thank you," Aamir said. "But you should have warned me that he was going to knock me out like that. It hurt."

Brian chuckled. "I didn't know he was going to do that either. Didn't think the old man had it in him."

"I don't know how I'm going to go back to school after this," my brother said shaking his head.

"That's right," Brian realized. "You're going back in a few days."

Aamir nodded.

"Have a safe flight back." Brian extended his arm for a handshake.

"Thank you," Aamir said shaking his hand.

"When do you go back?" I asked Brian. "You get your life back now."

"Wow I hadn't realized." Brian took a deep breath. "I don't know. I barely remember what my life was before this."

I nodded. "Two years is a long time."

"Especially in this town," Aamir said.

He chuckled. "Thank God that's almost over now."

He reached into his pocket and handed us cards. "This is my card. If you guys ever need anything or cause any trouble, contact me."

"Thank you," I said taking the card from him. "But I think after all of this, I'm never doing that again."

Brian laughed. "I don't believe you. I'll give you a few months until you're back at it again."

"Heads up," he said suddenly.

We stopped talking when I saw my parents approaching.

"Let's go," mom said passing us by.

I waved goodbye at Brian and ran after her—Aamir quick on my tail.

We stepped outside the flashing lights blinding us. A crowd had already formed.

I picked up the pace and walked alongside my mom.

"What did you guys talk about?" I asked her.

"None of your business," she said sternly.

I dropped it immediately. No need to anger her more.

We drove back in uncomfortable silence. I was so thankful we arrived home in less than five minutes because I couldn't endure the silence anymore.

I jumped out of the car and walked to the front door.

"We're going to call it a night," mom suddenly said after entering the house.

Aamir and I exchanged a glance.

We nodded not knowing what to say.

We stood in the entryway as we watched our parents go upstairs disappearing into their room.

"We're dead," I said quietly to my brother.

"Yup, a hundred per cent," he sighed.

Chapter 33

I woke up the next day momentarily forgetting everything that happened the night before until it all rushed back like a tidal wave.

"Oh no," I gasped.

I reached over to my bedside table and grabbed my phone.

I had three missed calls from both Matthew and Brianna and over fifty messages from them in our group chat.

I called them back and put them on a three-way call.

"Are you alive?" Brianna asked as soon as she picked up the phone.

"I don't know yet. My parents didn't talk to us last night. What about you guys?"

"My parents were pissed, but after I explained everything they understood. We went to sleep like 2 am. I got the longest lecture of my life. They said they'll discuss my punishment," Brianna told us.

"Same," Matthew said. "They were more shocked about the entire situation more than my involvement. They were mad that I put myself in danger, but they couldn't get over the fact that the principal was a part of this.”

“My mom cried because she couldn't believe it. She's thinking of moving from this town after I finish high school,” Brianna said.

We talked for a few minutes until my brother barged into my room.

“They're waiting for us downstairs,” he told me.

I nodded. “I gotta go.”

“Good luck. Let us know how it goes,” Matthew said.

“I will.” I hung up the phone and ran to the bathroom to quickly brush my teeth and wash my face.

“Let's go,” I told Aamir who was laying on my bed waiting for me.

We ran downstairs and entered the living room.

“Eat some food,” dad said to us. “We're going to be talking for a while.”

I nodded and walked to the kitchen and poured myself some cereal, Aamir doing the same.

We sat down at the dining table, and our parents sat across from us.

My parents looked at each other.

“Tell us where it all started,” dad said. “Don't leave a single detail out.”

I took a deep breath. I told my parents that after our club room got vandalized and they shut down the newspaper for the rest of the year, we decided to enter this competition. I told them how we investigated for a while and gathered information and filmed a KKK meeting in the forest. I let them know about our real motive for going to the school dance. I told them about the real reason we went to Washington.

“Everything happened so fast after we found out Brian

was an undercover cop. We realized we couldn't submit the article, so we decided to help him instead," I finished.

My parents stayed silent for a few moments.

"So, this was about a competition at first?" mom asked.

I nodded.

"She dragged you into this?" dad questioned my brother.

"No. She was trying to hide everything from me, but I made her tell me," Aamir explained.

Mom suddenly burst out laughing.

I looked at her scared and confused.

"This is so crazy," she said laughing.

Aamir and I chuckled along with her.

"Don't you dare laugh," she silenced us.

I stopped and lowered my head.

"Listen." She sighed. "What you guys did is just...I don't even have words to explain this. But, after your father and I talked last night and tried to understand the situation, we realized what you two did was brave and selfless. We were mad because you are our babies, and we never want to see you get hurt. We are proud of you both. You solved a case even the police couldn't. Without you, they probably would have never even gotten close to cracking this case. That is very impressive.

"I can't imagine how hard this must have been for you Aaleyah. Knowing your principal was responsible for something so heinous. Going to school every day and pretending nothing was going on," she continued.

"It's not about me," I sniffled. The emotions I've been suppressing spilling over. "All those people..."

I shook my head.

"Lewis. I never knew him, but my friends did. He's

probably dead, and they probably will never find his body. His parents won't be able to give their son a proper burial. I just can't believe something like this exists in the world. I can't believe people would sell other people. It's so messed up," I continued.

My dad looked at us proud. "You guys put a lot of bad people in jail. People who deserve to never walk this earth again. I don't think you understand how big that is. Aamir, the police told us how you were a target for these people. I can't even fathom the thought of losing you. What you did was so incredibly dangerous, but we're so glad you're safe."

"I never thought this is how my time here would turn out." Aamir shook his head.

"That old man. I never imagined he could be a part of this." Dad sighed and put his head in his palms. "To think that you were going there every day makes me sick to my stomach."

I let my tears flow unable to stop myself. "I don't know why he would do something like this."

"The police said he preyed on his victims," mom said. "Most of these kids didn't have an adult they could confide in, and he exploited that."

"Nobody would have ever suspected him," dad added.

"You should probably know that this is all over the news. All the major news outlets are covering this," mom said.

"Did you check social media at all?" dad asked.

Aamir and I both shook our heads.

Mom got up and walked to the lounge room.

I followed behind her and sat down on the couch.

She flipped through the channels until she settled on one.

I leaned forward and watched carefully as they talked

about the events of last night.

"Wow they're fast," I said.

We continued watching since the news was unfolding, and they were receiving updates regularly.

"How did they get our pictures?!" I yelled.

I watched carefully as pictures of me, Aamir, Matthew, and Brianna appeared on the screen.

"They're talking about us!" I yelled grabbing my brother's hand and shaking it.

"I know. I can see that," he laughed.

"I can't believe this," I whispered.

I listened carefully as they reported our story. They left nothing out except the part where Brianna hacked into the FBI database. They talked about how a few months ago, we made the school and town go viral on Twitter and how problems in this town were nothing new.

"I can't believe they're giving us credit for this. I really thought they'd take all the credit," I said in disbelief.

"Why aren't you guys shocked?" I asked my parents who didn't seem the least bit surprised.

"When we were talking to the officer last night he asked if they could mention you guys in their news release. He said they wouldn't include you guys if we didn't want them to. But we told them to disclose everything as it happened and to give you the credit you all deserve," dad explained.

"Thank you," I smiled.

"We have to call Brianna and Matthew," I said jumping up grabbing Aamir by the arm.

"By the way," mom called after us.

I turned around.

"You're both grounded."

"Today is New Year's Eve," I said to my parents later that night.

"You're right," dad realized. "Where is the time going?"

"Let's go around and rate how our year went," I suggested.

Chapter 34

I hugged my brother tightly as tears streamed down my face. "I'm going to miss you so much. More than the first time."

He chuckled and hugged me tighter. "I'm going to miss you too, but I have four months of summer remember? I'll be back before you know it."

I let go, and my parents hugged him.

"Okay," he said letting go of mom. "I should get going."

He smiled and waved at us. He walked away turning around one more time before he disappeared into the crowd.

"Let's go home," mom said hugging me.

I pulled into the school parking lot and parked my car near the front. Even after everything that happened, they decided that school would start as scheduled.

I took a deep breath and got out of my car.

I walked towards the school and opened the front door.

I walked down the hallway, and just as usual, everyone was staring at me. Some people even stopped what they were doing.

This time their stares weren't filled with hate, but with another emotion I wasn't used to seeing from them. Some people even cracked the teeniest tiniest smile. If you blinked, you would've missed it.

I stopped by my locker to grab my stuff. I turned around to walk away but was blocked by someone.

I rolled my eyes. "What the hell do you want Chad?"

I crossed my arms in front of my chest and glared at the boy and his friends in front of me.

"We just wanted to tell you we weren't a part of any of that. That was all Garrett. The rest of us had no idea this was going on," he said quietly.

I dropped my arms to my sides. "You didn't need to tell me that."

"Yes, I did. What they did was all kinds of messed up. I don't want you associating us with that."

I nodded and walked away to find my friends.

"Hey guys," I greeted them.

Brianna turned around giving me a big hug.

"Group hug," Matthew said joining in.

I laughed and hugged my friends back.

"I feel like we haven't seen each other in forever," I said letting go.

"Everything has been so crazy. My Twitter has been blowing up," Brianna said.

"Mine too," I told her. "I keep getting messages from journalists asking me to make a statement."

She nodded, "It's overwhelming, but in a good way."

"Have you talked to Brian?" Matthew asked.

I shook my head. "He's probably really busy. They're uncovering everything from the disappearances."

"I wish we knew what they found. The news is not saying much. I guess we'll have to wait like everyone else," she sighed.

"Have you talked to Lewis' parents?" I asked.

"Yeah, they got a call from the police explaining everything," she said.

"How did they take it?" I asked.

"Not good." She shook her head. "Mrs. Wiremen cried a lot on the phone. I can't imagine what they're going through. They're reopening the investigation, and they have to relive everything."

"But hopefully this time they get the answers they're looking for," Matthew said.

I nodded and leaned on a locker staring at the students walking by.

"This is weird," I said.

"What is?" Brianna asked.

"All of this," I told them. "Just going back to school like nothing happened after everything that happened."

Matthew nodded in agreement. "At least our college essays will be a banger."

I laughed.

"Do we have any classes together?" I asked.

"I didn't even look at my schedule. Wow, I am not prepared for this at all," Brianna said.

"Same," I agreed.

"At least we have one class together," Matthew said after we examined our schedule. I looked at my phone and noticed the bell was about to ring.

"We should start heading to class," I told them.

"I'm not ready for this," Brianna whined as she closed her locker.

We walked down the school hallway with everyone's eyes on us.

"I can't get used to this," Matthew said. "They're staring more than usual."

I linked my arms with theirs and dragged them along. "Who cares."

Matthew looked at me and smiled. "Amen to that."

I smiled. "I think this year will be a good year."

"*InshaAllah*," Matthew said.

I laughed. "Yes, *InshaAllah*."

Authors Note

You've made it to the end, or maybe you just skipped to this page, but either way, you're here. If you're reading this, thank you. An author only exists because of their readers.

I wrote this book because I noticed voices missing from the publishing industry. Voices like mine–and maybe–voices like yours. I decided to take control of my narrative, from the writing to distribution, because I believed in my story when others didn't, and when others wanted to change it.

Our stories matter. They're wanted and needed regardless of how it may seem when looking at the books in bookstores. I look forward to the day when I can walk into a bookstore, and the books are an accurate representation of the world we live in. We've got a lot of work to do, but that doesn't mean it can't get done.

Acknowledgments

Making this book a reality could not have been possible without my family. I thank my sisters Juweria, Samia, Maymuuna, Xafsa, and Salma. Thank you for your encouraging words. Thank you for believing in me, and most importantly, thank you for being the best team an author could ask for. Thank you for telling me the truth when I needed it. Thank you for brainstorming with me for hours for the design ideas of this book. Thank you for being there every step of the way. I honestly would not have been able to do it without you.

Bio

Aisha Yusuf is a 23-year-old Somali-Canadian author and publisher. As a young teen, she was an avid reader, but as she got older, she noticed there was no representation of people who looked like her and had her shared experiences. In high school, she decided she was going to write the book she always wanted to read. She started her writing journey at 15 and hasn't stopped since.

Visit her online at www.aishayusuf.com